MARY TANT

Don't Come Back

Threshold Press

First published 2012 by
Threshold Press Ltd, Norfolk House
75 Bartholomew Street, Newbury
Berks RG14 5DU
Phone 01635-230272 and fax 01635-44804
email: publish@threshold-press.co.uk
www.threshold-press.co.uk

British Library Cataloguing in Publication Data
A catalogue record for this book is available from the British Library
ISBN 978-1-903152-30-0

Designed by Jim Weaver Design
Printed in Great Britain by the MPG Biddles, King's Lynn

For Jane
A friend for all seasons

ONE

In spite of her thick coat Lucy Rossington shivered as an icy draught struck her. It passed on to the rood screen in front of her and was thrown back from the painted panels she was examining to send cold fingers creeping over her face as well. She tugged her Fair Isle hat more tightly over her chestnut hair, pulled her scarf further up her neck and snuggled her chin into it as she turned round, curious to see who had come into the church.

But there was no one in the nave behind her. It was badly lit beneath its high barrel roof as they had not turned on the main lights, but she could see that the main south door was still firmly shut against the cold outside. There was no sound of movement, no rustle of coat or tap of footsteps on the stone-flagged floor. But her friends in the chancel were talking, their voices clearly audible beyond the screen, so perhaps other noises would not be noticeable.

Lucy's gaze ranged round the interior, passing the dim outlines of benches and the sturdy pillars that lined the nave until it was drawn to a glimmer on her right, near the chantry chapel in the south aisle. As she stared she saw a slight movement, the rippling of a heavy curtain held back by a gloved hand that was faintly outlined against the dim light coming through a lancet window nearby. The hand released its grip on the curtain, which fell smoothly back into place, leaving a solid dark patch against the whitewashed wall. Strain her ears as she might, Lucy could catch no sound beyond the curtain.

She shrugged, studying the aisle as she walked into it. No doubt there was a door there behind the curtain, probably once private to the long-established Ballamy family, benefactors of the church since the sixteenth century. Whoever had been coming through that door now clearly did not want to disturb the visitors. Nothing unusual in that.

The chantry chapel itself was dedicated to its founders, Daniel and Susannah Ballamy, progenitors of all the other Ballamys whose memorials lined the aisle. Embedded in the floor was a worn granite stone commemorating their son, Captain Richard Ballamy, who had sailed with Drake to fight the Spaniards when they tried to invade England. The brass figurine that dominated the stone showed a typical Elizabethan, with his pointed beard and puffy doublet. His wife's image lay beside him, a perfect match in a moderately wide farthingale, but the face framed by her lace ruff was haughty.

Lucy was touched to see their carved hands were entwined. She bent to see which of them had created the memorial design, bending her head in an effort to read the wording on the plaque. Richard Ballamy had survived his wife, Catalina de Mendoza, by nearly thirty years. Lucy's lips pursed in thought, realising that Richard had presumably married an enemy, a Spaniard. How, Lucy wondered, had the appearance of a Spanish woman gone down here on the moor? And what had Catalina thought of the place?

Lucy crouched to peer more closely at the weathered lettering on the next stone. Richard and Catalina's son Charles lay here, close to his parents. In fact, Lucy worked out, he must only have been a year old when Catalina died, so could not have remembered his mother at all. Did he, Lucy wondered, show any trace of his Spanish inheritance? She read on, with difficulty, to find that Charles had, for a time at least, moved away from the moor. He had accompanied Raleigh when he was released from the Tower of London to set out on his ill-fated venture to find El Dorado for James I. Charles had obviously returned and survived, faring better than Raleigh, but there was no sign that he had ever married or had children. The Ballamy line seemed to descend through his cousins.

Richard and Charles appeared to have been the only adventurers in the Ballamy family, or at least the only ones to have returned home to die and be commemorated. Otherwise the Ballamy stones and plaques listed the lives and deaths of a series of local farmers and their wives. The men were churchwardens in this place of worship through the years of religious turmoil in the seventeenth century, the couples were fathers and mothers of large families through the later Georgian and Victorian eras.

Lucy turned back to where Daniel and Susannah's own tomb lay in pride of place at the centre of their chapel. Lucy wondered briefly what they had made of their two adventurous Elizabethan scions, a son and then a grandson who broke away from the farming mould of their ancestors and the others who came after them.

She had already been shown the stone effigies on the lid of the weathered tomb, which were remarkable for their age and state of preservation. The figures lay flat on their backs, Daniel smart in a belted gown, Susannah beside him neat in a robe that even in stone seemed to fall in soft pleats around her body. Simple collars framed their necks, but Susannah's had a delicate feminine frill of lace edging it.

Lucy was fascinated by the faces of the effigies, convinced they represented the originals more accurately than usual. After all, why else would Daniel have such large warts on his nose and chin, and such neatly brushed back hair? Why else would Susannah have such a wide mouth, with a dimple in her plump cheek? It was still tantalising, almost at odds with the smooth hair just visible under her coif and the square hands with their blunt-tipped fingers. Lucy bent closer to examine the flowers they clasped. Rosemary, she identified at once, sage, mint, and oddly, aconite and rue. She straightened up, wondering at the choice. Susannah obviously used herbs in her cooking, but the latter plants seemed to indicate she made her own remedies too. No doubt she had been a capable woman, making a jolly couple with her Daniel, and a happy one too, or they would not have chosen to be represented so realistically.

The real attraction of the tomb for Lucy, though, was the animals. Daniel and Susannah had been the owners of a local farm that still bore their family name, and their wealth had been based on its bounty. No swords and lap dogs for them. They chose instead to represent their sheep, whose faces peered out from carved woolly ruffs on the side of the tomb as their lambs gambolled behind them, frozen forever on a representation of the moor that lay above the farm. And in pride of place beside the couple lay their dogs, collies at their feet, smaller terriers in the crooks of their arms.

A movement beside Lucy made her glance down as her own collie, Ben, shifted impatiently against her legs. She touched his head gently. 'Alright,' she said. 'We won't be much longer.'

She walked back to the centre of the rood screen, her eyes passing quickly over the headless figures on it whose clothes still bore traces of their original colours. The brightness in the chancel was dazzling after the dimness of the nave and aisle. The lights were switched on here, revealing the rich gilding on the roof bosses. These had attracted Lucy too, especially the leering Green Man peering out through the screen of leaves that seemed to grow from his head, and the snarling red dragon spitting orange flames.

Her friends were near the pale beech reredos, a modern replacement whose newness was still obvious. They were examining yet another tomb close to the altar. The brilliant colours of the stained glass window shone out above Anna Evesleigh. She was Lucy's oldest friend, an ebullient beauty whose long dark curls fell over the shoulders of her scarlet duffle coat as she leaned forward to peer at the wording on the tomb.

Lucy smiled to herself. Anna, an actress and director of considerable ability, was always open to ideas that she could transform into characters or scenes. She would undoubtedly be interested in the adventurous Ballamys, her imagination easily creating a story around Catalina's brief life on the moor.

Church history was not of particular interest to Anna, but her companion knew so many details of the lives of the people commemorated in this church that she was keeping Anna fascinated. Lucy looked at Berhane, a tall thin woman whose finely cut dark features were silhouetted against the pale wood of the reredos as she moved Anna on to the brass plaques on the south wall. Berhane was a long way from her native Ethiopia, but knew her way around this church as if it was her home territory. As indeed it was, Lucy reflected. After all, Berhane was only a year older than she and Anna, and had lived here with her adoptive family since she was eight years old. So that's about seventeen years, Lucy realised.

They had all been at senior school together, but Lucy and Anna had seen little of Berhane since then. University had held no attraction for her, in spite of her undoubted ability. Until fairly recently she had been travelling widely, now and then posting internet accounts of her explorations to keep her friends up to date with her activities. She had originally set out to explore her birthplace and then found she wanted to see more countries, other ways of life. So it was four years, Lucy calculated swiftly, since all the friends had last met.

And now Berhane was back in the moorland village near the farm where she had grown up with her adoptive sister, Edith. Back to stay, for a while at least, now that she had bought the local Church House. Perhaps that would depend on the success of her current plans for a dining club.

Edith was the same age as Lucy and Anna, and Lucy pondered on how strangely things turned out. It should have been Edith, their contemporary, who was their closest friend,

but that had never been the case. Tall too, but heavily built
and gawky, Edith could not have provided a greater physical
contrast to her adoptive sister. The difference extended to their
characters too, Lucy thought. Edith had always been vague,
hiding her thoughts under a blank mask, living in a world of
her own that the others had never penetrated, nor wanted to.
It was Berhane, calm and straightforward Berhane, possessed
of an endless joy in being alive and always interested in other
people, who had formed the third in their teenage trio.

And it was she who had brought them to the church this
wintry afternoon. Edith had merely shrugged in disinterest when
invited, preferring to stay at home and watch the snow falling
past the windows of the Church House. And yet it was Edith
who was the direct descendent of the Ballamys, to whose tomb
Berhane had led them with such fond familiarity. It was Berhane
who had pointed out to Lucy the tiny flowers hidden among
the grass of the sheep pasture. Perfect little bluebells, poten-
tilla, milkwort, harebells, all growing together without regard
for seasons. By profession a botanist and now involved with
local heath and moor ecology, Lucy was riveted, as Berhane had
known she would be.

'Come on, Lucy,' Anna said, appearing suddenly right in
front of her and making her start in surprise. 'Stop daydreaming.
We're going back for tea now.' She shuddered dramatically. 'I'm
frozen to the bone and could eat a horse.'

Ben sprang forward, delighted to be moving as Lucy began
to follow her down the centre of the nave. Behind them Berhane
switched off the chancel lights. 'I wish I could think you were
joking,' she said huskily, 'but you always have had a good appetite, Anna.'

'I'm surprised you asked her to stay,' Lucy said over her
shoulder as she approached the wide south door. 'She'll probably eat you out of house and home.'

'That would be your brother's role, unless his interest in
food has shrunk as he's grown. I remember Will as always being

hungry,' Berhane said. 'I'm sorry he couldn't come for New Year as well. I'm looking forward to meeting him again. And,' she added, catching up with Lucy who was struggling with the door handle, 'it's Anna's gourmet knowledge that will make her useful. I want you all to comment on my meal, and help me be sure I'm providing food that will appeal to local people. Here, let me. The handle is awkward to turn.'

Lucy stepped back and Berhane grasped the handle, turning it with a deft twist. Still the heavy door did not move, and Berhane turned the handle again, more slowly and carefully. She released it, a slight frown on her forehead. 'I think it's locked,' she said, sounding puzzled. 'Somebody must have come down and closed up without checking to see if there were visitors inside.'

'Oh,' Lucy remembered, 'somebody did look through the little chantry door while you and Anna were in the chancel. I didn't see them, because they only opened the door a crack.'

'Then I expect they've left that door for us,' Berhane said, her frown disappearing as she turned into the south aisle and led the way unhurriedly along it.

Near the chapel she pushed the brocade curtain aside, revealing a narrow arched doorway and the faded oak of an ancient door. She twisted and turned the handle to no avail as the door stayed unmoving, oblivious to her efforts.

'How stupid,' Berhane said, standing back and staring at the door. 'This one is locked too.'

'How do we get out then?' Anna enquired. 'Do we need to ring the bells to summon the village? How exciting!'

Berhane shook her head, a slow smile lighting her face. 'There's no need for extremes, Anna. There's a spare key to this door hidden in the vestry, in case of situations like this. Wait here while I get it.'

They watched her go along the aisle and into the room at the base of the tower, its entrance almost hidden by the long bellropes hanging in a silent cluster. Ben watched her, but waited near his mistress, sniffing curiously around the foot of the chantry door, breathing in deeply now and again.

'It sounds as though it's been a problem before,' Lucy commented, suddenly aware of a pervasive smell of wax creeping over them from the candle stand against the wall of the chapel.

'I suppose the churchwardens are elderly and forget to look in,' Anna said, 'or maybe they just don't think there'd be anyone inside. After all, there's no service tonight and they wouldn't expect tourists to be visiting in this weather.' She glanced out of the lancet window by the door at the large wet flakes of snow swirling past in the gathering dark of early evening.

Lucy was doubtful. 'But somebody did look in,' she said. 'They must have seen the chancel light was on even if they didn't notice me by the rood screen.'

Anna lifted a shoulder in an elegant shrug. 'Then they need to change their glasses, or they've just been drinking too much over Christmas,' she said.

A soft footfall heralded Berhane's return, and they watched her coming back along the aisle, her tall figure obscured by the increasing darkness in the church. She bore a large iron key that she fitted skilfully into the hole beneath the ringed door handle. It took both her hands pressed hard against the key for it to turn. 'I think it's probably more difficult to turn from this side,' she commented, withdrawing it and pulling the door open.

'Even so,' Lucy began, breaking off to draw in her breath sharply as the cold outer air rushed into the church. The snow was now falling so hard that it obscured the graveyard in a white haze.

'Come on, let's get home quickly,' Berhane said, ushering them out. She looked around assessingly. 'I don't know how long this is going to last, but it certainly looks as though it's setting in.' She pushed the key into the lock again, turning it with more ease from this side before withdrawing it. She reached beneath her black and gold patterned poncho to pull her gloves out of the pockets of her woollen trousers. Drawing them on, she held the key more securely in one hand as she bent her head against the swirling snow. Pulling her wide purple shawl more closely over her face, she led the way past the south porch and round the tower towards the main path to the gate.

Ben pattered off as Lucy tugged her hat more firmly over her ears, awkwardly tying the flaps under her chin as she followed her friends. Blinking hard against the flakes that were landing on her eyelashes, she peered at the narrow track that led through the gravestones. Although the snow was melting almost as soon as it landed on the ground, still it obscured any marks there may have been on the wet grass.

Gravel crunched underfoot as they reached the main path and hurried towards the gate to the village green. Ben danced around, exhilarated by the falling snow, snapping at the flakes that floated tantalisingly towards him before settling on his nose and disappearing as he squinted at them. Ahead of Lucy the others were already dim shapes under the tree by the gate, where Anna's scarlet duffle coat was a beacon of colour.

Berhane ushered Lucy and Ben through the gate, letting it bang shut behind them, bringing down a shower of drop-lets from the branches overhead to plop softly on the ground. Heads down, the three women turned left away from the green that stretched westwards in front of them. Almost immediately the dark bulk of the Church House rose up through the swirling whiteness, only a faint glimmer of light showing from the lamp above the front door.

Anna opened the door as soon as she reached it, grateful for the unfashionable local habit of leaving doors on the latch. The others came in quickly behind her, and there was a communal shaking off of snow and peeling off of hats and coats.

Lucy glanced down at her dog, whose excited golden eyes were watching her, the tip of his pink tongue just protruding between his parted lips. His black and white hair was very wet and the crust of snow along his back was melting too. 'What a good job I brought loads of towels,' she commented. 'Where's the best place to dry Ben?'

Berhane looked round the hall, created by a high oak screen across the main room on the ground floor of the Church House. Wrought iron coat stands stood in both corners by the front door. Boot and shoe racks edged the screen on the left, a low wooden bench was against the right-hand wall between the front door and the narrow stairway that led up to Berhane's apartment. Soft light from two columns of branched lamps gave the hall a warm atmosphere, accentuated by the brown and gold Arabesque swirls of the specially commissioned Axminster rug on the stone floor.

'Here will be fine,' Berhane said. 'Just avoid the rug as much as you can.' She bent down as she spoke and rolled up the nearest end as far as the bench. 'That'll do. I only want them to look good for the opening night. After that any wear and tear will be okay.'

Lucy shook out her hair, letting it fall back into its long bob, as she held on to Ben's collar, knowing he would be keen to follow the other women out of the hall. With her free hand she pulled a couple of towels out of his travelling box, which she had left beside the china pot that acted as an umbrella stand beside the bench. Ben squirmed for an instant as Anna and Berhane moved towards the screen, opening the door in the centre of it and passing into the room beyond.

The collie glumly resigned himself and stood still while Lucy began to rub him with a towel. Occasionally he turned to lick her face, but his attention was really fixed on the room that was out of sight, where he could hear Anna and Berhane.

Beyond the screen Anna was looking around appreciatively. She was in a square open room of a reasonable height in spite of the uneven beams that supported the ceiling. The floor was stone here too, but the rugs that lay over it were more intricately patterned and deeper in colour, predominantly in shades of green. The thick granite walls were painted a rich shade of burnt umber, continuing the warm relaxing appearance created in the hall. They were only broken by the door under the pointed arch that led to the kitchen at the rear, and by three sets of small diamond-paned windows with matching arches. Two of the windows were in the front wall, with a view over the green, at least when the weather was good. The other was in the back wall overlooking the garden, with a glimpse of the solid bulk that Berhane said was the outside stairs that led to the upper floor, creating a private entrance to her apartment. Otherwise the walls were quite bare, except for an occasional woodcarving.

Anna stared at the one beside the wide hearth in the end wall. She walked towards it to examine it more closely and realised suddenly that the stylised shape was a line of running deer. 'This is lovely,' she commented, her hand hovering over it, longing to touch.

'Go on,' Berhane urged. 'Handle it, that's what it's asking for.'

Anna gently stroked the soft wood, feeling the curve of the deers' backs, almost sure she could feel their living warmth. 'Where did you get it?' she asked.

Berhane was watching her, pleased at the reaction she saw. 'They all come from a local craftsman,' she replied. 'Look, that's my favourite.'

Anna's gaze followed her pointing finger and saw an owl, wings spread as it attempted to fly off the back wall near the window. 'Yes, he looks as though he'll be passing overhead at any moment,' Anna said. 'You were lucky to find such a skilled woodcarver.'

Berhane shrugged. 'We've known him for years. I expect you met him when you and Lucy came from school to stay at the farm. Do you remember Phil Avery? His family worked for Gil and Mary for years and lived in the tied cottage beyond the farmhouse.'

Anna frowned in an effort of memory, recalling almost

immediately that Berhane had always called the Ballamys, her adoptive parents, by their Christian names. She shook her head. 'No, I don't think I met him.'

'He was about our age,' Berhane said. 'A secretive boy, so he wasn't around much. Not,' she added reflectively, 'that you could see, anyway. I sometimes thought he watched us without being noticed.'

'He doesn't sound very nice,' Anna said.

'He was just shy and curious, I think,' Berhane said. 'Anyway,' she added ruefully, 'I was lucky to get the woodcarvings, and I'm sure I wouldn't have done if he'd known I wanted them. He dislikes us, me particularly, for turning his parents out of their home.'

Anna drew her attention away from another woodcarving, a leaping otter so realistic that she thought she ought to be able to see the fish it was clearly chasing, and looked at Berhane in surprise. 'What happened?' she asked.

Berhane's grave face showed no sign of concern. 'Well, you know Edith and I sold the farm as neither of us would have worked it or wanted to live there. Well, the cottage was part of it, and of course we had to include it in the sale.'

Anna quirked a beautifully shaped eyebrow, wondering which of the sisters had actually wanted to leave the moor. It seemed far more likely to her that it was Edith, who despite the blood tie never seemed to belong there.

Berhane ignored the unexpressed question. 'We paid the Averys a generous final bonus, and they found work on another farm nearby. I'm sure they were happy with the arrangement, but their son, Phil, resented losing the cottage and expressed himself very bitterly.'

'Why did he blame you more than Edith?' Anna asked.

'Because I agreed to sell. He thought she'd have stayed put if I hadn't. And now I've probably added salt to the wound by coming back to live here. I'm sure he won't understand why I'd live here in the village if I wouldn't live on the farm.'

'Why do you?' Anna was curious.

'I'm not a farmer,' Berhane said. 'And I didn't know then what I wanted to do or where I wanted to be. Now I do.' She shrugged. 'I suppose a dining club would have worked on the farm as well as here, but this is the way it turned out. It is a better place, of course, and easier to leave to itself when I need to be away.'

'So how did you get the carvings?'

'Phil rents a smallholding right up on the high moor, near the prehistoric village at Riven Tor. It's very lonely up there, but I'm sure it suits him. He was always whittling away at pieces of wood, and now he's developed his hobby into a nice little business. Some of the shops in the local towns are selling his work, and I picked up these that way.' She glanced around at them. 'I needed something to bring the outdoors inside, with only the three small windows in this room. But I got the carvings because I love them, their look and their feel. And I think Phil's going to go farther than he realises, and these will eventually become collector's pieces.' She smiled at Anna. 'My insurance if my plans don't work out.'

There was a pattering of paws as Ben hurried over to them, his wet nose nudging against Anna's leg. Lucy was approaching too and was close enough to hear Berhane's last words.

'I never thought you were so fond of cooking,' she commented. 'You are doing it all yourself, aren't you?'

'Pretty much,' Berhane agreed. 'A couple of local women are coming in to prepare the vegetables and do the clearing up, but I'll do the actual cooking and serving. That's the idea, you see. It's a membership club, and people come to dine here as a social occasion with me as their hostess. That's why I've arranged the tables like this.'

One long wooden table ran along the width of the room, and at either end there was another shorter oak trestle table at right angles. These seated eight people each, and the centre one had places for twelve. Ben sniffed underneath them purposefully, before following a scent to the kitchen door in the back wall.

'Are you expecting people to eat together?' Anna asked in surprise, looking away from the dog. 'I thought it was just like this for us.'

'This is the standard layout,' Berhane said. 'And yes, communal eating is the idea. It's a longstanding tradition in rural areas in large parts of Europe and Africa, and I'm sure it was common here once too.'

'Are you providing traditional rural food?' Lucy asked neutrally.

'Oh no,' Berhane said, a hint of amusement in her husky voice. 'That's where the fun comes in. I've learned such a lot about different ways of preparing food. That's what I enjoy you know, the excitement of using good raw materials and creating something magical. And each time I can choose to use them differently. I can keep them simple in a pie or tagine, or I can jazz them up with more elaborate recipes.'

'But she's going to experiment on us first,' a soft voice said behind them, 'in case what she does is disgusting to English palates.'

They all turned, Ben pricking his ears up alertly, to stare at the woman who was standing in the screen doorway, bulky in a long cotton skirt and layers of thin mismatched jumpers. Edith looked little more than a girl, although she was in her early twenties like Lucy and Anna. Taller than either, but heavily built, with wet frizzy brown curls falling carelessly over her pale rounded face, Edith had an air of vague otherworldliness that Lucy had often though she deliberately accentuated.

'Hello, Edith. I thought you were going to doze off when we left you, but you look as though you've been outside,' Berhane said as Ben went over to the newcomer for a perfunctory inspection of her bedraggled skirt before continuing his tour of the room.

'Oh, I couldn't sleep,' Edith replied, not appearing to recognise the humour in Berhane's voice. 'It looked so nice on the green that I had to go out. I'd been at the window upstairs, just watching the patterns in the snow, you know. Then I thought I'd like to see them from underneath. They would be so pretty if only I could work out how to put them on canvas.'

'Why don't you have a go?' Berhane suggested. 'I've put an oil heater in the empty outbuilding at the back. I think it was the old pigsty but it's perfectly clean, so you could use that. Or if it's too cold you could work at the end of the sitting room. As long,' she added, 'as you're not working in oils. I don't want the smell to get down here.'

'Well, I don't really know what I'd use,' Edith said, as she pulled out one of the chairs and sat down at the centre table, oblivious to the drops of water that occasionally ran down her face from her wet hair. 'That's the trouble.' She traced an imaginary pattern on the wooden surface with one finger as she spoke.

Anna cut in, impatient with Edith's rambling. 'How many people are you expecting for New Year's Eve?' she asked Berhane.

'I'm not quite sure,' Berhane answered. 'Let's see, there's us four, Aunt Susannah and Lucy's grandmother, that's six.' She held up her hands, counting on her long fingers as she went. 'And Lucy's Hugh, and his friend.' She glanced at Lucy. 'What's his name again?'

'Mike,' Lucy said reluctantly, watching Ben as he settled down on the flat stone in front of the hearth. She had not told Anna this news yet.

'What?' Anna exclaimed, looking at Lucy in disbelief. 'Mike Shannon? What on earth is he coming for?'

'Dear me,' Edith said, glancing up. 'Don't you like him, Anna?'

'He's the most irritating man I've ever met,' Anna snapped, unusually perturbed. 'He's a complete boor, he'll ruin the party.'

'How exciting,' Edith almost whispered, her protuberant light-coloured eyes fixed on Anna's face. 'What does he do?'

'He's an archaeologist,' Anna said shortly. 'I think he's working over at Ravenstow Abbey.' She sighed, looking again at Lucy. 'I suppose that's it. Hugh's there too, isn't he? Talking to Brother whatsisname about a book.'

Lucy nodded. 'Yes. Brother Ambrose is planning to write about monastic herbal remedies. Ravenstow isn't far from here, just over the moor.'

'Lucy was talking about them,' Berhane cut in, 'and it seemed a shame not to invite Hugh's friend too when he's nearby.'

'You should have wondered why nobody else wanted Mike for New Year,' Anna said caustically. A sudden thought struck her and she glanced pleadingly at Lucy. 'Please tell me he isn't staying at the inn as well.'

'He can't be that bad,' Berhane said placatingly. 'I haven't met the man you can't charm, Anna.'

'I think we're about to,' Edith said, almost to herself.

'I'm so glad,' Lucy said quickly, 'that you'll both have chance to meet Hugh at last. It's over a year now since we were married. As it was a very quiet wedding we've been trying to see all our friends ever since.'

'It was very sudden, wasn't it?' Edith asked.

Lucy looked surprised. 'I suppose so, although it didn't seem like that to us.'

'What does Hugh do?' Edith persisted.

'Well, he was a barrister, but when I met him he'd just set up his own publishing company, concentrating on academic books. He writes a little himself, and takes photography commissions too.'

'A man of many parts,' Edith said. 'I wish I could meet one like that.'

'Have you got one in tow at the moment?' Anna asked, tired of Edith's inquisition.

Edith pouted. 'Not really. Only Taylor.'

'Who's he?' Lucy queried. 'I thought your bloke's name was Pete.'

'Oh, Pete was a long time ago,' Edith said dismissively. 'Though he's Dixon's father, of course.'

'Dixon? Your son?' Lucy asked, racking her memory.

'Yes, he's six now. He's with Pete in Orbridge for New Year.'

'That's sad for you,' Lucy said. 'You must miss him.'

'I suppose so,' Edith murmured. 'He's very energetic,' she added.

'Not like you then,' Anna said.

'No, he's not,' Edith agreed. 'He's probably like Pete. Aunt Su thinks he's like my dad, a real Ballamy. I can't see it myself, but then I didn't know Dad at that age.'

'Is Taylor coming for dinner?' Berhane asked, a slight frown on her face.

'I don't really know,' Edith admitted.

'Can you find out?' her sister demanded.

'I don't know when I'll be seeing him,' Edith answered. 'I think he's got a couple of gigs up near Bristol, but I can't remember exactly where.'

'Phone him then,' Anna urged. 'He must have a mobile.'

'Oh yes,' Edith agreed. 'Though it's so difficult getting reception here. There's just one spot on the green where I get it, if I stand on a tree root. It's patchy though. But,' she concluded vaguely, 'he'll get here sometime.'

Anna felt her jaw clenching but Berhane simply said, 'Well, we've got eight definites. And Gil Hannaford is coming too, so that's nine.'

'Berhane's bloke,' Edith murmured, her eyes on the repetitive pattern she was tracing again.

Berhane ignored her. 'I don't know if you ever met him. He lives in the house at the foot of the green and farms most of the land around here and up on the moor. It was Gil who bought the Ballamy farm.'

'He's so good looking,' Edith said softly. 'But so boisterous. I always feel weary after a few minutes in his company. Yes, of course,' she added, 'that's why I'm so tired now. Gil came looking for you.' She peered obliquely through her straggling curls at Berhane. 'He's worried about the weather for some reason. Something to do with the horses.'

Berhane considered her calmly. 'It'll be the New Year hunt.' She turned to the others. 'Gil is master of the local hunt and keeps the hounds. Not for the old-style hunting now, of course. He arranges treasure and drag hunts, and has actually kept nearly all of the old members. There's to be a drag hunt on New Year's Day, but if the weather is likely to be bad he'll want to bring it forward.' She glanced at her sister. 'Is he coming back or should I ring him?'

'I can't really remember,' Edith admitted. 'But I shouldn't worry. He's always here, isn't he? I'm sure he'll be around again soon. And if not, we'll probably see him at the inn.'

Berhane glanced at her watch, a tiny jewelled face on a narrow blue leather strap. 'We'd better get a move on. I've arranged for us all to have dinner at the inn tonight. I hope that's alright?'

'Of course,' Lucy said. 'I hope the landlord doesn't mind. He seemed a bit distant with us.'

'Joe Triggs doesn't like you,' Edith said, 'because you're Berhane's friends.'

Lucy stared at her in astonishment, which faded as comprehension dawned. She glanced at Berhane, asking, 'Because of the dining club? Are you competing with him?'

'I'm aiming at a different market, but the idea bothers him,' Berhane said, unperturbed. 'It shouldn't really affect him, and he may even benefit. After all,' she added, 'he's letting three rooms to my friends for a long weekend, and providing a meal for six tonight. And his food,' she said, a note of laugher in her voice, 'is nothing like mine either.'

Anna sighed as she registered the number of booked rooms. 'So Mike is going to be at the inn,' she said resignedly. 'What fun we're going to have.'

'It'll be fine, Anna,' Lucy reassured her. She turned to

Berhane. 'What about your aunt Susannah and Gran? Aren't they joining us?'

'Not tonight,' Berhane said. 'Aunt Susannah wanted to spend the evening with Isobel, catching up on all her news. They haven't seen each other for quite a while, and it sounds as though your gran has been up to all sorts of exciting things.'

'I hope she gets here in good time if the weather is going to get worse. And Hugh and Mike too. They've got to come over the high moor.'

Berhane glanced out of the window at the back of the room. There was a faint glow outside, lighting the narrow garden where a thin layer of snow covered the shrubs and lawn. 'It's stopped snowing and it isn't really settling,' she said. 'I'm sure they'll all get here without any problems. Why don't you get back to the inn and see if your men are there? You can see if Isobel has arrived too because she'll leave her car in Aunt Susannah's drive. It's just on the other side of the green from here, the old school where she used to teach, added to the original house where she lived. You'll easily know it, the only detached house on that side, at the end of the terrace of cottages below the inn.'

'Okay,' Lucy said, as the collie got up and sauntered towards her. 'What time are you coming over?'

'About 7.30,' Berhane replied. 'I booked a table for 8.00, so that'll give us the chance for a drink first.'

'Then 'bye for now,' Lucy said, walking towards the screen door with Ben at her side. Anna followed, looking unusually glum. Edith got to her feet and wandered along too, but took no notice of their departure as she meandered across the hall towards the stairs.

Berhane went with them to the front door, her dark eyes lit with laughter as she saw Anna's expression. She waited while they pulled on their coats and boots, saying idly, 'I hope we'll be able to do some walking over the weekend. I don't know how well you remember this part of the moor, but apart from the tors there are also some interesting historical sites.'

Anna closed her eyes in horror as she fumbled with the toggles on her duffle coat. 'If they're archaeological Mike will expect us to tramp to all of them and inspect everything in detail,' she groaned.

'Maybe we'll learn something from him,' Berhane suggested, opening the door to the outside world. Night had fallen, but the sky was clear of clouds now, leaving the darkness overhead sparkling with stars. A patchy white blanket covered the village green, etched immediately ahead by stark shadows as the light from the Church House doorway shone on the oaks that lined the lane.

The black outlines of the trees themselves were softened by an upper edging of frosty white. An owl in the branches nearby stirred, a conspicuous shape, watching as Lucy and Anna kissed Berhane goodbye and set off cautiously across the open space, Ben leaping excitedly ahead of them. Their faces tingled with the cold and their footsteps crunching the snow were the only sounds in the stillness as they headed towards the inn.

It lay at the north-western corner of the green, past a few cottages set back in their gardens from the lane that ran in front of them, the main lane that came through the village. Smoke rose from all the cottage chimneys and lights shone out from uncurtained windows, marking bright stripes across the black and white landscape.

The inn was a low irregular building, its thatched roof dipping and rising over whitewashed walls, which looked oddly creamy against the snow overlaying the hedge and bushes in front of it. A series of windows looked towards the green, their varied sizes and shapes highlighted by the golden light streaming through them.

Lucy's attention was caught by the glimmer of other lights on the western side of the green. She hesitated, looking down the row of terraced cottages to the house beyond, shaped like a sideways T, much further back from the smaller lane that ran round the western, southern and eastern sides of the green. Her gaze fell on the black Mini that stood in the drive, lit by the outside lamp that shone from the house wall.

Anna turned to glance at her enquiringly as Ben stopped too, staring over his shoulder at them. Anna's eyes followed Lucy's. 'Is that Isobel's car?' she asked.

'I think so,' Lucy said. 'I'm glad she's arrived safely.' She glanced at her watch. 'I suppose I'd better not go over to see her now. I'd like to have a shower before dinner, and really it will be a relief to see that Hugh's got here as well.'

'And Mike,' Anna said glumly.

'I knew you wouldn't be keen on him coming,' Lucy admitted, swinging round to look down the length of the green, back the way they had come, as Ben came up to her side. 'But I couldn't say that when Berhane offered to invite him, could I?'

'I don't see why not,' Anna retorted, stopping too. 'But I expect it wouldn't have made any difference. Berhane was never easily put off from her own plans.'

Her gaze fell on the dark bulk of the Church House on the east of the green, the rugged granite walls unpainted and stark against the snowy landscape. Unlike the bright welcoming inn the house seemed to stand back, looking older, sturdier, more part of the land. Beyond it stood the church, its nave and aisles only dim outlines behind the more conspicuous white-painted render of the tower, which looked almost disconnected and ghostly as it rose upwards.

'I'd never have thought Berhane would go in for something like this dining club,' Anna commented, her breath sending icy swirls up into the cold air. 'Did you?'

Lucy shook her head, feeling Ben shift impatiently by her legs. 'No. I thought she'd be involved in the international scene, an interpreter, something like that. How many languages does she speak? Six?' She frowned. 'It seems a waste to be stuck here.'

Anna glanced at her, conscious of an unusual note in her

voice. She remembered that Lucy had planned a different life
away from the West Country where her family had lived for
centuries. Lucy had been on the verge of achieving her ambi-
tions too, when she was offered a post surveying rain forest
plants in Peru after leaving university. But her father, Francis
Rossington, had died suddenly, leaving Lucy's younger brother
Will as heir to the family home, an Elizabethan manor house on
a small estate. Lucy had chosen quite freely to stay and put it
on a sound financial footing for Will, who would soon be able
to run it completely by himself now.

Anna studied her friend covertly as Ben wandered off to
sniff round the base of the nearest tree. Lucy still would not be
following her dream though, because she had met Hugh and
married him, and had just moved into the ancient farmhouse
they had renovated. Did Lucy, Anna wondered uneasily, regret
her choices?

Lucy turned, conscious of Anna's fixed stare. 'What is it?'
she demanded.

'Do you feel stuck? Being married and a house owner and
all that?' Anna asked, using the licence of long friendship.

Lucy turned away, staring across the green to the south
where the fringe of trees opened a little, leading the eyes to the
house that stood there, screened behind a bank of laurel. Beyond
it was the dark shape of the moor, high above the village.

'Not really,' Lucy said slowly. 'But sometimes I feel I've
missed out a bit. There was so much I was going to do, and now
everything's different. Berhane's lifestyle seems a big contrast.'
And so, she thought, does yours, Anna.

'Well, life did become serious for you rather suddenly,' Anna
said carefully. 'The rest of us have had more chance to follow
our fancies.'

Lucy's gamine smile lit her pointed face as she turned to
Anna. 'Is that what you're doing?' she demanded. 'I guess I did
too. I met Hugh and that was it. The rest is just a dream of what
might have been. What I want is different now, but the dream is

perhaps more enticing because of that. I shan't be testing it, so it can't be spoiled.'

A small frown appeared between Anna's arched eyebrows, but before she could speak Lucy gestured towards the house at the southern end of the green. 'Do you think that's where this Gil lives?'

'Who?' Anna demanded, puzzled.

'Gil Hannaford,' Lucy said. 'The bloke who came to see Berhane. Didn't you see what Edith was hinting?'

'Her,' Anna said shortly. 'She was forever hinting and sniping at school. Miserable little madam, I never did like her and she hasn't changed at all. I don't know why on earth Berhane puts up with her.'

'Berhane always did look out for her,' Lucy said. 'She was constantly standing up for her at school.'

'She should have left Edith to get on with it,' Anna said. 'Maybe then Edith wouldn't have stayed so helpless and hopeless.' She turned her head up to gaze at the stars, her long dark curls streaming down the back of her duffle coat. As she looked down again she muttered, almost under her breath, 'Gil. That's strange.'

'What?' Lucy asked.

'This bloke Gil. Wasn't Edith's dad called that too?'

'Yes, I think he was. But it's not really that strange. Even now the moor families stick to traditional names. I've come across a few of them in the last couple of months, now I've started the heath plant survey for the Wronham Trust. If this Gil is local he's probably even related to the Ballamys one way or another. Most of the old families are connected.'

'I suppose so,' Anna agreed. She turned back towards the inn, her eyes passing over the Schoolhouse. 'Yes, you're probably right.'

'In fact,' Lucy went on, remembering the effigies that had interested her in the church, 'Edith's aunt Susannah has the same name as the woman on the Ballamy tomb. I bet this one is named after the old one.'

Anna lifted her shoulders slightly. 'It's creepy in a way. All those ancestors still affecting people today.'

'Only by passing on their names, and perhaps the occasional physical feature,' Lucy pointed out. 'I think there was some resemblance between Aunt Susannah and her ancestress, but although I haven't seen Aunt Susannah for years I don't remember her having that satisfied look of the stone Susannah.'

Anna laughed and began to walk on, Lucy falling into step beside her, Ben sauntering off ahead of them. 'I remember her as very upright and rather stern,' Anna said. 'Terrifyingly firm, too, but always interesting. I bet she was a good teacher.'

'It seems right that she managed to buy the Schoolhouse when it was put up for sale. She must have taught there all her adult life, and I expect she went there as a child too. Susannah of the Schoolhouse,' Lucy tried it out. 'It sounds very Anne of Green Gables, doesn't it?'

'Only Susannah is more like the old lady. Marilla, wasn't it? Imagination was never her strong point, but discipline was a hot favourite.'

Lucy smiled, but said pensively, 'I wonder where Edith got her imagination from then.'

'Maybe she has all the family share for generations,' Anna suggested. 'If it is imagination. I reckon she's just hopeless.'

'More likely she got it from her mother,' Lucy said. 'I once caught Mary looking off into the distance, perhaps dreaming, although she always seemed so practical. Maybe her imagination just disappeared under the weight of work she did on the farm.'

'She probably wasn't dreaming, just exhausted,' Anna said cynically. 'There's always a lot to do on farms, and the work must have been even heavier ten years ago. She died first, didn't she?'

They had reached the hedge that separated the inn from the green. From beyond a man's voice said loudly, 'She's talking about death again.' He stalked through the garden gateway, a bulky figure in his thick donkey jacket, and stood still, arms akimbo, glaring at them from under the woollen beanie that was pulled low over his forehead. Ben fell on him joyfully as he said, 'We could hear you coming, bellowing and cackling as if you've already been partying.' He stroked the dog absentmindedly, his eyes narrowing suspiciously as Lucy kissed his cheek. 'Perhaps you have.' He sniffed ostentatiously.

'Hello, Mike,' Anna said sweetly, air kissing beside his face as he shied nervously backwards. 'We've so been looking forward to seeing you. How could we start a party without you?'

He scowled at her. 'Hugh's only just told me you were here,' he growled crossly.

'Lucy kept quiet about the treat in store too,' Anna said. 'Perhaps they didn't want to spoil the surprise.'

'Something like that,' another man said cheerfully, releasing Lucy from his hug and bending briefly to fuss Ben, before skirting round Mike to kiss Anna on her snow-flushed cheeks. 'You both seem to be having a good time.'

'Girl talk,' Anna said, regarding him fondly. He was of medium height and build, looking more solid than usual in a thick jumper and Barbour as he raised a quizzical eyebrow at her.

'Have you registered yet?' she asked, as she linked her arm with his, leading him towards the inn door. In the small squares of garden on either side of the path the tables shone wetly in the light from the windows.

'No, we've only just arrived,' Hugh said. 'Have you been with Berhane since you got here?'

'Pretty much,' Anna said. 'We've got a lot of catching up to do.'

Mike caught this comment and turned gloweringly to Lucy. 'How many of you are here?' he demanded.

'The three of us, as well as Gran and her friend,' Lucy said, skirting past him.

'I meant,' he said crossly, falling into step beside her, 'how many women.'

'All of us,' she said simply.

Mike clutched his head. 'God almighty. Five of you?'

'Six actually, with Berhane's sister Edith. She's staying at the Church House too.'

'No wonder Hugh wanted me to come,' Mike muttered. 'The poor bloke would have been completely swamped.'

Anna glanced over his shoulder as Hugh opened the door into the inn. 'I'm sure you'll more than make up for the shortage of men, Mike,' she said as she stepped past Hugh across the threshold. 'You always seem to fill a room.'

'There's another bloke around too,' Lucy said quickly. She held onto Mike's arm and pointed down the green to the south, where a faint light flickered beyond the screening trees and hedge. 'He lives down there and he'll be coming to Berhane's New Year's Eve dinner. I expect we'll see him before that. In fact, I think he may be joining us tonight too.'

Mike tugged his arm free and turned towards the inn, but Lucy continued, 'And that's the old Church House, down there on the left. Berhane's done a lovely job on it, barely touching its structure.'

Mike stood just behind her, breathing heavily. 'I should hope so. I'm interested in these Church Houses.'

'Surely they aren't your responsibility, are they?' Lucy asked, surprised. 'I thought your job only involved archaeological sites in the West Country.'

'It does,' he said shortly. 'But I do have other interests.'

'Really,' Anna said from the inn doorway, where Ben hovered undecidedly, torn between the cooking smells inside and the outdoor world where his mistress lingered. 'You do surprise me. Perhaps you could pursue them later. Mr Triggs wants us to close the door and keep the heat in, so are you staying out or coming in?'

'If the weather weren't so bad,' Mike said, looking towards

the car park beside the inn, where the back of his battered red Passat estate was just visible, 'I'd probably go back home.'

'Oh Mike, don't be so childish,' Anna snapped. 'Just get in here so that we can all have a drink.'

She turned on her heel and disappeared. Lucy went after her, suddenly feeling the cold infiltrate her coat. Mike followed reluctantly, his shoulders hunched, his expression gloomy.

TWO

Susannah Ballamy ran a finger appreciatively over the embroidered pattern on the purse in her hands. They were capable
hands, blunt fingered, short nailed, and well kept. The hands of
a sensible woman. But they lingered with pleasure on the lovely
purse they held. It was brightly lit by lights concealed in the
ceiling of the Schoolhouse kitchen, which shone down on the
glittering threads of gold that wound through the stitched green
leaves and pale yellow flowers.

'I thought of primroses,' Isobel Rossington said, watching
the other woman, 'because of a spring walk you and I once had
on the moor, when the girls were in their early teens. I came
over to collect them all, Lucy, Anna and Edith, at the end of the
Easter holidays. And Berhane too. It must have been a few years
after Gil and Mary adopted her. You and I walked up from the
farm to that prehistoric village near Riven Tor.'

Susannah glanced up, her grey eyes soft with memory. 'Of
course. It was one of my favourite routes. It still is for that
matter, although I come at it differently now. I go across Gil
Hannaford's fields beyond the village.' She smiled, her firm lips
relaxing a little. 'Perhaps we'll have chance to do it again while
you're here, even if the weather will be rather different.'

She looked down at the purse. 'Thank you for bringing me
such a beautiful thing,' she said, laying it on the corner of the

worktop near her cat. It was a large cat with thick creamy fur tipped with mink, and bristling eyebrows over big amber eyes. Right now those eyes were fixed on the small spaniel that lay at Isobel's feet, her back to him.

'Let's go into the sitting room and be comfortable over our sherry,' Susannah said. 'I'm eager to hear all your news.' She turned towards the glass doors on her right, opening one and walking into the room beyond.

The spaniel got awkwardly to her feet and ambled after her mistress, almost bumping into her as Isobel stopped in the doorway. While the dog got her bearings the cat slipped down from the worktop. He landed lightly on the tiled floor in spite of his bulk and stalked deliberately past Isobel and through the doorway, turning for a moment to look over his shoulder at the dog.

Susannah was watching this byplay with approval. 'Solomon is making it quite clear this is his house,' she commented, 'but your Juno is very good.'

'She's fine with cats,' Isobel said, 'and really too old to chase much anyway.' She moved forward into the room, a small slight woman in her late sixties wearing a black pleated woollen skirt and a high-necked jumper in her favourite burgundy. She was similar in build to her granddaughter Lucy, but her iron-grey hair was cut in a short bob to frame her face, whose sallow skin was a legacy of hot sun in India during her married life.

Isobel was looking round the open space in front of her with amazement. 'It's stunning,' she said. 'I can't even picture it as it was.' She frowned slightly, trying to remember. 'I think it was small classrooms, crammed with students at desks, wasn't it?'

Susannah was pleased. She was older and taller than Isobel, with the plump cheeks of her ancestress and namesake whose effigy in the church had interested Lucy. Although the modern version lacked the dimple her current expression of satisfaction softened the normal severity of her face as Isobel sat down on one of the upright armchairs near the wood-burning stove on the hearth.

Susannah took her own seat and began to pour sherry into finely chased glasses. 'I planned it all myself. After all,' she said dryly, passing a glass to Isobel and settling back in her seat as Solomon sprang into her lap, 'I lived in the teacher's side for most of my life. There was plenty of time to think what I'd do with the whole property if it came up for sale. I opened out the rooms of the school, throwing the old classrooms and staff room into this one large room for living. With these windows it would be wasted on anything else.'

As the cat settled on her knees, claws extended slightly to hook into her thick trousers, Susannah gestured at the rows of tall windows that lined the two main walls. 'You'll see in the morning. There's a view across fields to the moor at the back and another over the green at the front.' She smiled. 'On the one hand I can watch the changing seasons, on the other there wouldn't be much I'd miss in the village if I spent my time looking out.'

She glanced round the room with satisfaction. 'I brought as much as I could from the farm when the girls cleared it out. It would have been a shame to see it go to waste when I had room for it here.' The two women sat in velour-covered armchairs that were pulled up to the table in front of the hearth. Similar chairs were dotted around the room by smaller tables, which were burdened with memorabilia, china figurines and pillboxes, small silver pieces and overstuffed pincushions. Dark oak bookcases lined the walls between the windows, stacked with books, well worn paperbacks, faded leather-bound tomes, the occasional gleaming new hardback. A sideboard was backed with green cabbage-leaf plates, propped carefully on stands against the wall, but almost hidden by the framed photographs that covered the wooden surface.

Isobel accepted a cheese biscuit from the plate that Susannah held out, and leaned forward to look more closely at the pictures. 'Isn't that Gil and Mary?' she asked, pointing to the largest one.

'Yes,' Susannah agreed. 'It's one of the best. Edith has kept a few of her parents, of course, and Berhane has some too, but neither of them wanted the rest.' Susannah waved a hand at her collection. 'Family pictures going back to my great-grand-parents in the 1890s, and some of workers on the farm then too.' She smiled. 'I'm researching the family history, the modern fall-back of the retired, so it's fitting they find a home here with me.'

'One of my grandson's friends would be very interested in them, and I'm sure she'd love to hear all you know about the farm,' Isobel commented, her eyes lingering on the farming photographs. 'She's studying the social history of rural workers. I might get Will to bring her over one day, if you'd be interested in talking to her.'

'Of course,' Susannah said readily. 'There are some good photographs at the inn too. I always like to see young people recognising the value of the past. After all, it shapes what we are in the present.'

Isobel was looking around again, appreciating the cool cream of the walls and curtains, and the rustic oil paintings of people she guessed were Susannah's family. The rounded cheeks featured repeatedly, both in the men and the women. 'You were lucky to get the place,' she commented, sipping at her sherry, turning her eyes on Juno as the spaniel finished pottering curi-ously around the room and sank heavily down in front of the stove. 'People moving down from the cities will pay a lot for something like this, in such a superb position too. Even the little mews house I have in Coombhaven cost me far more than I expected.'

'I was curious when I heard you'd moved out from the manor,' Susannah said, drinking a little of her sherry. 'It's been your home for so many years.'

'My husband William and I were in India for even longer, and in some ways it was harder to leave there and come back to

England. But by last year it was clearly time to move on again. We knew then that Will has a good chance of keeping the manor and working the estate, and it was time to leave him to make his own choices,' Isobel said. 'He leaves school this year and I'd like him to be free to do what he wants. Anyway I was planning to travel more to research embroideries for ideas for my own bag designs. A small modernised house in town is much more convenient.'

'You clearly have an eye for design work,' Susannah commented, passing the plate again.

'I enjoy it,' Isobel said simply, accepting another biscuit, 'and enough people like what I do to make the work worthwhile. I spend part of my time in Italy, so I get the designs made up by local embroiderers in Florence. They're very skilled.'

'Where do you stay there?' Susannah asked.

'I leased a small apartment in an old convent earlier this year, in a village outside Florence,' Isobel said. She opened her bag, also embroidered with an intricate design of flowers, but in shades of rose. 'I normally plan to spend the winter months there, but I came back this year for Christmas in Lucy and Hugh's new house. I'll be going over to Italy again next Wednesday and staying until the spring.' She pulled a small album out of her bag and handed it over. 'These are pictures of the place. You must visit sometime; I'm always keen to see my friends there. Or use the place during the summer when I'm back in England.'

'That would be nice,' Susannah said, as she held the album above the cat and turned the pages slowly. 'I don't travel much these days, but I've always loved Italy.'

'Perhaps you'll be tempted to come and live there too,' Isobel teased. 'My apartment is in one of the artisan quarters, so you can potter along the alleys looking at craftsmen working as they have for centuries. It looks out on one of those little squares with plane trees and a very good coffee shop.' She bent forward to glance at the album, and Solomon turned a watchful eye towards her. 'Further on are the pictures of the garden. That should really appeal to you. There are orange trees above beds of flowers and herbs, and small avenues of vines leading to an arbour smothered in bunches of purple grapes.'

She leaned back, sipping her sherry, as Susannah reached the garden photographs. 'If it weren't for Lucy and Will,' Isobel said quietly, 'I sometimes feel that I'd settle out there for good.'

Susannah shook her head. 'I couldn't do that. It looks beautiful,' she said with feeling as she closed the album and passed it back, 'and I should love to visit you. I like seeing foreign places, but this is my home. And I enjoy my garden here. You haven't seen it yet, but it's the old playground in front of the schoolroom, just big enough for me to maintain myself. It's not much work, mainly bulbs and shrubs, but I'm rather proud of it and I couldn't imagine being away for any length of time.' She looked round the room. 'You were right though. I was lucky to get this place. The price was far beyond anything I had dreamed of. But Gil helped me. You know, my nephew, Edith's father.'

'I remember him,' Isobel said. 'He always seemed a good man.'

'Yes. And he knew that eventually it will pass back to his daughter.' Susannah's lips tightened. 'He would have turned in his grave if he knew his farm had passed out of the family.'

'Of course, Edith sold it, didn't she?'

'She and Berhane sold it to Gil Hannaford,' Susannah replied levelly. 'I was sorry to see it go. Of course Gil is local, which is something. He's come to own most of the land round here, but doesn't farm much of it himself.' She picked up the sherry decanter, offering it to Isobel, who shook her head. 'He's a very keen rider and more interested in those hounds he keeps than working his land. He's got tenants in all the farms he's acquired. The one at our place is a pleasant enough man. He's trying to make a go of it with rare breed sheep and cattle, but I think he's struggling. I shouldn't be surprised if he doesn't renew his lease.' Susannah shrugged, putting the decanter down with a little bang. 'It's hard for farmers, proper farmers, these days. He's got a shop out there, and that helps a little, but not enough. I buy most of my meat from him. The chicken in tonight's casserole came from there.'

'That sounds good,' Isobel said, brushing a few crumbs from her skirt. 'I didn't realise,' she continued, as Juno got stiffly to her feet and came over purposefully, 'that Berhane was involved in the farm sale.'

'Gil left it equally between them,' Susannah said flatly.

'I see,' Isobel said, as Juno lay down heavily across her feet. 'I know he always regarded Berhane as his own child, but it must still have been a difficult decision.'

Susannah sighed and the cat kneaded his paws against her trousers, his claws extending and retracting, pulling more of the black threads into tufts. 'I think he hoped Berhane would influence Edith and that they would run the farm together.' She shook her head ruefully, looking at the plate of biscuits she had picked up. 'Edith could never have managed it on her own, she's always been a woolgatherer. Berhane, though, is intensely practical, but her mind was fixed on travel then and she had no idea of anything beyond that. And yet here she is, back again, settling into the village as if she plans to stay.'

'No, they're very tempting, but I mustn't have another,' Isobel said, as Susannah held out the plate. 'I remembered how good you are at baking.'

As Susannah put the plate back on the table, Isobel asked, rather puzzled, 'Is Edith living with Berhane now?'

'No, that would never work. She's only here for the family opening of Berhane's dining club. Edith paints rather fey pictures which tourists seem to like,' Susannah's tone was dispassionate, 'and she lives in one of those arty villages outside Orbridge. She's probably closer to you in Coombhaven than she is to us here.' Susannah turned the conversation. 'Of course, you've had better luck with the manor.' Seeing Isobel's enquiring look, Susannah said, 'It's still in the family.'

'Yes, that's true,' Isobel agreed. 'Although it was touch and go when my son Francis died. And I wasn't happy that Lucy gave up her planned career to keep things going for Will. I really didn't see how it could be more than a gallant attempt to stem the inevitable tide that generally overwhelms family places. Death duties, taxes, farming difficulties, there are so many problems to face, without even thinking of running the house. Still,' Isobel sipped again at her sherry, finishing it and putting the glass down on the table, 'it turned out for the best, quite fortuitously really.' She looked across at Susannah. 'My grand-children and their friends have developed a tendency to fall into, let's say, unexpected situations. As a result of one of these they found the Rossington chalice, and during another they uncov-ered a number of valuable things in the attics. Will can sell them and fund the estate if he wants to. It's profitable enough at the moment, maximising the use of grants and moving into the tourist market. But I doubt if it will survive long term without extra money, especially with all the plans Will has.'

'What does he want to do?' Susannah asked curiously.

'I'm not really sure,' Isobel said. 'He's full of enthusiasms. The latest is Shire horses for ploughing and general working on the land. That has the support of both our estate manager and Jack Leygar at the Home Farm, so the stables are being reno-vated and Will travels all over the country whenever he can to look at possible horses.'

'That sounds good,' Susannah commented approvingly. 'He's taking advantage of the opportunities he's got. And that's really the best thing any of us can provide for younger people. Opportunity. Then you just have to hope they take it.' She finished her own sherry and stood up, lifting the cat and putting him onto the floor. 'I'd better have a look at the casserole. Come through with me, we'll be eating out there anyway.'

Isobel followed her back to the kitchen, Juno struggling along behind her. 'Can I do anything to help?' she asked.

'Just lay the table, please,' Susannah said, gesturing towards the far end of the room.

'This is clever,' Isobel said, looking around as the other woman bent down to the oven. The front door opened directly into the right-hand side of the kitchen. Plain modern units ran left across the front wall, turned right to line the far wall, then right again to form a partial waist-high barrier across the room. Beyond this was a tiny dining area, with just enough space for a small round table and four chairs, and a worn painted pine dresser filled with blue and white plates and bowls. 'This was two rooms before, wasn't it?'

Susannah put a covered dish down on top of the cooker and opened it to stir the contents, releasing a delicious aroma of meat and spices. 'Yes. The smaller rooms didn't fit well with the increased space in the schoolroom next door, so I took down the wall here and extended the kitchen into the old sitting room. The rest of that is now a little dining area with French windows onto the garden. I eat out on the small terrace in the summer.'

She put the lid on the dish and put it back in the oven. 'This is ready, so we can start on the soup. You'll find the tablecloth in the left drawer of the dresser, and the cutlery in the right.'

Isobel walked over obediently and began to lay the table, admiring the lace cloth she was spreading out. 'This looks old,' she commented.

Susannah looked up from the soup she was ladling into delicate china bowls. 'It belonged to my great-grandmother, so that makes it Victorian. It is pretty.'

'So is the dresser,' Isobel said, taking out the heavy silver cutlery. 'This painted wood furniture is very popular again.'

'Ah, I think that's even older than the tablecloth. It came from the farm. Edith didn't want it, and I couldn't see all these handmade things just thrown away. So many of them had been in the family for generations.' She cast a fond glance at the dresser as she brought the bowls over to the table. 'It's parsnip soup,' she informed Isobel, gesturing her to a seat. 'I'll fetch the bread. I got it from the Women's Institute market this morning.'

Susannah brought a breadboard and knife over to the table and placed it on one side. 'Just help yourself,' she said, sitting down and picking up her napkin. 'It's very good, made by a local farmer's wife. They're all diversifying into whatever they can, and I think Angie is doing well with this.'

Isobel broke off a piece and tasted it, watched myopically by her spaniel who stood hopefully nearby. 'Mmm, sourdough. It is good.' She bent her head, drinking the soup, and silence fell for a moment or so.

'What about Lucy?' Susannah asked, as Juno sank down with a disconsolate grunt and laid her head on her front paws. 'Has she picked up her career again?'

'To an extent,' Isobel replied. 'She's a botanist, and she's doing work for the Wronham Trust in the West Country. Her role has just been expanded, but it doesn't match the work she could have done in the Peruvian rain forest.'

'And she's married now, isn't she?' Susannah questioned.

'Yes. To Hugh Carey. He's a well-known barrister, although these days he's more involved in the small publishing company he's set up. You'll meet him tomorrow.'

'Still, women don't allow marriage to stop their careers now,' Susannah said dryly. 'I often wonder how they think they can have everything. Marriage, children and a career seems a lot for any one woman.'

'It's very different these days,' Isobel said. 'How about Edith? I seem to remember there was a man in her life.'

Susannah laid down her spoon. 'That was probably Pete. She knew him in some artists' colony, but when he found accountancy paid better than making felt she lost interest in him. Would you like any more soup?'

'No, thank you. It was delicious, but I really can't eat any more.'

As Susannah collected the bowls Isobel asked, 'Is there somebody else on the scene now?'

'It's always difficult to know with Edith,' Susannah said,

walking round the partition into the kitchen. 'If she wasn't such a naturally vague person I'd actually say she was secretive. But I think Berhane is expecting a friend of Edith's, some man, at the dinner tomorrow evening. He brought Edith over a couple of days ago, on a big noisy motorbike of all things. But I couldn't see what he's like, he was covered in black leather. Certainly he wasn't local.'

Susannah opened the dishwasher and stacked the bowls neatly. 'I do wonder sometimes about Gil Hannaford. He could certainly do with a wife. When he's not fussing over his hounds, he's always up at the inn for his meals.' She took the casserole out of the oven. Beyond the partition Juno lifted her head, sniffing. Solomon strolled in purposefully from the sitting room and jumped onto the worktop. 'That reminds me, Isobel. Gil called in on his way across the green just before you arrived. He was on his way to the inn then; perhaps he's meeting up with the girls. Anyway, he arranges the New Year hunt. Drag now, of course. Today's snowfall wasn't heavy and it'll be gone by morning, but the long-range weather forecast is ominous and Gil's bringing the hunt forward a day. So tomorrow I'll need to be up early to help with the hunt breakfast. It's something I've always done, even when I stopped going out myself.' She tapped her left hip. 'I broke this badly a few years ago, so now I generally follow the hunt with one of the older farmers on his quad bike.'

'Don't mind me,' Isobel said, watching over the partition as Susannah ladled casserole onto two plates. 'I can find something to do.'

'Oh, I'm not going out tomorrow,' Susannah said, replacing the lid on the dish. 'No doubt Berhane will be riding though. She keeps her horse in Gil's stables, and sometimes I think she's as besotted with the hunt as he is.' She shook her head a little. 'Anyway, I'll slip over to her place when we've eaten to see what I can do during the day to help for her dinner. Edith doesn't like riding, but she doesn't like cooking either, so she won't be any use.' She came round the partition and put the plates down on the table. 'Gil used to be sweet on Berhane before she went away, but he seems to have been spending a lot of time with Edith recently. If it does come to anything it would be good to have her and the boy back on the moor.'

'The boy?' Isobel queried as they sat down again.

'Edith's son,' Susannah said. 'Dixon. Such a name to give a child. Not even a second family name. Still at least he has her surname. Dixon Ballamy.'

'This is a very good casserole,' Isobel said. 'I must call into your farm shop on my way home. I need to stock my freezer before I go away again. Though,' she added ruminatively, 'I can't quite identify one of the flavours in this.'

'I cook everything in one pot now, potatoes, vegetables and meat,' Susannah said. 'It saves so much extra washing up. But I added a little harissa, something Berhane recommended that I find enhances the flavour of most meat dishes.'

'I must bear that in mind,' Isobel commented above Juno's gentle snoring. 'Is Dixon here with Edith for Berhane's dinner?'

Susannah shook her head. 'No, he's with his father. A pity. I'd like you to meet him. He's the image of Edith's father, although she can't see it.' She looked up from her meal. 'It's something to look forward to, the new generations, you know.' She picked up a forkful of chicken and chewed it, before asking, 'Will Lucy have children, do you think?'

'Who knows,' Isobel replied, thinking bleakly of that barely conceived child her granddaughter had lost earlier in the year during one of those eventful situations she got into. Lucy seemed fully recovered now, with barely a trace of a limp from her injuries, but the lost baby was never mentioned.

Mike was the first to come down from his room that evening in The Seven Stars, looking very little different from when he had arrived a short time earlier. He had run a comb through his red curls, simply making them stand up more, and changed from his working clothes to another similar pair of trousers and thick jumper. These, though, did not yet bear the trademark tears and mud stains of an active archaeologist, and Mike was feeling rather satisfied that he had inadvertently thrown into his bag things that were not worn threadbare. Not that he cared, but Anna did carp so.

His foot hesitated on the last step before coming down heavily. Now, he thought crossly, she'd probably think her moaning had been effective. He glowered round the hallway, its corners littered with walking sticks and shooting sticks, riding crops and hats, all so worn that it was not clear whether they were still in use or not.

A movement under the stairs made him swing round in time to see the landlord appear from the cellar, rolling a barrel awkwardly in front of him and across the back hall into the bar. Mike was about to follow him when his attention was caught by a couple of shelves piled high with stones.

He peered at them curiously, muttering crossly to himself as he spotted a shaped piece. He picked it up and turned it over in his hands, blowing away the cobweb strands that dangled from it, appraising the neatly shaped flint edges. Prehistoric, he would swear. He put the stone down and studied the others, noticing that they were all shaped or carved in some fashion. They were generally prehistoric, apart from a couple that appeared to be parts of a mediaeval doorway. Mike ground his teeth, wondering how many more artefacts were scattered among collections in the neighbourhood without any indication of their original sites.

He looked round the hallway more carefully, paying closer attention to the moorland pictures hanging on the walls. They showed several generations of locals in all their modes of life, generally farming in many forms, but also in their brief leisure hours on the cricket pitch. Mike found himself growing absorbed in the sepia-tinged pictures of raking, mowing and ploughing, where the men stared solemnly at the camera, almost identical in their trousers, waistcoats and pork pie hats. Their frequent companions were moor ponies, pulling equipment, bearing a rider, laden with packs, and almost overwhelmed by wagons piled high with hay.

Women featured too. There was a milkmaid immaculate in white cotton with a pail in either hand, her face under its bonnet slightly turned away from the camera. The 1920s postmistress with her neat Marcel wave, her twinset and pearls, was among the later photographs, staring confidently into the lens, the postmen flanking her in subordinate positions, leaning against their bicycles.

Most of the village pictures were from the early decades of the twentieth century, and Mike's eyes ran over them more cursorily. The blacksmith in his leather apron holding his hammer over the anvil outside his forge, the travelling salesman on a motorbike with a sidecar laden with suitcases, the open carrier's truck with villagers sitting on wooden seats, none of these held any interest for Mike.

The pictures were scattered higgledy-piggledy on the walls and the higher frames had definitely not been cleaned for some time. Mike's spirits lifted. This seemed like a place that would suit him. Now if only the beer was decent and the food good, not all messed around with sauces, he might be glad he had come after all.

He swung away from the photographs, brushing clumsily against the coats that hung in an untidy mass on a coat stand. The stand swayed and Mike caught it, holding it in place with an effort, but unable to prevent several of the coats from falling in a cloud of dust to the floor.

Muttering irritably under his breath as moths fluttered anxiously away from the scene, Mike gathered the coats up, wondering how long many of them had been there. Certainly the hacking jacket at the bottom of the heap had been around long enough to feed the moths generously.

He turned to hang everything back up and stopped short as he saw the picture they had concealed. Larger than the others, it showed a group of men in flat caps and waistcoats over their shirts, sleeves rolled up in a business-like way. They bore picks, shovels and trowels as they waited stiffly for their picture to be taken. They were the chorus for the main act, the men who stood in the foreground, formal in suits and broad-brimmed hats, standing proudly beside the round house that was evidently being reconstructed.

Mike swore loudly as he leaned forward, trying to read the handwritten label at the foot of the photograph. He could make out the words *Field Club*, but the names of the men in the tiny crabbed script were not at all clear. He dropped the coats again and reached for the picture, lifting it carefully off the wall to peer at the words, but they were too faded to be legible.

He put the picture onto the hook again, careless that it hung at a drunken angle as he heaped the coats onto the stand. Standing back, he rubbed his dusty hands down his trousers, leaving black marks on the light brown cotton. The sound of male voices drew him to the door straight ahead of him that led into a small room, dimly lit and unheated. The bar was beyond, at the back of the inn. As he entered it the three men leaning against the counter, deep in conversation, looked up briefly and nodded at him before returning to their discussion.

Mike took two purposeful steps across the room and looked along the bar counter to where the landlord waited, the dour man who had greeted him earlier. 'You've got a picture out there,' Mike began abruptly, 'of the Field Club. Do you know anything about it?'

The landlord shrugged. 'It was before my time. They're all dead now.'

'I know that,' Mike said impatiently. 'Did they leave any records? I'm,' he swallowed hard, moderating his tone, 'interested in the work they may have done.' He added belatedly, 'I'm an archaeologist, you see.'

The innkeeper's face grew surly, but he merely shrugged again.

One of the men from the neighbouring trio turned round. 'Come on, Joe,' he said, 'you know you're always sounding off about those digs your granddad worked on.'

'Great-granddad,' Joe muttered. 'There's not time to talk now.' He glowered at Mike. 'D'you want a drink then?'

Mike struggled with his impatience, shoulders tense with the effort. He scanned the pumps behind the counter and relaxed a little. 'Ah yes, Dartmoor ale. I'll take a pint of that. Maybe we can talk when you're less busy. I'm here for a few days.'

The landlord served him without a word. Then the man asked truculently, 'You having dinner too? With Berhane?'

'I don't know who she is,' Mike said, 'but I'm certainly eating here.' He looked round appraisingly. The room appealed to him. It was only slightly larger than the dining room, but better lit and warmed by the fire in the small blackened hearth. The walls were clean but a plain utilitarian white, the wooden tables and chairs were battered and scarred with long use. Little attempt had been made to decorate or brighten up the surroundings. Mike's chest swelled with satisfaction. A proper pub. And surely they did proper food too. 'Have you got a menu?' he asked.

Joe shook his head. 'Nope. There's three choices. Steak. Fish. Tonight that's sea bass. Chicken.' He added defiantly, 'With chips and peas.'

Mike's square face bore a rare smile. 'Just what I fancy. Real pub grub. You don't often get it these days.'

The man who had spoken earlier nodded approvingly. 'There you are, Joe,' he said. 'That's what I say. Those are your strengths. You should build on them. Good local beers, and plain decent food. Everyday meals, not special occasion ones. You and Berhane will complement each other.'

Joe snorted. He was a thickset man with the muscular build and stance of a wrestler. The heavy bristles on his chin seemed to prickle at the man's words. 'Alright for you to say, Gil Hannaford,' he muttered. 'You want it both ways, to keep

Berhane here and gobble up my food every night.'

Mike demanded, 'Who is this Berhane?'

The man next to him considered Mike in surprise. 'She's starting a dining club in the Church House, on the side of the village green here,' he said. 'I thought you'd come for her first dinner tomorrow.'

'I think I have,' Mike said slowly. 'But I don't know her yet. What's her food like?'

'Fancy,' Joe snapped.

Mike's expression darkened and he took a long draught of his beer.

Gil Hannaford laughed. 'It'll be good,' he said. 'You're lucky to be getting it too. There was some mix-up over Berhane's food orders, and she only found out by chance that they'd accidentally been cancelled. So you can thank your lucky stars the food's come. If you're out on the moor for the day you'll have a rare appetite by the time you sit down to dinner.'

'If weather holds up,' Joe said gloomily. 'There's already snow on the ground.'

'It'll soon be gone and tomorrow will be fine,' Gil said. 'That's why I'm bringing things forward. The forecast is bad for quite a while after tomorrow evening. Did you manage to get the message through?'

The landlord grunted, and Gil explained to Mike, 'Joe's one of the local amateur radio buffs. Him and his nephew, they pretty much set up the local network. It's handy when we want to get messages through in a hurry, much faster than ringing round everyone. And Joe enjoys passing on difficulties.' Gil ran his eyes over Mike's sturdy form. 'Do you ride? We've got a hunt on tomorrow. It's usually on New Year's Day, but with the weather worsening I don't want to risk having to cancel it or chance damage to my horses and hounds. It's a drag hunt these days, but I can mount you if you like.'

'Not me,' Mike said bluntly. 'I prefer to stay on my own feet. But I want to get over to the prehistoric village at Riven

Tor.' He glanced at the landlord. 'That's an interesting collection of stones you've got out in the hall. Do you know where
they came from?'

'My great-granda collected them,' Joe said shortly. 'He was
interested in local history. A load of rubbish, if you ask me.' He
wiped the counter top with a damp cloth, making the drinkers
quickly lift their resting elbows. 'I'll get rid of them one of these
days. Give them to Susannah Ballamy most likely, her's interested in them too.'

'If you want to know more about them Susannah's the
person to ask,' Gil said. 'She's doing a family history of the
Ballamys, but I think it's developing into a local history.' As
Mike looked blank, he added, 'She's Berhane's aunt, step-aunt
really. You'll meet her at the Church House dinner. But if you
want to get to Riven Tor you'd better go tomorrow. You can
walk down the lane past my place at the bottom of the green,
keep right, and follow the bridleway sign past the back of a
large house, Holly Cottage it's called. It's a shortcut that cuts
off a couple of miles from the lane route. I don't take the hunt
that way, because the bridge over the brook is too narrow. It's
usually okay for pedestrians, but there's been damage to one
of the struts. A bloke who lives up on the moor spotted it.' Gil
glanced at the landlord, who was polishing the pump handles
in a desultory fashion. 'Phil mentioned it when I saw him at his
smallholding this afternoon. D'you know he's got a damned fox
in one of his runs up there? With a broken leg.' He lifted his
tankard and took a great gulp of beer.

'Anyway,' Gil turned to Mike, 'I checked the bridge on my
way back. There's no chance of getting it repaired before the
bad weather hits us, so I've arranged for a barrier to be put
across the approaches. It's to stop walkers using it, but there
shouldn't really be a problem unless there's more damage.
Heavy rain swells the brook in no time, and it's only going to
take one misplaced boulder or log washed hard against it and
that strut will give.' He shook his head ruefully. 'There's never

any end to the work if you've got land.'

'I'll check it before we cross,' Mike said. 'But if the weather's turning bad later on I'll make sure I get up there tomorrow. There's no point coming here if I can't see the place.'

Gil grinned. He was a big man, tall, broad-shouldered, with a fair weather-beaten face and thick brown hair. 'That's right. You get out there and you'll probably see us in action anyway. There's always a fine turnout.' He looked at the landlord, who was silently cleaning glasses and returning them to their shelves under the counter. 'Since I saw you at the Schoolhouse I've rung the people I know are coming, Joe, but pass the word on when you can. Susannah has got the breakfast organised, so it'll all be as usual, just a day early.'

Footsteps pattered on the uncarpeted stairs then tapped lightly through the front room. Anna's entrance into the bar was heralded by a cloud of scented air. Gil got to his feet, admiration plain on his face as he noticed her creamy complexion, the long black hair that curled over her shoulders and the nicely rounded figure, elegant even in jeans and a jumper. 'Hello,' he said cheerfully. 'You must be one of Berhane's friends.'

'Hi. Yes, I'm Anna Evesleigh. I was at school with Berhane, and so was Lucy Rossington.' She glanced over her shoulder at the sound of voices. 'And here she is with her husband, Hugh Carey.'

Lucy and Hugh came into the bar, and Gil greeted them, bending to stroke Ben's head as the collie pressed eagerly against his legs. 'Hello. I'm Gil Hannaford.' He grinned at Anna. 'I've probably known Berhane as long as you have, even if I wasn't at school with her. All girls, wasn't it?'

'Yes,' Anna said, her blue eyes sparkling with mischief. 'But most of the girls had brothers.'

Mike grunted, draining his tankard and putting it down on the counter with a bang. He gestured towards the landlord, who came reluctantly towards him.

'I see you've already met Mike,' Anna said to Gil.

'Not exactly,' he said, looking expectantly at Mike. 'We were just blokes talking.'

'He's Mike Shannon,' Anna said, knowing the archaeologist was unlikely to bother to introduce himself.

But Gil's attention had moved on, over her shoulder.

'Berhane,' he said, 'I thought you'd never get here.' He paused, staring at her, noticing the scratches on her cheek and the slight limp she could not quite conceal as she crossed the bar.

'What happened to you?' he demanded.

'I slipped on the outside steps down from my apartment. As I was coming up here anyway I went on to Freda's cottage to talk to her about arrangements for tomorrow's dinner. We chatted for a bit, I suppose; you know how she likes to pass on all the news. Then I remembered I'd got the spare key to the chapel door, which I'd meant to give to her husband as he's a churchwarden. So I went back home and found Aunt Susannah on the floor of my sitting room.' Berhane frowned. 'She'd just disturbed an intruder, who knocked her down and got away down the outside stairs as I came up from the hall.'

'What!' Gil exclaimed in disbelief. 'Who on earth would do that?'

'Somebody just taking a chance,' Berhane said slowly, 'because there's nothing valuable there.'

Gil's expression had hardened. 'Is that how you got hurt? He went for you too?'

'No, I didn't see him, but once I was sure Aunt Susannah was alright I went down the stairs after him, hoping to get some idea of who it was. I didn't see there were traces of oil on the steps and I slipped down the last few. Anyway,' she looked ruefully at Gil, 'I think he'd already got what he'd come for, before he tried for a bit more. My oil tank has been pretty much drained, earlier on, I suppose. Having got away with that I guess he came back to try his luck in the apartment.'

'Have you rung the police?' Gil demanded.

Berhane shook her head. 'Aunt Susannah didn't think there was any urgency. She said there's been a spate of oil thefts recently, and she doubts the police would get out here in time to find any important traces, given the weather.' Berhane shrugged. 'I think she just doesn't want a fuss while our friends are here, but I didn't want her to get any more stressed, so I agreed I'll ring up after the New Year. After all, she was alright and I've only got a few bruises, nothing serious. But there's very little oil left to keep the heating going. That's going to be a problem.'

Gil heaved a sigh of relief. 'I've got plenty, I'll get some sent over. Thank God you can still ride. I'm bringing the hunt forward to tomorrow. It sounds as though the weather's going to turn nasty by the evening, and I want to get the hounds out while I can. They're raring to go and all fit as can be.'

'Edith said you'd been over,' Berhane said, 'so I guessed that's what you'd be doing. Have you got hold of everyone?'

'What was Edith doing when the intruder was in your apartment?' Anna asked curiously, watching the collie sniffing under the stool Lucy had pulled out at the bar counter. 'Surely she must have heard something.'

'She was out somewhere,' Berhane replied. 'She's constantly trying to get in touch with her bloke, and you know what mobile reception is like around here. She'll join us soon.'

'How was Aunt Susannah?' Anna asked, accepting the glass of red wine Mike held out to her.

'A bit shaken,' Berhane said. 'I was worried, of course, because she's got a bad heart. But she's tough, and luckily she fell on one of the rugs, not onto the floor, so it could have been worse. She wouldn't have a fuss made, or even take one of her pills, so I just walked her over to the Schoolhouse on my way back up here.'

'Between us Joe and I have got hold of pretty much everyone to tell them about the day change,' Gil said, leaning back against the bar, supremely uninterested in anything except the hunt. 'I'll ring the last few people again when I get back.'

'You are staying to eat with us, aren't you?' Berhane asked.

'Sure,' he agreed, 'but I can't stay long. I've still got to work out where to lay the scent.'

'What a shame,' Edith said, coming through the door into the bar, her long skirt dangling unevenly around her ankles. 'I expect the hounds will enjoy the company though.' She reached the counter and said pointedly, 'Hello again, Gil.'

'What?' Gil broke off from the conversation he was having with Berhane. 'Oh hello, Edith. Long time no see.'

'You still wanting to eat here then?' Joe demanded truculently. 'Only Betsey won't be here all night, you know. She wants to get off home, like some of the rest of you.' He stared morosely at Gil.

'Sorry, Joe,' Berhane said. 'You know what it's like once Gil gets talking about his hounds.'

'You're as bad as him,' Joe grumbled.

Berhane smiled slowly at him. 'I know,' she agreed. 'But we'll order straight away.' She swung round to the others. 'It's steak, fish or chicken with chips and peas,' she said succinctly. 'What's the fish tonight, Joe?'

'Bass,' Mike answered before the landlord could open his mouth.

Berhane turned her eyes on him, realisation visibly dawning. 'You must be Mike,' she said. 'I'm so sorry. I just dived into hunting talk with Gil.'

'No problem,' Mike said. 'We'd been discussing the moor ourselves.'

'And archaeological sites on it, I expect,' Anna interposed. 'Mike,' she explained to Berhane, 'is obsessive about his work.'

Berhane was looking round, her gaze settling on Lucy and Hugh. 'Lucy, how dreadful of me. And you must be Hugh. I'm so glad to meet you at last.' She took his proffered hand, but leaned forward to kiss him lightly on the cheek. 'Mike might be obsessive about his work, but I think Gil and I share the same love of working his hounds. Watching them follow a scent is amazing. You must come out and see them.'

'What about these meals, then?' Joe said belligerently. 'If Betsey goes off, you'll all have to get home and cook your own dinners.'

'Okay, let's concentrate,' Berhane said. 'Gil, I know you'll have steak. Who else will?' She counted. 'Mike and Hugh. So that's three steaks, Joe.' She looked at the others. 'Those for fish. Anna, Lucy and me. Three again, Joe. And that just leaves one for chicken.'

Edith smiled vaguely. 'Oh yes, I suppose that's me.'

Lucy crossed to her side, the collie at her heels. 'Edith, this is Hugh.'

The vague smile remained on Edith's face as her pale eyes considered Hugh. She shook his hand limply. 'I'm sure you're not interested in the hunt. Aren't you something literary?'

'In a way,' Hugh said, 'but I expect I'm pretty obsessive about my books. I'm sure Lucy thinks so.'

'Of course you are,' his wife agreed amicably. 'But don't you think we all have a degree of obsession?'

'Surely,' Hugh agreed. 'What do you think yours is?'

Lucy sipped her wine, pondering. 'Well, once I would have thought it was the manor. Keeping it going for the family, and all that.'

Mike snorted. 'It is for that brother of yours.'

'Will is interested in a lot of things,' Lucy said, 'and the manor is certainly a priority. But,' she added slowly, 'I don't think he would struggle indefinitely to keep it, so I don't think it classes as a true obsession.'

Hugh nodded. 'He's got too many interests for it to matter above all else. If he's going to obsess, he doesn't yet know what about.'

'Is that your definition of obsession?' Gil asked. 'A single all-absorbing interest.'

'Yes, I think it's as good as any other, that one particular thing matters more than anything else,' Hugh said.

'That's a no-brainer, then,' Gil said. 'My hounds and my horses above anything. In fact, I've just made sure they'll be alright if anything happens to me. I signed my will today so they'll be kept safe.'

'Gil,' Berhane chided, 'that can't be necessary.'

'You can't be too sure these days,' Gil said firmly. 'I wouldn't rest in my grave if I thought they were at risk.'

Edith's pale eyes wandered from his face to Berhane's. 'That's unusual, isn't it? To will your hounds away?'

Gil shrugged. 'Who cares?' He looked demandingly at Hugh. 'Would you class me as obsessive?'

'Do you know,' Hugh replied, 'I rather think I would.'

Gil grinned. 'So that's us blokes, true obsessives. What about you women? Come on, Lucy. We know it's not the manor for you. Your family home, is it?' When Lucy nodded, he carried on, 'What's your fixed interest then?'

'I don't really think I fit that particular mould,' she said thoughtfully. 'Unless wanting all the aspects of my life to work together counts.'

'I don't think you do either,' Berhane said. 'You're too rational. Like me. My biggest interest is maintaining communities on all scales, family, friends, neighbourhoods.'

Gil glanced past her to the counter, where Joe hovered, a black expression on his face. The landlord pushed another pint of beer towards Mike as Berhane continued, 'Maybe it could become an obsession in itself, but I think there are too many things involved in it for fanaticism.'

'That's you women counted out then,' Mike said, 'because nobody could see Anna as an obsessive. She's always dancing from one thing to another. First it was acting, then it was directing. God knows what it is now.'

'You're an actress?' Gil asked Anna, impressed.

'Yes,' she said, pulling her angry glare away from Mike.

'And a very good one,' Lucy said. 'She was a great success in Paris last year in a play about Marie Antoinette.'

'What are you doing now?' Gil asked Anna.

'I've got a part in a play in London in the New Year, but I've spent the last couple of months helping a friend design the clothes and set for a 1920s revival. The fashions were fantastic then,' she said enthusiastically. She looked ruefully down at her own well-rounded shape. 'Although they wouldn't have suited me at all.' She considered Lucy's slender figure. 'You'd have looked wonderful.'

Mike snorted.

Hugh said mildly, 'What about you, Edith? Is there something that interests you obsessively?'

She looked at him in surprise. 'Oh no. Don't you think that would require a lot of effort?'

Hugh considered her thoughtfully. 'Yes, I think it would.'

'Well, then, what's the point? I prefer to just watch for the patterns in life.'

Mike stared at her, his glass halfway to his mouth. Anna caught sight of his expression and felt a bubble of laughter rising in her chest.

'You're eating in here,' Joe announced abruptly, banging cutlery down on a table behind them. 'I'm not opening up another room just for you.'

'For God's sake, Joe,' Gil expostulated, 'what on earth would we want to eat in either of those chilly holes for?'

'It's not my fault the oil tanker hasn't got through,' Joe snapped. 'And I'm not wasting the logs on a fire for you when you'll be off to the hounds as soon as I've set the food on the table.'

He walked off angrily to the kitchen as the group moved to the table and began to sit down. Ben followed Lucy with alacrity and slipped under the table to lie across her feet. Anna sat down next to her and Mike hurriedly moved to the far end of the table on Lucy's other side, his expression darkening as he saw Edith take the seat beyond him.

Gil pulled back a chair for Berhane and said apologetically

across her to Hugh, who was seating himself on Anna's other side, 'Joe's not always as bad as this. He's a worrier, you see. And the hunt means a great deal to him. He'll be a lot happier by tomorrow evening.' He glanced at Berhane as he sat down between her and Edith.

She met his gaze with her slow smile. 'Then his main worry goes back to being my presence.'

Gil grinned. 'Nobody else is complaining about it. And once he's seen you riding and remembers how good you are, he'll tone down. That matters more to him than anything else. His obsession.' He laughed suddenly. 'One of many.'

'Perhaps,' Berhane conceded, 'but I'm going to have to make my other plans public soon.'

'Are they controversial?' Hugh enquired politely.

'Not really, unless someone's looking for trouble.' She looked over her shoulder towards the kitchen. 'I expect Joe will be, but what I hope to do should benefit him.'

'I'm not so sure,' Gil said. 'They're not likely to be in here eating and drinking, are they?'

Anna leaned across the table. 'Don't be so mysterious,' she said firmly. 'Tell us what you're up to, Berhane.'

'There's no mystery,' Berhane said, 'but I still have to find a site.'

'What for?' Anna persisted.

'An international training centre for long-distance runners and riders,' Berhane said quietly. 'I got the idea in Ethiopia. There are so many running clubs for young people, who are all very good and very dedicated. It's a potential way of improving their lives, of getting a measure of success, and they train very hard to succeed. The images I had of them swam around in my head while I was travelling, and gradually I realised I wanted to set up a training centre for young people like them, an international one that would bring people of all races together.'

The whole table was listening now, their attention fully on Berhane. So the plates that Joe thrust in front of them made

Anna and Lucy flinch. 'Fish,' he said succinctly, putting the plates down with exaggerated care. Beneath the table, the collie sniffed the air curiously before lowering his head with a sigh.

As Joe walked away Anna raised her delicately arched eyebrows, looking across at Berhane. Berhane smiled back at her. 'The food is good,' she said. 'And Gil's right, the manner's likely to improve by tomorrow evening.' She sat back slightly as her own plate arrived in front of her, while the second plate was whisked behind Gil's back and plonked down before Edith on his other side.

The steaks arrived promptly, followed by three large bowls of fat chips and a couple more of vegetables. Frozen, Anna assessed them immediately, as she leaned forward to take a couple of chips. 'Mmm,' she said. 'These are good. Hand-cut.' She surveyed the bowls ruefully. 'I have a weakness for good chips. Still,' she glanced at Mike out of the corner of her eye, 'I expect I'll walk them off tramping over the moor tomorrow.'

'You don't have to come,' he growled from his place at the end of the table. 'I don't expect you'll be up to it anyway. It's going to be a long walk, and no resting for the idle.'

To his left, Edith was watching him curiously, her pale eyes fixed on his face as he reached for the nearest bowl of chips and tipped some onto his own plate.

Before Anna could respond Lucy spoke to Berhane. 'How far have you got with your training centre plans?'

'They're pretty much sorted.' Berhane said, dissecting her fish. 'Once I thought about it, I realised the moor is such a fantastic place for runners to train, and then of course I couldn't leave out long-distance riders. I came to know a lot of people on my travels, and began to make contacts, create interest in the idea, so I've got a lot of support, financial and organisational, in place. I've even got world-class trainers who are prepared to give up the odd week of their time to help.' She ate a piece of her bass, then looked around. 'So really I can do all the things I like best, and here where I feel at home. I'm very lucky.'

'There's still the site to find,' Edith said. 'You'll need accommodation and a fair bit of stabling. Places,' she added generally, 'are much more expensive on the moor now.'

'I'm sure something will turn up,' Berhane said placidly. 'In fact I've already got a place in mind.'

'You know it won't be a problem,' Gil said, his attention on his steak. 'I'd like to help. I'll find you one of my places. In fact, I was looking at a possible site today. The tenant at Ballamy's Farm has given notice as well, and I think a couple more will be moving on when their leases end. It's a difficult time for farmers, but I'll try to keep the land in use. Or,' he grinned at Berhane, 'you can have it for your training centre.' He looked up as he raised his fork to his mouth. 'Delicious, Joe,' he said as he put the food into his mouth.

They all became aware of the landlord, standing at a distance behind the bar counter, obviously trying to hear what they were saying. Beyond him the kitchen door swung open, revealing a small woman, thin of body, but bristling with energy, who spoke sharply to the landlord.

'More chips?' Joe demanded abruptly, leaning over the counter.

Anna looked guiltily at the empty bowl in front of her. 'I'd better not,' she said. She looked enquiringly at Lucy who shook her head.

'Yes,' Mike said loudly. 'We can manage more down here.'

Gil grinned. 'Definitely,' he said, scooping the remaining vegetables onto his own plate. 'I'll surely be working them off tomorrow.'

'No, Gil,' Berhane said, as Joe came round the bar and cleared the empty bowls from the table. 'Not horses and hounds again. Give them a break. They've listened endlessly to you and to me. It's somebody else's chance to talk.' She turned to Hugh as the landlord went out to the kitchen with the empty bowls. 'Tell us about your books. It isn't just that you read them, is it? You're a publisher too.'

Hugh nodded, his mouth full of steak.

'Really?' Gil said, chasing the last peas round his plate with his fork. 'What do you publish?'

'Mainly academic books,' Lucy said for Hugh. 'But he's edited historical papers for publication too. We found a series of letters in my family home a year ago and Hugh has made them into a book.'

Gil looked at Hugh with interest. 'That's a coincidence,' he said. 'I don't know what sort of thing you look for but I've just found some old diaries that may be up your street.'

Hugh's expression remained imperturbable, but his heart sank. This was always a problem when people knew what he did. 'Have you read them?' he asked noncommittally.

Gil laughed. 'They're not my scene,' he said. 'I've skimmed through a couple. My great-grandfather wrote them, back at the end of the nineteenth century. He seemed to have a finger in all the moor pies of the time, and an avid interest in every bit of gossip he picked up.' He glanced at Berhane. 'I don't suppose you've read the ones I gave you yesterday.'

Berhane shook her head. 'No time,' she said. 'I may start the first one this evening when I get to bed, but I won't have time to read much of it before next week.'

'There are some Ballamy bits in them,' Gil said. 'I was telling Joe and Susannah when I saw them.' He snorted with laughter. 'Joe wants to read them all, can you believe that?' he demanded of Berhane. 'He thinks there'll be a clue to that treasure his own great-granda hinted about.'

At the end of the table Mike's head jerked up. His eyes focused on Gil, who was saying, 'Joe hasn't seen them. The diaries are actually small notebooks with dated entries. The handwriting is tiny, scrawled across the pages, and in places the words run up the sides as well. Susannah's keen to see them, too, but I expect she'll be able to read them. I thought she might like to include them in a village history, but maybe Hugh'd fancy casting an eye over them first.'

'Let me have a look at one of them,' Hugh said, resigned, 'and I'll tell you if they're likely to appeal to a wider market.'

'Gil's lent me three. I'll let you have one of those,' Berhane offered.

'Fine,' Hugh said. 'I'll pick it up tomorrow.'

'I rely on Berhane's judgement,' Gil said, 'but I'll be interested in what you think too.'

A poorly suppressed grunt of derision startled them. Joe Triggs stood at the end of the table with another bowl of chips. His dark brows were lowered and the bristles on his chin seemed to prickle more than ever. 'Chips,' he said shortly, banging the bowl down.

The group was silenced. All except for Edith, whose vague voice was heard clearly as she said, 'The Moor Diaries, Scandal and Secrets from a Hundred Years Ago. I wonder if it will be a bestseller.'

The village green was still and silent as they came out of the inn later in the evening. Hugh closed the door on the faint hum of male voices in the bar and fell into step beside Lucy as the women walked down the path to the gate.

'I am sorry to break things up so soon,' Berhane said as they crossed the lane and passed through the trees onto the open green, where there was no sign of the earlier snowfall. 'But having the hunt tomorrow means an early start.'

She led the way diagonally across the green towards the Church House. The grass was slippery under their feet as the collie trod gingerly over the cold ground. Their whitened breath rose in clouds towards the diamond brightness of the stars. They walked in silence for a few minutes, Edith falling back to drift along behind the others.

A slight movement beside the trees on their right caught Ben's attention. Hugh paused, calling him to heel, looking to see what had attracted him as the women came to a halt too. The nearly full moon cast stark black patterns across the open space but there were few lights in the buildings edging the lane beyond the trees, so at first Hugh could not see anything. Then a low russet form trotted out of the shadow under one tree to be briefly visible in the moonlight before it disappeared into another patch of darkness. Hugh seized Ben's collar as the dog's nose twitched excitedly. He squirmed as Hugh latched his lead on.

'Will the hunt make things difficult for you with the dinner in the evening?' Lucy asked Berhane as they set off again. 'I can come and give you a hand when you get back, if you like.'

'Thanks, Lucy. Freda, one of the local women who lives near the inn, is generally going to help out with my dinners. This time she's going to do all the vegetables, with some help from Aunt Susannah. So I think I'll be okay, but if the hunt goes on for hours I'll be glad to know you're there to call on.'

'I suppose it's difficult to know how long you might be out,' Hugh said. 'Where do you start from?'

'Here,' Berhane replied. She pointed down the green to the house whose bulk was visible in the gap between the trees, a couple of lights still shining out above the hedge that screened it. 'That's Gil's place. He keeps the hounds there, and his horses, so we all meet on the green. There's usually about twenty-five riders, and three times as many followers.'

'Isn't it unusual to keep hounds so close to the village?' Hugh asked curiously. 'Surely they must make a lot of noise.'

'A bit,' Berhane agreed. 'But nobody minds.'

'It's traditional,' Edith murmured. 'Gil's father and his grand-father and his great-grandfather all kept the hounds there.' Her words faded as if her energy had drained away. 'And now Gil has no son to leave it to, so the tradition will die out.'

'He's got years yet to have a son, or a daughter for that matter,' Berhane said.

'Mmm,' Edith said. Her voice suddenly strengthened. 'Why did your friend Mike stay behind?' she asked, turning to Hugh. 'He said it was for another drink, but he really wanted to talk to

Joe, didn't he?'

'I expect it was both things,' Hugh said, rather taken aback.

'Why did he want to talk to Joe?' Edith persisted. 'He doesn't know him, does he?'

'He's interested in Joe's great-grandfather's collections,' Berhane said. 'Mike was telling me about the stones in the hall, and I mentioned that the old man had been part of a group that was involved in examining and excavating some of the early settlements on the moor. I think he kept most of their findings.'

Edith nodded. 'Oh yes. That's why Joe always thought they'd found some kind of treasure. His granddad was forever dropping peculiar hints about it when we were children.' As they passed the Schoolhouse on their right she added vaguely, 'Perhaps Joe will think that's what Mike is after. Maybe that's why Anna stayed behind, to protect Mike when he gets into trouble. Or to tell him how stupid he's been.'

Hugh closed his eyes briefly. Lucy took his arm and shook it affectionately. 'What time will the hunt set out?' she asked Berhane.

'Susannah organises the breakfast at the village hall from eight,' Berhane gestured toward the church as they passed it. 'You can't really see it from here, but it's to the left of the church gate, behind that high hedge. Then Joe provides the stirrup cup and off we go at about ten. Gil's going out early to check on the team of lads laying the aniseed trail. There was a bit too much fooling around last time Gil took the hounds out, so he wants to keep an eye on things. The lads need to keep well ahead of us, they've to lay a good number of false leads as well as the main trail.'

'Gil will have an early start,' Hugh commented. 'It'll still be quite dark; won't it be difficult for him?'

'Not really. Gil and his horses know this ground like nobody else. He'll be keen to join the hunt as soon as possible, at least by the time we get up onto the moor,' Berhane said as she reached her front door. She glanced up at the sky. 'Unless cloud comes over again by morning the light won't be too bad for him.'

Ben sniffed at the step and turned back to face the green, sitting down with a resigned grunt.

Berhane looked at him. 'He'll enjoy a good run if you go walking with Mike tomorrow. It's quite a distance to Riven Tor.' She glanced at Lucy. 'You'll probably remember the route when you get higher up on the moor. We used to take picnics over there from the farm in the summer holidays.'

Lucy nodded. 'I know. But I expect it'll look different at this time of year.'

'It will,' Berhane said, 'so watch where you put your feet. The rocks may well be wet and there are old mine workings you don't want to fall into.'

'We'll be careful,' Lucy assured her.

'Keep an eye on the weather too,' Berhane said. 'It's supposed to be okay until the evening, but you can never be sure. You don't want to be up there in a snowstorm. It's a fair distance to go, you'd best get off as early as you can.' She loosened the wide shawl that sheltered her dark hair, allowing it to fall back onto her shoulders. 'Betsey, Joe's cook, lays on lunch for the riders whenever we get back. Join us if you're here, although it'll be pretty rowdy. You'll probably want to take food with you too. Betsey will pack something if you ask.' She smiled. 'Joe'll moan but don't take any notice. Betsey's his sister-in-law as well as the cook, and she really runs the inn. She's even learned to do the accounts online. Really, if it weren't for Joe's manner they'd be doing very well at the inn.' She glanced at Hugh. 'There's a real nature versus nurture situation with Joe and his brother Eli. Their father was an elder at the local chapel, very outwardly religious, even in the naming of his sons. Joe is actually Joshua and Eli is Elijah. But old Mr Triggs, from all I've gathered, was a cantankerous person, who specialised in setting people against each other. And his sons have either inherited or learned the trait. Mr Triggs' biggest success was with his sons, right up to his dying day, when he left the inn to Joe, the younger, with no mention of Eli. Eli's never spoken to Joe since, so it's rich that it's Eli's wife who's really keeping things going. Left to Joe I suspect the inn wouldn't last long. Anyway, Joe'll be harassing Betsey at the moment, he's put out at having the hunt arrangements changed, but she takes him in her stride. She's had plenty of practice. He and her husband are like twin peas in a pod.'

'That wasn't the only reason Joe was grumpy tonight,' Edith said dreamily. 'He's all upset about everything right now.' She drifted past Berhane into the churchyard without another word and Hugh looked after her, surprised.

Don't mind Edith,' Berhane said. 'She likes being out in the starlight. Sometimes she lives in a different world to us.'

'She always did,' Lucy said. 'She hasn't changed at all.'

'Have any of us?' Berhane asked. 'Maybe we just know ourselves better as we get older.'

Hugh had only been listening with half an ear, his eyes running appreciatively over the Church House. 'I don't know much about these buildings,' he commented. 'Were they used for something in particular?'

'Mainly for sustaining parishioners who came in from a distance across the moor for services in the church. I guess bread and home-brew featured strongly,' Berhane said.

Ben whined and put a paw up against Hugh's knee.

'We'd better let you get in,' Lucy said to her friend, 'and take Ben round the green. I don't want him waking up too early tomorrow and upsetting Joe even more.'

'Joe'll be up before it's light,' Berhane assured her, opening the front door. 'He's riding too. He's as keen on the hunt as Gil, and has been its treasurer for years, well before Gil took it over. Joe will want everything in order at the inn before he sets off, although it'll be Betsey who makes sure it is. So don't worry about disturbing him when you get up. Sleep well, and I'll see you sometime tomorrow.'

'Goodnight,' Lucy said. Hugh raised a hand in farewell and they turned away, hearing the door close behind them.

Lucy tucked her hand in Hugh's arm. 'Let's go round the green,' she suggested. 'It's a lovely night.'

He looked at her, enjoying the pink tinge the cold had put into her cheeks and the sparkle in her hazel eyes.

She pulled the flaps of her woollen hat more tightly together, pushing a loose strand of chestnut hair out of her eyes as she smiled at him. 'Come on,' she tugged gently at his arm. 'It's too cold to stand around any longer.'

'I suppose I shouldn't let Ben off again,' Hugh said uncertainly as the collie jerked his other arm, pulling hard on the lead.

'No,' Lucy said firmly. 'We don't want him wandering off on a scent. That fox trail is so fresh it will be far too interesting.'

They began to walk over the green towards Gil's house, Ben doing his best to drag them forwards through the blackness under the trees. 'I would have thought it's too cold for more snow,' Lucy commented. She looked up at the sky. 'And there are no clouds anyway.'

'But who knows how long it'll stay like this,' Hugh said. 'I think Berhane's right, we'd better set off in good time tomorrow to get to Riven Tor. Do you have any idea how far it is?'

'It's about four miles from Ballamy's Farm,' Lucy said, 'and I guess it'll be a bit more from here. But most of it's uphill.'

'I suppose we could take a car part of the way,' Hugh mused, as Ben yanked him to the edge of the lane.

'That's not a good idea,' Lucy said, waiting as Hugh allowed Ben to cross to the hedge that screened Gil's house. 'If we get caught up with the hunt followers we could be delayed for quite a while. And we don't want one of our cars stranded out in the wilds if it does come on to snow again.'

Hugh sighed, letting Ben sniff eagerly along the laurel trunks. The dog paused frequently, cocking his leg industriously. Nearby a hound yelped, setting off others in a chorus of barking. Gil's voice could be heard quietening them and Hugh guiltily pulled a reluctant collie back onto the green.

'Oh well,' he said resignedly. 'I suppose we'll have to make the best of it. We can't let Mike go alone, and there's no chance that he'll change his mind.'

'Not the slightest,' Lucy agreed as they began to walk back across the green. 'And at least if we're with them there's not so much opportunity for him and Anna to argue.'

'Hmm.' Hugh sounded unconvinced.

'Really,' Lucy insisted. 'They won't have the breath, anyway, let alone the energy.'

'Let's see,' Hugh said noncommittally. 'I was surprised Anna wanted to come too. I know she's a strong walker, but even so...'

His voice tailed off as Lucy's laugh rang out, silvery in the icy night.

'When it's a choice between walking with Mike and staying around here with Edith, then the first option could look almost attractive,' she said. 'Anna's such a happy-go-lucky person that it seems particularly unfair that she's stuck with that kind of choice here.'

'Edith is...,' Hugh hesitated, searching for the right description. 'Rather odd,' he finished lamely.

'She's alright,' Lucy said. 'She's always been like it. She's there with you but never obviously part of the scene. Although,' Lucy added thoughtfully, 'I'm beginning to think she's more aware of what's going on around her than I once realised.'

'Do you think she's putting it on, this vagueness?' Hugh asked curiously.

'No,' Lucy answered, considering the idea, 'but perhaps it isn't as all encompassing as it appears. She's always been woolly-minded, and that does get under Anna's skin. I sometimes wondered at school if Edith enjoyed that. Look,' she said, gesturing to the house set back beyond the foot of the terraced cottages, 'that's the Schoolhouse where Edith's aunt Susannah lives. Gran's car is in the drive.' Lucy's eyes ran over the house. 'It looks like they've gone to bed. I expect tomorrow's going to be a busy day for Susannah from the sounds of it. She's running the hunt breakfast first thing. I hope she's going to be up to it, after this evening's shock.'

Hugh looked puzzled for a moment. 'Ahh,' he said, realising what Lucy was referring to, 'Berhane's intruder. Somebody does seem to have targeted her. Expecting the newcomer to be vulnerable, perhaps.'

'Still, it is odd,' Lucy said thoughtfully. 'I wonder if it had anything to do with locking us in the church.'

Hugh shrugged. 'It's hard to tell. Come on, Lucy, we'll have an early start in the morning too.'

They moved on, pausing now and again for Ben to sniff around. 'It's going to be an interesting weekend. I like Berhane. She's got quite a personality.'

Lucy smiled happily. 'Yes, she's a great person.'

'Did Edith mind having an adopted sister?' Hugh asked.

'Not that I ever knew,' Lucy replied. 'Of course, Berhane was already on the scene when Anna and I first went to boarding school and met her and Edith. It was quite a romantic story, you know, and Anna and I were fascinated by it and Berhane when we were girls.'

'Why?'

'Well, Gil Ballamy, Edith's father, was involved with a farming charity that was trying to help in Ethiopia after some war or famine. While he was out there he came across Berhane's family. Her parents were dead and she was being brought up by her older brother, who was well known to Gil. Something happened to the brother, and Gil decided to bring Berhane up with his own daughter. He brought her back to England, and the first anybody knew about it was when he turned up at the farm with her.'

Hugh whistled softly. 'Not a recommendation for a happy family,' he commented.

'I don't know,' Lucy said thoughtfully. 'You see, Berhane is very like him in personality. I don't think I was aware of that before. But you can see what made him want to give her an opportunity.'

'Oh yes, particularly with Edith drifting along in counter-point,' Hugh said dryly. 'What about his wife, Edith's mother?'

'Mary.' Lucy pursed her lips briefly. 'I think she just accepted whatever Gil did. She always seemed to take everything in her stride.'

'Is Edith like her?'

'No, not at all,' Lucy said, her voice trembling with laughter. 'Anna and I were talking about her earlier and we decided Mary was eminently practical, with not an ounce of imagination in her body. Edith isn't like anybody in the family, as far as I know.'

'A changeling,' Hugh commented idly.

'She is rather like that,' Lucy admitted. 'A bit fey and other worldly, but,' she finished slowly, 'with odd flashes of aware-ness. I think, you know, she may always have had those. I just didn't notice when we were younger.'

Ahead of them a figure trudged away from the pub along the side lane, turning in at the gate of the second cottage in the terrace above the Schoolhouse. A light sprang on in the cottage, but its neighbours lay in darkness. In the inn the brightly lit windows darkened one after the other as Joe presumably went round turning the lights off. At last only the outside light shone like a beacon in front of the low thatched building, which seemed to be settling itself down comfortably behind the trees for the night. The starlight seemed even brighter, the Plough constellation hanging directly above the pub.

Hugh paused, drawing Lucy to a halt too as he looked up at the arc of the sky. 'There's Cassiopeia, like a giant sideways M,' he said. 'See, and that little cluster is the Pleiades.' He spun round. 'So Orion should be behind us. Yes, there's his sword belt, right above the moor.'

Lucy followed his pointing hand, admiring the glittering bar of stars, before she tugged at his other arm. 'Come on. Let's go in. We don't want to upset Joe even more by making him wait up for us.'

THREE

Horses and hounds milled around the village green in a state of excited anticipation, their hooves and paws churning up the wet ground into muddy mush. Voices were loud as riders called to each other over the barking of the hounds, greeting friends, commenting on the weather, exchanging news. A pigeon homing in on its usual perch in one of the oaks only landed briefly before beating its wings hard to rise again, startled by the din and movement.

Isobel was glad to be in the inn garden, warmly wrapped in her green loden coat, well away from the general hubbub. She was even more glad that she had left Juno in the Schoolhouse. The little spaniel was ageing noticeably, her eyesight and hearing both failing, and she would have been upset by the turmoil on the green.

Glancing at her watch, Isobel was surprised to find it was only a quarter to ten. She had risen at seven, concerned that Susannah might be suffering after her encounter with the intruder at Church House the night before. Susannah had been physically intact, bruised perhaps, but she had still seemed unusually shaken when Berhane had brought her home. Nonetheless she had shrugged off Berhane's persuasive attempt to get her to hand over the hunt breakfast to somebody else, determined not to allow the intruder to affect her plans.

Entering the kitchen that morning, Isobel was not much surprised to find Susannah had already gone to the village hall, leaving a note to encourage Isobel to follow at her leisure. After a cup of tea and a slice of toast in the Schoolhouse, it was not quite eight o'clock when Isobel had left Juno ensconced in her own small fleece-lined bed. The spaniel had lifted her head curiously as her mistress ate and pottered to the door when Isobel had put her coat on, but she had shown no sign of wanting to go with her mistress into the cold world outdoors.

There had been quite a few horses tied to the long rail outside the village hall when Isobel had passed it. A tall, broad-shouldered man had just been coming round the hedge that screened the rail from the hall, calling over his shoulder to somebody behind him.

He was bright-eyed and alert as he greeted Isobel cheerfully. 'Hello, you must be Susannah's friend. I'm Gil Hannaford, from the foot of the green.'

'Yes, I'm Isobel Rossington. I'm just going to see if I can help Susannah.'

'She's got everything well in hand,' he had said, 'but I'm sure she can always use a bit more help. I've just had the right breakfast to set out on, and it's a lovely morning for riding.'

The horses tied to the rail had shifted impatiently, a grey in the trio nearest to Gil stamping from hoof to hoof. Gil had grinned. 'They can't wait to go, and my Java is going to be peeved. I only got him recently and Berhane's trying him out today, so I'm taking her Acer instead.'

Isobel had stood to one side, watching him untie the reins of a tall bay gelding and mount in one swift movement. Gil was certainly an impressive figure in his hunting pink, his brass buttons so brightly burnished that they gleamed like his highly polished boots, even in the dull morning light. As Gil had turned the bay, raising a hand to Isobel, the grey horse who was still at the rail had whickered, tossing his head, fretful at being left behind. The chestnut beyond stood still, glancing sideways from one liquid dark eye.

In the hall the organisation had been formidable, just Susannah and two other village women providing scrambled eggs, sausages, bacon, black pudding and fried bread for the men and women who were just beginning to drift in. Berhane was there, her dark hair in a loose ponytail hanging above the neck of her white shirt. She dispensed endless supplies of tea and coffee, chatting easily as she filled the cups, moving between the crowded tables without haste.

Isobel had made herself useful passing out full plates, especially to the people gathering outside, and collecting in the empty ones, grateful that she was not needed to play a part in the actual cooking. Betsey, the inn cook, had brought over a mountain of eggs from her own hens, and Isobel had watched it diminish rapidly in a large chipped bowl with a slight feeling of disbelief.

In a brief pause in the plate relay she had looked out of the door as somebody else came in on a draught of cold air. The space between the hall and the hedge that screened the rail was full of people, scooping up their breakfast from plates balanced on one hand as they chatted animatedly. Nobody there seemed to feel the cold, warmed perhaps by the animated buzz that filled the air. Or perhaps by the stirrup cup that seemed already to be circulating, handed round by a dour-looking man, immaculate in a dark-blue coat and tan breeches. The inn landlord, Isobel guessed.

It was with a sense of great relief that she had finally helped to stack the dirty plates in the hall's dishwasher, clattering in the cutlery as the last riders left, banging the door noisily behind them. Sent to the inn garden by Susannah to help pass the stirrup cup round, Isobel had found the village green was already full of mounted riders. The rail outside the hall stood unused and looking around Isobel had seen Berhane's tall figure very erect on the back of the grey who had been tied there earlier.

As Isobel stood now in the inn garden, glad to be able to relax, the scene that lay before her was a colourful one. The hunting pink of a few of the riders' coats was vivid against the blue and green of the majority and the darker shades of the horses and hounds. The sun was brightening, but it brought no warmth to the morning so clouded breath rose in swirls above the masses of people and animals. She sipped gratefully at the hot wine in the small metal cup she had been handed by the landlord, who was now mounting his own gelding.

Susannah was on horseback now, riding the chestnut who had been one of the early trio of horses at the hall rail. She mingled with the riders, her face glowing from the cold as she spoke to one person, then another, swinging round to respond to calls from all sides. Isobel, watching, realised that Susannah probably knew and was known by everyone there. Perhaps, Isobel thought, many of them had been taught by her. Although, she realised, there's such a range of ages that can't be the only way they know her. I suppose they're all locals.

As the speculations crossed Isobel's mind Susannah pushed her horse through the crowd and brought her up to the inn garden gate. 'I'm just going to take Raine off for a ride, away from the hunt,' she called, leaning down a little as she patted the horse's arched neck. 'Otherwise she'll want to go with the others when they move off. I won't be long, and when I get back we'll have coffee at home.' She sat back and edged her horse through the throng along the main lane, past the cottages tucked back in their gardens and out of the village to the east.

Susannah had only been gone a few minutes when a horn sounded, blowing a long clear blast and two pink-coated riders, the whippers-in, collected the hounds into a seething pack at the southern end of the green. When another blast of the horn came the hunt moved off along the lane that led towards the moor beyond Gil's house.

Within a few minutes they had gone, followed by the crowd of onlookers in Landrovers, 4x4s and on quad bikes, and the green fell strangely silent. Isobel squeezed her empty cup onto a crowded tray on a garden table and began to walk slowly round the edge of the open space, under the trees that lined the encircling lane. She looked at the cottages that ran along the top of the green, but the doors were shut and nobody was to be seen. By the time she reached the churchyard Isobel felt she was the only person left in the village. She looked over the church gate, admiring the fine white rime thatching the lichened stones that stood crookedly above the wet grass. Moving on, she caught a faint movement in the window of the Church House next door. Glancing up she saw a pale blurred face looking down at her. Edith, she guessed, raising a hand in greeting. There was no response, so Isobel walked on.

The sound of hooves on the lane behind her made Isobel turn round. Susannah was coming up to her, clearly holding Raine in as the mare trotted eagerly along.

Isobel waited until Susannah reached her, but the mare did not stop. As Susannah passed she pointed ahead with her crop and called, 'I'm taking her to Gil's stable. I keep her there.'

Isobel raised a hand and followed on, crossing the bottom lane and following the line of the side hedge to the yard beyond a large sprawling house. Edwardian, Isobel guessed, but perhaps a bit earlier, with lots of additions. The field opposite the yard was full of Landrovers, 4x4s, horseboxes and trailers, all in neat rows across the turf, which was scored black with tyre tracks.

The yard that Isobel entered was lined with stables, all the stalls eerily empty now, except for Raine who stood in front of one of them. Her saddle already hung over the half door and Susannah was rubbing her down as Isobel approached.

Susannah lifted her head without ceasing work. 'It was a poor imitation of a ride,' she said, 'but I can't use Raine to follow the hunt. We're both of us too old, but we'd still be tempted to join in. But,' she added, moving round to the mare's other side, 'I had her out for a good hack yesterday, so we'll have to be content with that.'

'Gil's got quite a set-up here,' Isobel commented, looking round with interest.

'Yes, he has,' Susannah agreed. 'He keeps quite a number of horses on livery, like Raine and Berhane's Acer. Other people leave their horses here overnight before the hunt. It was crowded with people saddling up by the time Gil left this morning. And of course Berhane inveigled him into letting her ride his new grey, so he's gone out on her horse. They arranged it when she went down to the stables to saddle up. She's very persuasive.' She smiled. 'I'd have done that once; I was always keen to ride a new horse.' She shrugged a trifle ruefully. 'Joe Triggs, the land-lord from the inn, was down very early; he keeps his gelding here too. Gil told me when he came for his breakfast that Joe had already been and gone, taking his horse up to the inn to be ready in good time. It's the only occasion any of us see Joe looking happy, when he's going out with the hunt.' Susannah jerked her head backwards. 'The kennels are over there. State of the art, and Gil's always doing something to improve them. Nothing's too good for his hounds.'

Isobel walked over the yard, picking her way carefully between the litter of straw, horse dung and dog droppings. A faint sound of barking and voices made her look up towards the high moor. There, half way up the slope, the hounds were racing ahead with the horses strung out in a line behind them, the few pink coats vivid like drops of blood on the dark background.

The sound of the hunt, hounds baying and faint wordless shouts, assailed the four walkers who had just reached the high moor. They had set out from the inn at eight o'clock that morning and found the wide village green already full of people, streaming up from Gil's stables towards the hall next to the churchyard. The hall was not visible from the green, hidden by its thick hedge. But horses were tied to the rail in front of the hedge, reminding Lucy of a scene from a Western transposed to the English coun-tryside, watched as they were by somnolent pigeons perched in the branches of the nearest oak. She caught sight of Isobel going round the hedge, just before a solitary rider came out and rode away down the lane, against the flow, exchanging greetings with other riders as they passed.

The walkers had found the lane past Gil's house was slippery with mud, so Lucy had picked her way along it with care. Anna kept pace with her, glowing in her red duffle coat. She had risked wearing her fur hood, and the tassels at the end swung backwards and forwards as she walked.

Mike strode on without pausing, narrowly missing a group of people who appeared from the stable yard, clearly heading for their breakfasts. Behind them other riders had been bustling about, while their horses stamped impatiently in front of the stalls. The predominant noise, though, came from the hounds, barking in frenzied excitement in their kennels.

The sounds had died away as the walkers went on along the lane, keeping away from the stone walls on either side to avoid the fallen leaves, oak, hazel and ash mixed into a wet russet mush. The walls had been too high to see over, topped as they were with unkempt hedges. Hart's tongue fern was still green in crevices in the stone wall, and here and there long bleached grasses hung down, concealing the thorny strands of bramble that arched out to trap the unwary. Through occasional gateways Lucy had spotted rounded outcrops of rock in one of the fields, just like giant cottage loaves, and wondered if they had given their name to the field. Bun Meadow, perhaps. Something for her to look up, she had thought, as she had lengthened her stride to catch up with the others.

Rooks had cawed from their perches in the trees on the far side of the walls. Drops of water fell from the bare branches onto the heads of the walkers, occasionally slipping down an unguarded gap in scarves to chill their skin.

Hugh fell back at one point, watching a bullfinch feeding on the few desiccated remains of blackberries on one of the bushes. The bird's rosy pink breast was as bright a beacon as Anna's coat in the winter landscape. Mike's stentorian bellow brought his attention back to the group as they stood by a footpath sign, and he stepped out again to catch them up.

Walking was easier once they had left the lane behind, branching off on the footpath that Gil had mentioned to Mike, past the home-made sign warning of the damaged bridge. The wind was more noticeable though, blowing coldly from the west, and there had been little conversation as they had followed Mike's determined lead along the worn track that bisected the small meadows.

The only sign of life here had been the thin grey spiral of smoke rising from the chimney of the house at the foot of the high moor. Hugh had peered curiously at it as he passed a gap in the holly hedge that bordered the place. It was difficult to tell what the cottage was like as trees in the garden partly hid it. The house appeared to be large and modern, in what looked like a standard construction, probably with amazing views from the picture windows that looked on one side towards the village and, on the other, back up to the moor.

It was beyond the house that they had come to the bridge, forewarned by the sound of water tumbling, loud among the sallows and alders that fringed it. Mike had waved them to a halt before stepping cautiously over a wooden bar onto the planks, one hand grasping the single handrail.

Anna had bitten her lip hard to keep back a gurgle of laughter, avoiding Lucy's eyes, as Mike had bounced up and down, before walking backwards and forwards across it.

'It's fine,' Mike had announced from the far side. 'Come on over.'

They had followed and Anna could no longer contain herself. 'It does look as though other people have found it safe too,' she had said lightly. 'Look at all the footprints.'

Mike's eyes had flickered downwards, his brows contracting with fury. He had said nothing, but turned uphill, almost slipping on the slope as his heels dug into the wet ground.

From here on the gradient had increased swiftly from steep to very steep. Anna had kept her head down once they were out of the tree shelter, trying to avoid the biting chill that stung her face as they had climbed upwards. Mike had set a cracking pace, and Anna was damned if she was going to ask him to slow down, although the rucksack she bore seemed to get heavier with every step.

The summit had been reached at last, and Mike had finally stopped amongst the rocky clitter that was scattered beneath the rampart-like tor to their right. He had consulted his map, comparing it with the terrain ahead, turning his head from side to side as he picked out landmarks.

Careful not to show the relief she had felt at the pause, Anna stood next to Lucy on the rugged ridge of rocks that stuck like giant bones through the cropped grass. Lucy was watching Mike, but Anna stared around at the scene spread out before them.

The boulders were encrusted with silvery-grey lichen, which also grew in miniature rock gardens on the flatter lumps of stone. Below her on the left the slope was covered in hawthorn scrub, where a flight of fieldfares dipped into the bushes, feeding on berries the colour of dried blood.

On her other side the open moor stretched away like the flank of a huge animal, clothed in a wet bronze pelt of crumpled bracken. Isolated trees stood here and there, battered branches pointing the way back towards the village. Further away, stacks of heavy granite rose in bleak grey towers, stretching off to the south and west like ominous sentinels of the wilderness.

A kestrel hovered nearby, close enough for her to see his fierce eyes as he scanned the crevices for movement. Ben found these fascinating too as he pottered around, picking up new scents, wandering off on the trail of the various creatures that had trekked across the ground.

They were high above the village here and Anna looked down the way they had come. The path up to the ridge was lined with holly trees, their prickly leaves a shining green. Here and there one still bore bright red berries, flaunting the colour to attract passing birds. Beyond the path the brook was out of sight but she could see the fields that separated the village from the slope of the high moor. She drew a grateful breath as she tried to pick out the places she knew.

Although it was brightly lit by the sunshine the valley was a subdued landscape, dull green highlighted here and there with the black of trees and hedges. The village was marked by the whitewashed tower of the church, which stood out like a dirty cream beacon. Houses looked like a child's toys, and in the field beside Gil's house rows of tiny vehicles sparkled in the clear light. There was no movement to be seen there, but below the ridge Anna could see the hounds and horses streaming across the flank of the high moor, rushing full pelt towards a copse of trees to the west.

'Are they supposed to catch up with the people laying the trail?' Anna asked, wondering where the scent went as she looked round more generally. 'I don't think I'd like that lot finding me.'

Hugh shook his head. 'Not if they're smart. They had a good two-hour head start, time to lay several false trails. I don't know what the usual rules are, but in this case the hunt ends if they catch up with the trail layers. They win if they get across the finish line in one of Gil's fields before the hunt catches up with them. They aim to get there before two o'clock, I gather, giving the hunt a four hour run.'

Mike snorted angrily as he looked along the slope to the frenzied activity in the distance. 'I hope they watch where they're going,' he grunted. 'The damage they could do to sites up here is incalculable.'

Anna said sharply, 'Mike, you've been moaning about it for ages. Let's just get on to this place you want to see before the hunt gets there too.'

Before Mike could reply Lucy asked, 'Can we see the

prehistoric village yet?'

Mike swung round, pointing an arm towards a dimly visible tor that appeared to be on the distant horizon. 'There, those rocks are just above it. The site is on the far side.'

Anna drew in her breath and let it out again in a hiss as she studied the ground between them and their target, noting how the land in front of them rose and fell in steep slopes, but generally rising always towards that faraway tor. 'Mike, that's miles away,' she said in dismay.

'Hitch a lift on a horse then,' he snarled, 'or go back if you can't manage the walk.'

'It isn't as far as it looks,' Hugh said, considering the map in his own hand as Lucy called Ben back to her. 'If we circle round that way we'll avoid the worst of the terrain and come out beside Mike's site.' He gestured to his right, where a narrow gully ran south-westwards from the foot of the slope ahead of them. 'Otherwise there'll be a lot of going down and coming back up, and some nasty boggy areas. But watch where you're going along this bit by the gully. It's marked as a mine area, and the workings may be overgrown.'

'Mines would be pretty obvious though, wouldn't they?' Anna asked as Mike strode out ahead of them again. 'Surely they're fenced off, anyway?'

'Not necessarily. You're thinking of mines like the big Cornish ones,' Hugh replied. 'Here tin streaming was the more common form of mining. It involved digging trenches across deposits in valleys and making leats to bring water to wash through them, isolating the tin. That left a lot of ridges and pits, which are probably well hidden now. It's unlikely they could be easily fenced off, so that's why you need to take care.'

'I'd better keep Ben with me,' Lucy said as they strung out down the slope behind Mike. She called the collie, who had ranged ahead along a driftway between the rocks, and he came reluctantly back to her side.

Anna rounded a clump of gorse, still sprinkled with yellow

flowers, starting in surprise as she almost came face to face with a honey-coloured cow. The cow opened her huge eyes wide, still thoughtfully chewing the cud as she swung her heavy head slowly under the weight of wide horns, watching as Anna edged past.

Mike was already pushing through the scrubby gorse that ran along the top of the gully. He disappeared into a fringe of trees, mainly ashes. Long silvery grey strands of lichen hung like limp curtains from the branches, whose tips still had a few dried keys to rattle as Mike bumped into the trunks. Although he was out of sight the others could see the zigzag route he was following as the bushes shuddered and shook to mark his heavy passing.

'Let's hope Mike doesn't get lost in a trench,' Anna said, panting, as she saw him momentarily on the edge of the gully before he disappeared down into it. 'I wouldn't want to have to pull him out.'

As she spoke they heard Mike yell loudly in shock and surprise, the sound partly disguised by the crunching of branches and thumping of falling stones. Rooks exploded from the gully like black arrows, shooting through the air in different directions amidst loud alarm calls.

'Oh God, I didn't mean it,' Anna gasped, as she and Hugh quickened their pace anxiously. Lucy paused for a moment, clipping the lead on the indignant collie's collar, then hurried after the others.

They reached the bushes and pushed carelessly through them, snagging their clothes and gloves on prickly strands and sending water spraying into their faces as they slithered into the gully. Ahead of them they saw Mike's rucksack flung aside, and his figure bent over on the ground in a copse of small trees at the foot of the gully.

Anna's heart began to thump hard, and for a moment her vision blurred. When it cleared she saw that Mike had stood up and turned to face them, his square face white under the horrible black beanie that hid his red hair.

'He's dead,' Mike said, his voice unnaturally loud. 'Broken neck.'

Anna's glance fell to the figure at his feet, partly obscured still by the trees. A rider in tan breeches and a pink jacket lay awkwardly at the edge of the stream at the bottom of the gully. Beside one out-flung arm the oblivious water flowed gently over the rounded pebbles. 'Who is it?' she asked tremulously.

Lucy came up beside her, firmly holding Ben back. A pink coat, she noticed at once. Not many of the riders she had seen on the village green wore those.

'It's that bloke from the pub,' Mike said obliquely, his voice breaking into Lucy's racing thoughts.

Hugh shrugged his own rucksack off, dropping it on the ground against the trunk of a stunted sallow. He picked his way down the slope and bent over the body, peering under the hat at the face, half hidden by the clump of water mint in which it lay. Standing up again, Hugh glanced at his watch, noting the time. Eleven o'clock. 'It's definitely Gil Hannaford,' he said bleakly. 'He's broken his neck.'

He ignored the horrified gasps behind him and stood surveying the motionless body of the rider, taking in the drag marks on the clothes, the cuts in the once fastidiously polished boots and the broken branches of the bushes on the edge of the copse. 'He didn't fall here,' Hugh said shortly. 'Can you see his horse anywhere?'

They began to look round, spreading out in a wider search pattern through the trees as Hugh scanned the ground around the body, moving slowly. It was Anna who called out softly, 'Here he is. Don't come over. He's badly frightened.'

The others came back together beside Gil's body, standing still there, waiting, listening to Anna's voice, gentling, coaxing, for some time. It seemed like hours before she appeared, but Hugh, glancing again at his watch, saw that it was only a few minutes.

Anna was leading a tall bay gelding with some difficulty. The horse kept throwing back his head, the whites of his eyes showing, and Anna maintained a low flow of talk as she brought him over to her friends. He baulked as he got closer, and she stopped with him, reassuring him. 'Don't move suddenly,' she warned softly, 'or talk loudly. I can barely hold him as it is. And the saddle has come off. It's in a bush here, just above Gil.'

'What do we do now?' Mike demanded in a gruff whisper. 'We can't get the horse back like this, and we can't leave Hannaford here alone.'

Hugh's eyes were running over the horse. 'That's odd,' he said slowly. 'Why would the saddle come off? Wait here.'

Hugh cautiously skirted Anna and the horse before anyone could protest or question him. He moved slowly up the bank of the stream, branching off towards the spot where Anna had found the horse and walking carefully back towards the copse, following the route they had taken.

Behind him he left an oddly frozen scene. Only the horse moved, twitching and stamping nervously, while Anna murmured to him and her gloved hand moved soothingly over his sweating neck.

Hugh crouched down, disappearing behind a thicket. The others waited, wondering what he had found, restraining themselves from calling out to ask. Mike was beginning to shift restlessly from foot to foot by the time Hugh stood up again. It was only Lucy's hand on Mike's arm, and the warning glance that she threw him, that prevented him from speaking.

Hugh came back to join them, obviously picking his path with care. His pleasant face was set and hard when he reached them. 'The girth gave way,' he said harshly. 'I guess when the saddle slipped Hannaford must have fallen with his foot in the stirrup and been dragged along until the saddle came off the frightened horse. God knows at what stage Hannaford broke his neck.'

'Surely that's odd,' Lucy said quickly. 'Gil must have checked everything before he set out.'

'Yes,' Hugh said. Nothing more, but it was enough to make the others look at him sharply, as he got out his mobile, frowned at the 'no reception' symbol, and thrust it impatiently back into the pocket of his coat.

'You don't think it was an accident,' Lucy said quietly, her eyes widening.

'No.'

'Bloody hell,' Mike whispered, his tone angry enough to worry the horse, who shied nervously, 'not again. Not another bloody murder.'

'Be quiet, Mike,' Lucy said. 'Anna can barely hold that horse.' She stopped, cocking her head as Ben pricked his ears. The others heard it too, the sound of hounds baying, getting closer and closer.

'My God,' Hugh muttered. 'We don't want that lot down on us. Mike, come with me, we'll have to warn them off. Lucy, you stay here with Anna. Try to keep the pack off Hannaford's body.'

'Hugh, I can't,' Lucy said urgently to his retreating back. 'I don't want to be here with Ben when the hounds come down.'

Hugh and Mike were already scrambling in single file up the slope, carefully avoiding the crushed bushes that marked Gil Hannaford's last ride. Lucy looked around desperately and saw a faint wisp of smoke curling into the air above the firs higher up the other bank of the stream. 'Anna, there's a house up there. I'll see if I can stay there with Ben and call the police. You don't mind, do you?'

'No, get off quickly. I'll see if Dobbin and I can block the approach to Gil's body.'

Anna stood still, one hand firmly clutching the horse's reins, the other still stroking his neck, as she watched Lucy splash across the stream and pick her way hastily up the far slope, dragging a reluctant Ben with her. When Lucy disappeared behind the trees Anna tried to edge the gelding closer to Gil's body, but the horse tossed his head in terror, almost pulling the reins out of her hand. 'Alright, alright,' she said softly. 'That was silly of me, but we had to try.' She spent a few seconds calming the frightened animal, before she carefully pulled her mobile out of her duffle coat pocket, hoping against the odds that her mobile could pick up reception even though Hugh's could not. After staring at it for a few frustrated seconds she put it away again with a sigh of exasperation.

As Hugh and Mike came to a panting halt in the bushes above the gully the sound of the hunt was louder, audible above the pounding of the blood in their ears. Hounds were baying more frantically, people shouted, the ground reverberated to thudding hooves, and the noise was obviously getting closer.

The riders were strung out across two fenced fields to the south, while behind them a gaggle of vehicles made their way through a gateway, all heading towards the spot where Hugh and Mike stood. Just above the two men the sun was bright on the pink coat of a solitary rider, who was picking his way carefully over the rocky ridge the walkers had recently crossed. Patchwork hounds milled around him until one lifted its head, baying triumphantly, and led the pack downhill towards the gully, followed by the rider. The rest of the hunt was pouring over the last fence onto the open moor. They changed direction to join the hounds, crossing in front of the line of vehicles emerging from the field, which paused to let the riders pass.

Hugh had time to think how primeval the scene was, with the hunter on the horizon, the riders and hounds bearing down on the two men below. For an instant he felt the eternal fear of the hunted.

Beside him Mike swore fluently. 'Bloody hell, how do we stop this lot?' He did not wait for a reply, but began to run forward, stumbling over the roots of gorse bushes and heather clumps, a string of mumbled curses faintly audible through his heavy breathing.

Hugh joined him, waving his arms vigorously to attract the riders' attention as the horses approached, but the hounds poured past him, intent on the scent they were following. The first rider, a threatening figure in his dark coat, loomed up above the two men, and Hugh and Mike came to a halt, shouting to him to stop.

The rider's face under his hat was twisted with fury, and it was only as his raised arm brought a crop down heavily that Hugh recognised Joe Triggs. The landlord was bellowing abuse as the crop struck Hugh, who stumbled, raising his own arms to protect his head. Joe brought his horse round, barging against Hugh and knocking him down.

Mike grabbed the reins and dragged the horse to a stand, reaching up to seize the arm that Joe had lifted again. With a heave he brought Joe off the horse to land heavily on the ground, just missing Hugh's still form.

Mike fell on the innkeeper, seizing the crop and throwing it to one side. As Joe struggled to his feet Mike raised one fist and hit him hard on the chin. The landlord staggered, keeping his balance with difficulty, trying to fend off Mike.

Horses were milling all around the fighting men, their breath puffing out great clouds of mist. Riders were leaping to the ground, but it was Berhane who got to the struggle first, just as Joe fell to the ground and stayed down.

'Mike, what the hell are you doing?' she yelled, leaning across her horse towards him.

Mike swung round, his square face suffused with angry colour. 'For God's sake,' he yelled, glaring at the furious riders running towards him. 'There's a dead man down there. We're trying to stop you fools riding over him and this maniac attacks us.'

'We thought you were demonstrators, trying to disrupt the hunt. Even when it's a drag hunt we don't get any peace,' a man shouted. 'How do we know you aren't just here to make trouble?' He pulled Mike away as another rider helped the landlord to his feet, restraining him as he lunged towards Mike.

'I know them,' Berhane called, dismounting and looping her horse's reins over her hand.

She followed Hugh as he pushed his way through the circle of riders to stand next to Mike. Hugh's face was badly scratched on one side and he walked with a slight limp, cradling his left arm awkwardly across his chest.

Mike glanced out of the corner of his eye at him. 'The other fellow will look worse,' he muttered. 'Is it broken?' He jerked his head at Hugh's arm.

'No,' Hugh grunted. 'Thanks, Mike.'

Berhane barely noticed the exchange. 'Who's dead?' she demanded urgently.

'Gil Hannaford,' Mike said abruptly. 'His neck's broken.'

Berhane's eyes widened. Her grey gelding snickered, trying to throw back his head as Berhane's hand tightened involuntarily on the reins. 'Gil?' she repeated slowly. 'Are you sure?'

'Yes,' Hugh said. 'And the scene mustn't be disturbed until the police get here.' He groaned, using his right hand to wipe away the drops of water running down his face from his uncovered wet hair. 'I suppose the hounds are down there now.' He looked round as he spoke, spotting his fur-lined hat trampled into the ground beneath a sea of hooves.

'We'll call them off,' one of the whippers-in said.

'Wait,' Hugh said urgently. 'The damage has already been done, but don't trample the ground more than you have to.' He turned and looked back the way he and Mike had come up the slope and through the bushes. 'That's our route, you can see the marks on the grass. Keep to that as far as you can. Over there,' Hugh pointed, 'is where Hannaford was dragged when he fell. And it looks as though that's the way the pack went,' he said grimly. 'But nonetheless keep to our track as much as possible.' He scanned the land above the gully. 'I suppose the best thing is to take the hounds away down the stream. And for God's sake,' he looked round furiously as the two whippers-in went cautiously forwards, 'the rest of you keep back.'

Beyond the massed ranks of riders and horses came the sound of more voices. Hugh shifted, trying to see who was coming. Of course, he realised, the followers were wondering what was happening. 'Keep the others away,' he said sharply. 'We don't want any more people here. Get them all back down to the village and wait for the police. Somebody must ring them as soon as possible. Ask for Chief Inspector Elliot. Say Hugh Carey thinks he should be here.'

'Who are you to tell us what to do?' Joe demanded belligerently, shaking off the hands that held him back. 'We ought to see what we can do for Gil. It's not right to leave him there alone.'

'He won't be alone,' Berhane said huskily. 'I'll go down, but the rest of you do what Hugh says. He knows what he's talking about.' She saw the dark glances and heard the muttering. 'You know Gil,' she said, raising her voice to be heard by the others. 'All of you know Gil. Why would he be down there in the first place? It's not a good spot to ride. Can you believe that he fell just like that?' Heads were shaken slowly. 'Well, I can't,' Berhane continued. 'He was riding my Acer, and he's a sound horse. Gil and he knew each other and rode together often. There's something wrong about this and I mean to know what it is.'

The voices fell silent and eyes became wary as the riders considered what she had said.

Berhane had seen Hugh glance at her as she spoke and turned quickly to him. 'Acer?' she asked anxiously. 'Is he injured too?' She passed her reins over to another rider. 'Please take Java back with you, Liz. He shouldn't stand around in this cold.'

Berhane pushed through the hovering riders and began to walk quickly towards the gully behind the whippers-in, leaving a rising tide of voices behind her. Hugh and Mike caught up with her as Hugh said, 'The horse seems to be fine. Nervous, but uninjured. Anna's down there and she's got him. She was managing him well.'

'Poor Anna,' Berhane said. 'She really doesn't like horses.' She increased her pace. 'And the hounds won't be helping if they're all milling around. Although I can't believe the scent trail will take them down there, but Acer's hooves may smell of it if he crossed any of the aniseed.'

Mike grunted and muttered something inaudible. He lengthened his stride, almost catching Berhane on the heels as she followed Hugh, who had taken the lead.

Ahead of them they could hear the yells of one of the whippers-in, urgent above the excited whimpering of the hounds. 'I didn't think of that,' Hugh said guiltily as they reached the edge of the gully. 'I hope Anna's coping alright.'

Berhane glanced at him. 'She always manages. 'You do think there's something wrong about this, don't you? I knew as soon as you spoke.'

Hugh nodded. 'Yes. You'll see why for yourself.'

She stopped on the edge of the gully, staggering as Mike, taken by surprise, bumped heavily into her. Recovering her balance, she looked across the scrubby bushes and trees, raising one hand to shield her eyes from the sun reflecting brightly off the rocky outcrops. 'Gil certainly wouldn't have come down here deliberately,' she said. 'It's riddled with mine trenches, far too dangerous for horses. He knows that, he's ridden here all his life.'

'He didn't mean to come down,' Hugh said grimly. 'He fell up here above the gully, but must have had a foot caught in the stirrup and was dragged down towards the stream before the saddle came off.'

Berhane's hand dropped as she turned to stare at him. 'The saddle came off?' she repeated flatly. 'I just don't believe it.' She began to walk down the slope, spotting her gelding by the copse. Her eyes fell on Anna, standing next to him beside the stream, beleaguered by the hounds milling around her and the horse. The grey was sidling and stamping anxiously while Anna hung on grimly to the reins close to his bit. Just beyond her one of the whippers-in had dismounted, leaving his own horse tethered to a sallow some distance away, to straddle Gil's fallen body, pushing away any hounds that came too close.

Hugh looked down, wondering briefly where Lucy had gone, as the hounds at last began to run downstream, encouraged vocally by the other whipper-in. As Hugh led his companions down the slope he was dismayed to see how disturbed the ground was. The grass had been churned into a muddy slush, and hoof marks were intermingled with paw prints everywhere. The police, he realised, were going to have a hard job finding anything relevant here.

Lucy had to drag Ben with her as she scrambled over the stream to the far bank. She was glad to find that a narrow path had been trampled out here through the sallows. It had already been used this morning, the muddy ground was marked by footsteps and paw prints. Pushing through the bare whippy branches of the trees as she followed the trail, she brought down showers of droplets on her head and shoulders, soaking her woollen hat and trickling cold wetness inside the collar of her coat and down her back. The collie was anxious not to be separated from Hugh and hung back at the full length of his lead as Lucy picked her way up the slope, avoiding the gorse. When she reached the sheltering belt of firs above the gully Lucy paused to look back.

On the opposite bank of the stream beside the copse Anna seemed to have calmed the bay horse. But as Lucy watched the triumphal baying of the hounds suddenly filled the gully and the horse began to shift nervously again. Lucy hesitated, wondering whether she should go to help Anna. This was not the first time she had left her with a body, but on the last occasion Anna had at least had Mike for company and was not going to be mobbed by a pack of hounds.

The first of the hounds appeared over the edge of the gully, followed immediately by his comrades. They poured down towards Anna in a flood of colours, cream, tan and brown. She was struggling with the horse, who was now tossing his head in agitation. The pack swirled past her and rushed up to Gil's fallen body, sniffing eagerly around it. Ben pulled suddenly on his lead, keen to go back down, and caught Lucy by surprise so that she almost lost her footing. It was with a surge of relief that she saw two pink-coated riders picking their way carefully down the opposite slope towards the hounds.

'Come on,' Lucy urged Ben, 'let's go. I'm sure they'll come down the sides of the stream, and I don't want us to be in the way.'

The collie was still reluctant to leave the scene of so much activity, but Lucy persuaded him through the belt of firs to the high wire fence that ran behind it. She followed this, unable to see through the huge bushes that grew against it on the other side. Pausing at last on a tarmac drive that curved right, running below the perimeter of the garden and out of sight, Lucy found her way into the property barred by a pair of strong double gates.

She looked uncertainly through the gate bars at the bungalow beyond. A 1950s building, she thought, but definitely uncared for these days. It was small and ramshackle, the cream-painted walls dirty and damp-stained, with odd lean-tos propped against the original structure. The curved timber bargeboards on the centre gable were cracked and weathered, no longer providing a focal point above a picture window. This must once have overlooked the gully but now had its view blocked by the trees on the perimeter. Several sheds and wired enclosures of differing shapes and sizes straggled in a ragged line on both sides of a concrete garage, blocking any view of what lay beyond.

The bungalow sat among its satellites in the centre of what had once been a wide front lawn. This was now more like a rough meadow with untidy hummocks of grass. Here there were signs of activity, the grass criss-crossed with numerous tracks that had clearly been trodden over many times.

Loud barking startled Lucy as she stood on the outer drive, wondering what to do. She jumped back from the gates as three dogs threw themselves against the wooden bars, ferocious snarls twisting their muzzles. Ben's hackles rose and his lips rolled back, exposing his own white teeth as he stepped stiffly forward. Lucy began to retreat down the drive, her eyes on the dogs as she dragged Ben with her. She had noticed the gates were efficiently covered with wire netting on the inside, now she just hoped it was high enough to keep the dogs inside.

A man's stern voice called the dogs and they moved back from the gates reluctantly, their gaze still fixed on Lucy and Ben. At another command the dogs finally turned and trotted over to the figure who had come round the corner of the bungalow. He opened the gate of a nearby pen and shooed them in, closing the gate behind them. As the dogs prowled the perimeter of the wire-mesh fence the man strode towards the drive, looking just as antagonistic as his dogs. He was wrapped in a bulky jumper and fleece waistcoat, his shoulder-length black hair flopping over his face, which was tight with suspicion.

Lucy stood where she was, watching him cautiously. Ben waited too, his body stiff and his eyes alert. 'Quiet,' she cautioned him.

'What do you want?' the man called roughly as he approached the gates. 'If you're lost, follow the drive round to the lane at the back and turn right down to the village. Don't hang about here, the weather's going to get worse.'

'There's been an accident,' Lucy shouted as he stood on the far side of gates. 'Down by the stream, just below here. A man's dead.'

'You bloody hikers,' he said angrily, yanking one of the gates open. 'You'd better come in. We'll ring the police from the house. Mobile reception's patchy out here, as I suppose you've found.'

As Lucy led Ben through the gate the man said, 'What a

stupid place to walk. It's riddled with mine trenches, a right trap for the unwary. And it's insane to do it with bad weather coming.'

'It isn't one of us,' Lucy said. 'It's a rider.'

He stopped by the front door, looking over his shoulder at her. 'A rider,' he said, surprised. 'Who's that then? Not a local. None of them would take horses down there.'

'I'm afraid it is,' Lucy said, as he pushed hard at the door, heaving it across the scratched parquet flooring of the hall. She followed him reluctantly into the house, Ben close at her side, his body radiating tension. They were distracted for a moment by the sound of high-pitched bleeping from the room to their right, but an impatient movement brought her attention back to the man who had stopped in front of her. 'It's a man called Gil Hannaford,' she said, pulling off her wet hat and letting it dangle limply from one hand, 'from the village.'

'Hannaford,' the man repeated disbelievingly. 'You must be mistaken. I know he brought the drag hunt forward to today, but there's no way he'd risk any of his horses in the gully, even in better conditions.'

'I don't know what happened,' Lucy said, beginning to shiver as her guide moved on into the kitchen on the left. 'But we met Gil last night and my husband is sure it's him. Please, can you ring the police?'

He ran his eyes over her. 'You're wet through,' he said dispassionately. 'I'll get you a towel and one of my jumpers while you ring them. You can explain what's happened.' He pointed to the old-fashioned telephone, a black handset curving over a square base. 'I'll get you a brandy too. You look as though you need it. I'll take over when they want directions and you can go back to the hall and change.'

'Thanks,' Lucy said gratefully, letting Ben's lead drop as the collie leaned against her legs. 'But could you make it tea, please.'

He shrugged and went across to a kettle, filling it with

water and switching it on. He disappeared as she picked up the
telephone and began to dial the emergency number. By the time
she was speaking he had returned, dropping a thick blue jumper
and threadbare towel onto the worktop near her.

The kettle whistled and he turned, opening a canister to put
a tea bag into a mug before pouring in boiling water. From a
bowl he took three spoonfuls of sugar and stirred them into the
mug. He turned to Lucy just as she leaned across to hand him
the telephone. 'Lots of sugar in it,' he said. 'You need it. Go and
get dry.'

She was feeling very cold now, her teeth chattering uncon-
trollably as she picked up the jumper and towel and hurried out
to the hall. Ben pattered after her and watched as she hurriedly
pulled off her coat and jumper, running the towel over her hair
and body, before quickly pulling on the borrowed jumper. Still
rubbing her hair with the towel she returned to the kitchen and
looked at the strong brown tea in her mug. Lucy cautiously
fished out the teabag, looking round to find somewhere to
dump it, settling after a second's indecision on a plate she fished
out from a rack. She was half listening to the telephone conversation as she clasped her hands about the welcome warmth of
the mug and looked around her.

The room was an odd mixture. The formica doors of the
fitted cupboards, still bearing traces of their original pale pink
colouring, contrasted strangely with occasional well-polished
wooden tables, like the pie crust one on which the telephone
stood. The floor seemed to still have its original black and white
linoleum tiles, although they were cracked and split. It was
littered with wood shavings from the long bench that ran across
the far side, where the kitchen opened into what had once been
a small dining room. At the far end of this was a stove, a fire
crackling behind the glass door, golden flames casting a flickering light over the pile of logs and wood offcuts beside it.

The room now clearly served as a studio and as Lucy's eyes
ran over the bench she saw a wooden mallet, a small sharp knife

and a collection of chisels with varying gouges, their handles well worn. A piece of wood lay on the bench, clearly about to be shaped, but as Lucy's eyes moved on they fell on some finished pieces propped against a side wall. She recognised the head of a fox peering through branches, a rounded robin, perky as the relation she often saw in her garden, and a kestrel hovering, just as she had recently watched the one above the ridge.

She dropped the towel on the kitchen worktop and unconsciously stepped closer to look at the pieces, the collie keeping close to her. A slight movement startled them both, causing Ben to swing round swiftly. Lucy turned too, finding the woodcarver watching her from beside the telephone, the receiver now back in its cradle.

'They're lovely,' Lucy said quietly. 'How lucky you are to be able to make them.'

His face lightened and he smiled. 'I know. I spend hours watching birds and animals, and then sometimes the right one just seems to come out of the wood under my hands. I can't think of a better way of spending my life.'

A faint memory tugged at Lucy's mind as she studied him, particularly the crooked eyebrows that gave his face a comical look, which had at first been screened by his long hair. 'Don't I know you from somewhere?' she asked. 'Have you always lived round here?'

He stared at her, a mild frown on his forehead as he took in her damp chestnut hair and small pointed face. 'I used to live down in the valley, on one of the farms.' His eyes widened. 'The Ballamy farm. You used to come and stay there. You were at school with Berhane and Edith.'

'Of course,' Lucy exclaimed. 'Your parents lived on the farm, didn't they? You're,' she struggled for the name, retrieving it from her memory triumphantly, 'Phil, Phil Avery.'

He nodded, his face shuttered again. 'We'd lived there all my life, until Gil Ballamy's daughter turned us off. Edith was never cut out for farming, and Berhane didn't want to get involved.

They made a mint of money out of it, and Gil Hannaford extended his empire. So they were all happy.'

'Where are your parents now?' Lucy asked, aware she was treading on dangerous ground.

'They live on one of the other farms. They're happy enough,' he conceded grudgingly. 'They got a good final bonus, so they did well really.' He added, 'That was Berhane's doing. Thought it would be a sweetener, I suppose.'

Phil looked at his workbench. 'It worked out alright for me in the end too. I was doing odd jobs around the moor when I got this place. I've Susannah Ballamy to thank that I don't need to do them any more.' He looked at Lucy. 'She always encouraged me when I was at school here, never made me feel stupid. I hated it when I left. I wasn't really any good at book learning. But it was Susannah who got me a place with a woodcarver, persuaded me to turn up to the job and try it. I've never looked back. These,' he gestured at the carvings, 'are beginning to fetch good prices.' He grinned suddenly. 'I still don't really believe people will pay for them.'

'Where do you sell them?' Lucy asked, looking down at the carvings again. 'I'd really like to have that robin for myself and the kestrel for my husband's birthday.'

'Pick them up and feel them,' he said. 'Get to know the shape of them, the curve of their wings.' He glanced at her rapt face. 'I suppose you're here for Berhane's dinner. I've heard all about that. Strange she should come back.'

'Why?' Lucy asked, one finger running over the robin's plump carved chest.

Phil gestured at the carved kestrel. 'She was like that, needing to spread her wings and fly.' He shrugged. 'So she did, then returned to roost here after all. I didn't expect that.'

'Will you join her dining club?' Lucy asked.

His eyes went blank. 'She won't want the likes of me,' he said. 'But I'll bring these down to the Church House for you later today. Or the inn, if you're staying there.' He caught himself, coming back to reality. 'No, maybe not. Not with Hannaford dead. Tomorrow, if the weather doesn't change.'

'Will you be alright up here? We're supposed to be getting a lot of snow.'

He grinned again. 'I'll love it. I've got lots of logs for the stove, plenty of food in the freezer, the dogs and animals for company. No callers. Even the phone lines go down sometimes, so I'm just left with the radio network for contacting people.' He squinted sideways at her. 'What more could I want?'

Before she could reply Phil looked at his watch. 'We'd better get moving. I've still got the rest of the animals to feed, then we'll need to get up to the lane above my place,' he said. 'You'll have to be there when the police arrive. They'll need you to show them where to go.'

'Okay.' Lucy said. 'What animals? Not the dogs?'

'No, they'll stay in the pen until you've gone. No point in taking chances. They can be cautious with another dog on their territory.' He waved a hand to the rear of the bungalow. 'I've got a few injured creatures round the back. Come and see them if you like, but keep your dog well away.'

He picked up an old Barbour and tossed it to her as he walked out into the hall and opened the front door. Lucy pulled it on as she followed him out reluctantly, shivering as she felt the chilly air strike her again.

Phil slammed the door shut behind them and strode off round the side of the bungalow, behind the pen where the dogs prowled, watching Lucy and Ben closely. Here at the back, out of sight from the drive, the lawn was divided into long runs and Lucy stopped, staring in surprise as Phil picked up the bucket he had obviously put down when she arrived. In the closest run was the original of the fox in the carving, his black eyes staring at her out of his red fur as he paused in his pacing to watch Phil. As the creature moved again Lucy saw that he walked awkwardly, one front leg tightly bound in a splint.

'One of this year's cubs,' Phil said shortly, tipping food from

the bucket into a row of bowls. He picked up one and pushed
it through a low flap beside the gate of the fox's pen, leaving it
well away from the water bowl on the other side. 'He used to
play in the garden with his brothers and sisters, and must have
dragged himself back here when he broke his leg. That was a
couple of weeks ago.'

Lucy stayed well back, holding tightly to Ben, whose nose
was whiffling as Phil picked up two more bowls of food. As
he walked to the next pen and pushed a bowl through the flap
Phil said, 'There's a badger here. Hit by a car. He's got a nasty
wound in his flank, but he'll survive. You won't see him. He
won't come out while you're around. And there,' he jerked his
head to the far pen, 'a roe buck. I found him trapped in a wire
fence and starving. He'll only be here until I've fed him up a
bit.'

As Phil pushed the last bowl into the far pen they both heard
the faint sound of sirens. He stood up, brushing his hands down
his trousers. 'That's it then. Back to the big world. The living
and the dead.'

Horses thronged the village green once more, but the festive
mood of the morning had gone. There were no gregarious clus-
ters of eager riders, no loud boisterous voices. Riders stayed
astride as their mounts shifted uneasily, but hardly anyone
spoke. When they did it was in low voices, leaning in to one or
two other people, heads bent close together over their horses'
necks. Speculation had been rife, rumours wild, as they had
ridden soberly back down from the moor. But now, in sight
of Gil Hannaford's house, the clamour was stilled. The only
persistent sound was the yapping and whimpering of the hounds,
shut into Gil's kennel yard. And the riders were not keen to
notice the noise, generally keeping their shoulders turned away
from the house, but occasionally sending fleeting, almost furtive,
glances towards it.

Isobel stood in the centre of the green again, surrounded by the steaming horses, most of the people high above her head, so that they had to lean down to take the tots she offered from her tray. She paused for a second to look through the crowd up towards the moor, wondering what was happening, where Lucy was. Isobel shook herself mentally. There was no use in letting her thoughts wander. She should be used by now to her family and their friends getting into these kinds of situations. But, she bit her lip ruefully, nothing made the knowledge of sudden death easier. She offered the last of her little metal cups to the two men who were nearest her. They were accepted in silence and knocked back without hesitation, the cups returned almost immediately. Strange, Isobel thought, to be doing the same thing again, taking the drinks around on this tray, giving a weird sense of déjà-vu. Perhaps that was how the riders felt, for while some of the riders really seemed to need the brandy, others sat clutching their cups awkwardly, merely sipping absently at the contents from time to time.

Isobel picked her way carefully through the horses with her empty tray, glad to get back to the comparative space in the inn garden. She put her tray down on one of the tables, edging aside another two to create enough room, glad to be relieved of the weight. The inn seemed to have several old-fashioned wooden ones, capacious but heavy to hold for any length of time. No doubt they had been used at the inn for centuries, Isobel thought wryly, as she glanced across at Susannah who was weaving her own way through the riders with another tray. She watched Susannah for a moment, anxious about the other woman, who was moving more stiffly than usual, perhaps as a result of yesterday's fall.

The two women had been in the sitting room of the Schoolhouse late that morning, lingering over their coffees as they chatted in a desultory fashion. A light lunch was just being discussed when their attention had been attracted by the sound of vehicles and loud voices outside, clearly audible above the excited calls of children who had been playing on the village green. Susannah had gone out to investigate, returning white and shaking after several minutes to pass on the news that the hunt followers had brought. Unable to persuade Susannah to stay indoors until more was known, Isobel had gone back outside with her, hoping that rumour might have exaggerated the situation.

The followers were more than ready to repeat what they had already said, that they were sure that a rider had died up on the high moor. But the stories that circulated among them bore more than one name. Gil Hannaford. Berhane. Others that Isobel did not know.

She thought she would never forget the moment when the riders had finally trooped back into the village from the moor. The hunt followers were waiting, huddled into tight little knots, no longer speaking and speculating, just waiting. Those villagers who had not gone out with the hunt had joined them on the green, stunned by their unexpected return, shocked and anxious when they heard the news. The only person not there was Edith.

'Leave her in her own little world,' Susannah had said sharply, when Isobel offered to go over to the Church House. 'She can do no good here.'

Susannah's face had been the colour of dough. Her eyes seemed to have shrunk to the size of currants. But it was the blue tinge around her mouth that had worried Isobel. Susannah had thrust a hand into the pocket of her breeches and pulled out a small silver box. 'I always carry it,' she had said briefly. 'Heart.' She took out a pill and popped it into her mouth. A few minutes later she was herself again, briskly organising Betsey at the inn and marshalling the trays of brandy. 'Most of the people here are in a state of shock,' Susannah said briefly. 'And some of them will just want a drink. It'll be worse for the riders, and they should be back soon. Whatever,' she said, straightening her back, 'it gives us something to do. It's better than just standing around.'

It was not much later that the hounds had trotted up the lane by Gil's house in a neat pack, themselves subdued by the atmosphere. The whippers-in had urged them into the yard behind the house while the rest of the riders rode onto the green. The only noises that heralded their return were the thudding of many hooves and the jingling of bridles. The pigeons that had settled in the oaks around the green rose with a heavy flapping of their wings and flew away to watch from a distance.

Isobel thought it was a scene that would be forever engraved in her mind. If she could paint, it would be something she would record for posterity: *The Death*. The hunt bore with it the aura of disaster. The riders were silent, their faces shuttered, their bearing one of confused and sudden defeat. The contrast with their exuberant exit, when riders, horses and hounds were fizzing with excited anticipation, could not have been greater.

As the riders had approached the waiting crowd on the green, one person from each side had come to the fore. Isobel shivered, wondering how many times over the centuries mounted men had brought bad news to waiting villagers here. For a moment the scene flickered, a gaily caparisoned Cavalier rode glumly forward to the woman in gay silks and laces who stood waiting under the oaks, her uncovered ringlets framing a white frightened face.

Then reality was back, and the rider was the inn landlord, the waiting woman was Isobel's elderly friend. Joe Triggs had leaned over the neck of his horse to speak to Susannah who stood waiting, not moving, her face uplifted towards his. Not a horse moved, not a person shifted. Time stood still for an instant, moving on as soon as the landlord spoke.

'It's Gil,' Joe had said bluntly. 'Dead. Broke his neck, apparently. God knows how.'

Susannah had swayed and recovered herself quickly, putting out a hand to the horse's shoulder to steady herself.

She had scanned the riders, looking for another person. 'Berhane?' she had asked.

'She's with him,' Joe had said gruffly. His voice roughened.
'And those people staying here. They found him. Dead, so they
say. Makes you wonder though. I thought they were saboteurs,
the way the blokes came leaping out in front of us.' His face
darkened. 'Makes you wonder,' he repeated. 'I can't see how
Gil came to be there. Or how he'd fall. There was never a better
rider.' His scowl deepened. 'And one of those blokes telling us
what to do. Who's he to know? And we've gone and left them
all there. That can't be right. Just as well Berhane did stay. She'll
make sure there's no more monkey business.'

Susannah had said sharply, 'Don't make a fool of yourself,
Joe.' Her eyes had run over him, taking in his wet and muddy
coat. 'If you haven't already. Hugh Carey is a well-known
barrister. He'll know better than most what to do about an
accidental death.'

'The way he was going on anybody would think it was
murder,' Joe had said sullenly.

'Nonsense, Joe. The best of riders can be unlucky. Although,'
Susannah had said in suddenly weary tones, 'I would never
have expected Gil to be.' She had shaken her head, visibly shedding her tiredness. 'I suppose we need to wait here until the
police come, or Hugh gets back and tells us more. You get into
the inn and bring out something to warm the riders up. Not
much, mind,' she had warned. 'Just enough to keep the chill out
of them. The followers have already had their lot. I'm paying
for it,' she added, seeing his mutinous expression. 'Betsey's busy
with the lunch. It'll have to be eaten, and there's no knowing
anyway how long everyone'll be here. Make sure you don't
get in her way.' She gave him a wintry smile. 'Get on with the
drinks, Joe, I'll take Roman down to the stables for you.'

As Joe had walked his horse round to the yard behind the
inn, Susannah turned to Isobel. 'He'll be alright,' she had said.
'He only needs organising, then he manages very well. And
Betsey really runs the place anyway, she'll cope with everything.'
She had sighed, her shoulders slumping slightly. 'I won't be

sorry to get out of the crowd for a few minutes. It'll be good for Joe to be busy out here.' She glanced wearily towards the Church House. 'I suppose I ought to go and tell Edith the news. She'll have to hear it some time, so the sooner the better. But I'd better see to Joe's horse first.'

Susannah had straightened up, walking off purposefully round the inn. Now, half an hour later, here she was again, busy on the green.

Isobel looked at her face quickly as Susannah came into the inn garden. There was no sign of the blue tinge around the other woman's lips, although she was still pale and her eyes were strained.

'Let's slip into the kitchen,' Susannah said, propping her heavy tray against the table, 'and see how Betsey's doing.'

Isobel followed her into the inn and down the hallway. 'How is Edith?' Isobel asked quietly. 'Has she come out onto the green?'

'You can never tell with Edith,' Susannah said tartly. 'She didn't say a word, just sat staring blankly at me. I left her at the Church House. I don't know if she'll go outside or not.' She passed the cellar door and turned into the kitchen that overlooked the yard, enquiring, 'How are you managing, Betsey?'

'Such a business,' Betsey said, her face reddened from the heat of the oven as she lifted out a tray of turnovers. 'Just as well we've got all this food here.'

'It does smell good,' Isobel said. 'I'm sure people will be glad to eat.' Susannah glanced at her watch, saying, 'You've obviously got everything under control, so I'll go back onto the green. The police must be here shortly. We seem to have been waiting for ever.'

Susannah left the kitchen abruptly, and Isobel followed her, rather reluctant to leave the warm room and delicious scents, realising that she was hungry herself. Breakfast had been a long time ago.

Susannah was standing in the front garden, scanning

the crowd as Isobel pulled the inn door shut. A gap opened up through the horses and Isobel saw two marked police Landrovers pulling up at the far end of the green. Both came to a halt alongside the hedge that shielded Gil's house. The riders blocked Isobel's view, their horses turning towards the Landrovers, then all pausing to see what happened next, in a movement as neatly executed as if it had been practised.

Skirting the horses carefully Isobel hurried down the green. As she passed the Church House the door opened and Edith appeared, wrapped in a faded grey shawl, flowered rubber boots visible under her long skirt. Isobel hesitated fractionally, then nodded at her and carried on. She arrived at the bottom in time to see Lucy emerge from the first Landrover with Anna and Mike. Ben's face was pressed against the window of the back seat, watching his mistress anxiously.

Isobel grasped her granddaughter in her arms. 'Lucy,' she said, 'it's such a relief to see you.'

Lucy returned the embrace, rather startled. It was unlike Isobel to be so demonstrative.

Her grandmother drew back. 'The atmosphere here is getting to me,' she murmured. 'I've never been anywhere so laden with doom.' The occupants of the other Landrover were getting out too, and she recognised the square figure and rubicund face of Detective Sergeant Tom Peters, whom they had come to know well over the last two years. 'Where's Hugh?' she demanded quickly.

'He stayed up there,' Lucy said, as Anna and Mike hovered behind her. 'Rob Elliot, you know, Inspector Elliot, is there and Hugh will come down with Berhane a bit later.'

Susannah had reached them, Edith drifting along behind her. 'Where's Berhane?' Susannah asked, in the peremptory tones of a schoolmistress.

'She's bringing the horse back, the one Gil rode,' Lucy said. 'He's still very nervous, and Berhane didn't want to leave him with anybody else. And although we got hold of another saddle she decided not to put it on. She's going to walk him down with Hugh when the police have finished up there.'

Susannah frowned. 'Surely they could have got hold of a horsebox? There are plenty in Gil's field here. Joe could take one up.' She looked round, ready to requisition one.

'I think,' Anna said gently, 'Berhane wants to walk partly to have time to herself. Hugh will keep her company if she needs it. If not, he's very good at keeping quiet.'

Susannah stared at her, then nodded jerkily. 'Yes, of course.'

'Berhane offered the Church House to the police,' Lucy said, 'for interviews. She thought the inn and the village hall might be full of people getting out of the cold. They'll have to wait around for a while, because the police are sure to want to talk to everyone.'

Mike snorted as he stared round the green. 'That'll take all day.'

'So it was,' Susannah paused, then said stiffly, 'murder. Joe wasn't really very clear about what had happened.'

Mike snorted. 'That bloke's not capable of thinking,' he snapped. 'He's not safe out on his own.'

'I believe this is normal practice in the event of an unexpected death,' Lucy said evasively.

Susannah considered, then nodded again. 'I'd better take the police over to the Church House,' she said briskly. 'They'll want to get started, and the sooner we can get people away home the better.'

Isobel looked round from her conversation with Sergeant Peters and introduced him to Susannah. 'We've met Sergeant Peters many times now,' she said dryly.

'If you'd like to come with me I'll show you Berhane's house,' Susannah said. 'Edith, you'd better come too.'

'Oh no,' Edith said mildly, 'I'll go down to Gil's place and see how the hounds are. He'd want them to be okay.'

'There are plenty of people to see to them,' Susannah said sharply. 'And I'll look in on them when I check Joe's horse again.

I took Roman down a while ago, but he was rather unsettled.'

Edith was already wandering towards the hedge, oblivious to her aunt's comments. Susannah stared after her for a second, before turning back and walking over to the Church House, followed by Sergeant Peters and a uniformed constable. The crowd parted to let them through, falling in again behind them to stare. It was only the older children who actually followed them, pausing as the Church House door closed, shutting off the spectacle.

'Well,' Isobel demanded urgently, 'what happened?'

Lucy glanced around quickly as Anna and Mike drew in closer. Nobody else was nearby, and all attention anyway was focused on the police, but Lucy lowered her tone cautiously. 'Hugh thinks at least one of the straps holding the saddle girth was tampered with, partially cut, in fact. Gil's ride must have been strenuous, and eventually the strap gave way.' She winced. 'Gil didn't fall off directly. He might,' she said reluctantly, 'have survived if he had. But it seems that the horse may have bolted when the saddle slipped, perhaps when the strap gave way. That seems to have been when Gil fell.' She heaved a sigh. 'His foot was caught in one of the stirrups so he was dragged for some distance, probably until the saddle finally dropped off. By then he was already dead.'

'However it happened, he broke his neck,' Mike said roughly.

'So it is,' Isobel lowered her voice to almost a whisper, 'murder.'

'Oh yes,' Mike grunted. 'Again. I never know how we fall into these things.' He glared at Anna. 'It's as if we have a Jonah among us.'

Anna ignored him. 'And we don't know who was the intended victim,' she said softly. 'That's really why Hugh will come back with Berhane.'

Isobel stared at her in shocked surprise. It was Lucy who explained. 'Gil was riding Berhane's gelding. He had a new horse she wanted to try out and they exchanged in the stables at the last minute, just before breakfast.'

'Of course,' Isobel exclaimed. 'I saw him come out of the hall after he'd had his breakfast and he told me that himself.'

'Did he check the girth on his horse then?' Lucy asked quickly.

Isobel frowned, trying to remember. 'I don't think so,' she said, 'but I really couldn't swear to it. Perhaps he wouldn't check it again, though, if he'd only recently saddled up.'

'No, maybe not,' Lucy agreed reluctantly.

'But then,' Isobel said slowly, 'if the damage was done deliberately, was it Gil or Berhane who was intended to fall? Was it done in the stables or outside the village hall?'

'Those are some of the questions,' Lucy admitted. 'We don't know if Berhane's realised yet. She's still coming to terms with what's happened. She feels that if she'd ridden her own horse the girth strap would have given way when she had company. She'd probably have been bumped a bit, but the other riders would have been there to help her. That's on her mind now.'

Isobel looked round at the milling throng. 'But why on earth would anyone want to kill either of them?' She caught her breath. 'I suppose that's what the police will be looking into now.'

Lucy nodded. 'That, and opportunity.'

Mike snorted again. 'Anyone could have done it. There must have been opportunities in the stables. And there were several horses tied up to the rail near the church when we set off walking this morning. A number of people could have tampered with them while Berhane and Hannaford had breakfast in the hall.'

'They were both there early,' Isobel agreed. 'Their horses were at the rail when I arrived, Berhane's own bay that Gil rode, and his grey that Berhane was going to ride. And as well as Susannah's mare I think there were at least two other horses further down the rail. Some of the breakfast helpers were riding out with the followers later on.'

'Surely,' Anna said, 'the possibilities can be narrowed down by who knew about the horse exchange. No,' she amended in exasperation, 'of course, we can't do that until we know whether Berhane or Gil was the target.'

'Anybody could have done it,' Mike reiterated. 'And the bastard has made sure I won't get to the prehistoric village at Riven Tor today. I suppose,' he stared at the blue sky, 'there's always tomorrow. It's still too cold for snow.'

'Really, Mike,' Anna expostulated, 'there are other things to think about now.'

'I am not,' he growled, 'getting involved in this. You can play at detectives with the boyfriend if you want.'

'Rob Elliot is not my boyfriend,' Anna snapped, as Lucy turned to the Landrover, opening the back door to let Ben out.

'Her boyfriends were never boyfriends, even at school,' Edith said idly, making them all jump nervously as they had not seen her return. 'Look,' she gestured vaguely, 'there's Aunt Susannah waving from the Church House. I suppose the police want to start with you. After all, you were on the scene first, weren't you?'

Mike groaned theatrically, before he stumped after Lucy and Anna.

FOUR

The long oak table in the Church House dining room was covered with a woven sepia-coloured cloth. Embossed glass candlesticks of varying heights stood along the middle of the table, entwined with a thick rope of rosemary that scented the air. The candles cast a flickering light over the scalloped cream plates and the silver cutlery, sending erratic slivers of reflected brightness over the faces of the people who sat around the table.

The faces were sober, but the visitors were mainly festively dressed. Isobel was neat in a long black velvet skirt and patterned silk blouse in a soft red, Anna elegant in her favourite crimson and Lucy in the dress that Hugh liked so much, the golden jersey that brought out the natural highlights in her chestnut hair. His own contribution to dressing up lay in his embroidered waistcoat and the red and green bow tie his brother-in-law had given him for Christmas. Mike was the only one of the visitors who had made no effort, coming as a matter of course in the trousers and thick jumper he had worn the previous evening.

Conversation was spasmodic, and Anna broke the next silence by commenting, 'That's a nice jumper, Mike.'

He glanced at her suspiciously, tugging unconsciously at its neck. 'A present from my mother,' he growled. 'She sends me one every year.'

A flash of amusement crossed Anna's face. 'It must be nice for her to know for sure what you need.'

Mike glowered, letting his soup spoon drop noisily back into his empty bowl, causing Ben to look up quickly from his place under the table by Lucy's feet. 'I don't need them. I have plenty, but I can't get the message across to her.'

Silence fell again as the others lowered their own spoons. 'That was delicious,' Hugh said politely to Berhane, who sat opposite him between Anna and Mike. As Hugh looked round the table he appreciated the care that Berhane had put into the seating arrangements. Anna and Mike were separated, Edith was sitting on Hugh's right, a good distance away from Anna. With a twist of his lips he realised that left Lucy with the two most difficult people on either side of her. Still, he thought with relief, Lucy wouldn't let either of them bother her. It was odd that they should both get under Anna's skin so easily. Anna, who was normally so equable, could barely conceal her dislike of Edith, and Mike always seemed to irritate her.

Edith sat in a froth of wispy layers of grey and mauve cotton that fell in different levels over another of her thick full-length skirts, so washed out that it was almost colourless. A sprig of rosemary was pinned to her shoulder, brushing against her ear every time she moved. As he considered her, Hugh wondered that the sprig did not get entangled in the long hoop earrings she wore. A sudden thought struck him. Edith's colour scheme definitely wasn't festive. Was it a deliberate indication of mourning? No, he realised, she couldn't have known she'd need it. Could she? He glanced at her out of the corner of his eye. She was staring at her sister, her expression quite blank, her pale eyes seeming to protrude more than ever.

Berhane was immaculate in a long silk tunic over narrow trousers, both in a deep gold, that emphasised her slender height. Her thick black hair was laced with gold threads and tied back with a patterned scarf. She had clearly made as much effort as if they were actually celebrating the arrival of the New

Year as she had planned. Her cool face gave no indication of her thoughts as she stood up and collected the bowls together.

'Delicious,' Isobel echoed Hugh from her place at the far end of the table. 'Such a clever combination of flavours. I've never had pomegranate in soup before.'

Susannah, seated between her and Hugh, gathered herself together visibly. 'Yes, it is very unusual. Berhane tried it out on me a few weeks ago.'

Berhane looked across the table as she got to her feet, smiling affectionately at her adoptive aunt. 'It's always useful to have willing food samplers,' she said. 'Just because I like something doesn't mean other people will. Tastes vary so much. This is a nice meaty soup for the time of year, my adaptation of a Persian recipe.'

Susannah's eyes followed her as she walked to the pointed archway at the back of the room that led to the kitchen. Susannah was wearing a deep green woollen dress, a bright silver brooch at its neck, its simplicity suiting her severe features, and combining what she felt to be appropriate regard for Gil's death with Berhane's wish to carry on as she thought he would have wished.

Isobel hesitated, aware of her neighbour's preoccupation, then said quietly, 'She's a very good cook. I should think her dining club will be very popular.'

'Yes,' Susannah agreed, collecting her thoughts with an obvious effort. 'I never guessed she would be interested in doing something like this. She didn't seem to have much interest in cooking when she was growing up.'

Anna got to her feet. 'I'll just see if she needs a hand,' she announced, glancing inimically at Edith before following Berhane.

Edith seemed totally unaware of the animosity aimed at her. She gazed unconcernedly at the far wall, where the carved owl's face glimmered in the shifting light as the bird strained to fly out of the painted stone. One of her hands lay on the table, pulling at a piece of rosemary in the rope, gradually tearing off the needles and leaving them littered across the cloth. 'I hope Gil wasn't poisoned,' she murmured. 'Joe would be only too keen to blame Berhane's cooking.'

'I suppose it must be an interest she developed from her travels,' Susannah said, ignoring her niece. 'She was always good at meeting people, and seems to have got to know many cooks in different countries. Sometimes quite odd-sounding people,' Susannah added, 'from her stories.'

'She was always curious about how food was made,' Lucy said, leaning forward to talk down the table, keen to keep the conversation going. 'I remember how she liked to make the pastry for Mary's apple pies when we visited the farm.'

'With cinnamon,' Edith contributed unexpectedly. 'Mummy wasn't sure about it, but Berhane always liked spices. Isn't it lucky people do nowadays?'

Mike stared at her. 'Not everyone does,' he said irritably.

She looked back at him, quite unfazed, her pale eyes almost unfocused.

'I don't think it's a new trend,' Hugh commented, aware of Lucy's anxiety to keep people talking. 'The Elizabethans certainly used a lot of spices.'

'Wasn't that to cover up bad meat?' Mike demanded.

Hugh glanced at him, one eyebrow raised quizzically. 'You probably know more about it than I do.'

'It's not part of my field,' Mike snapped. 'Only general knowledge.'

Silence fell again, heavily. Ben shifted slightly, watching the old spaniel who sat over Isobel's feet, her own attention on the kitchen door. Lucy looked round with relief at the sound of it opening. She was glad to see Anna returning to the dining room, balancing a platter of bread that she put down in the centre of the table. Behind her came Berhane, and Lucy was taken aback to see that she bore a tray laden with tall glasses and a magnum bottle of champagne.

Berhane placed her tray on one of the serving tables that had been moved to stand in front of the back wall, next to the other, piled high with plates. She looked up tranquilly to face them, aware of the censure in Susannah's expression and the surprise on Isobel's face. 'This was to see the New Year in,' she said in her husky voice, 'but I feel it would be more appropriate now.'

Susannah opened her mouth, but shut it again as Berhane continued, expertly unpeeling the foil, 'I expected Gil to be here with us tonight. We all did. As he isn't, and never can be again, I would like us to celebrate his life in a way that he'd appreciate.'

She eased the cork out, releasing a spume of foam which she caught deftly in the nearest glass. Mike unexpectedly stood up and took two long steps to reach for the glass, which he passed over the table to Susannah.

Susannah took it with reluctance, but without saying a word. She watched forbiddingly as Mike passed more glasses round until all the diners had one.

Lucy stood up and the others rose to their feet too, even Edith, who only seemed to notice what was happening when Hugh tapped her elbow, bringing her attention back to the room. They faced Berhane who had come to her own place at the dining table. She lifted her glass, her hand steady, her eyes calm. 'To Gil, who loved the moor and his horses and hounds more than anything.'

Hugh was surprised to hear a whisper from Edith and glanced quickly at her. He could not be sure what she had said but that breath of sound had startled him.

Berhane put her glass down with a snap. 'And now, please let us talk about him, remember him, even if it means talking about his death. He should not be an unwelcome ghost at this feast.'

She walked swiftly back to the kitchen, Anna at her heels and the others resumed their seats. At the end of the table the collie sighed quite audibly.

'She's right,' Susannah said bleakly. 'We're all thinking about him. Strange, I seem to picture him most easily as a small boy. He was a cheerful child. You always knew what he was thinking then. He was competitive too, but always a good loser on the rare occasions when he wasn't first.'

'Did you teach him?' Isobel enquired, pouring herself some water from one of the jugs on the table.

Susannah nodded. 'Yes. He was a bright boy. He would have gone far if he'd had the interest.'

'His interest was here,' Berhane said, coming back into the room in time to catch this. 'It always was.' She was carrying a wide dish, piled high with rice, vivid with the colours of dried rose and marigold petals. Lucy gasped in admiration as Berhane put it down on the serving table, and turned to Anna who had come up with a tray covered with bowls, three large ones and several smaller ones. Berhane unshipped these, putting them around the central dish before she stood back.

She carried on speaking as she did this. 'Gil was lucky. All he ever wanted was here, and he was lucky enough to have it.'

This time Hugh was alert, waiting for a sound from Edith. None came. She simply sat staring at the tablecloth, one finger stirring the rosemary needles she had broken onto it.

'That looks stunning,' Hugh commented, looking appreciatively at the food. 'Are you going to tell us what we're about to enjoy?'

Berhane turned her slow smile on Hugh. 'Of course. Unless you'd rather guess as you eat it.'

'Not me,' he said.

'The main dish is basically Moroccan, with a few amendments of my own, and there's either plain sourdough or cardamon bread.'

Anna felt a bubble of laughter well up in her chest as she saw the horrified expression on Mike's face.

Berhane continued, 'It's chicken and rice with pistachios and apricots.' She smiled at Mike. 'It's only got cinnamon in it.

There's plain mixed beans to go with it, but you might also like to try the Spanish beans with ham and Serbian cabbage rolls. There are lots of herbs in both and a touch of cumin in the rolls. All the other dishes are really just for you to taste and tell me what you think.' Seeing Mike look at them cautiously she added, 'They're all much spicier than the main dishes.'

'A little of everything, please,' Isobel said as Berhane looked enquiringly at her, a serving spoon in her hand. 'That looks interesting,' she commented, pointing to a dish of small undistinguished-looking squares. 'What is it?'

'Pieces of aubergine omelette, an Egyptian recipe,' Berhane said, spooning a small amount onto Isobel's plate. 'There's harissa in them, which gives a bit of bite. But you like spicy things, don't you?'

Isobel nodded. 'A relic of my days in India. I'd be interested to find out more about your recipes when you've got time. I use spices a lot in my own cooking, and I'd like to hear about the ones you're using. I've only just come across harissa.' She nodded towards Susannah. 'Last night, in fact.'

'Try some of the sauce with the omelette pieces,' Berhane advised. 'It's mainly tomato and olive, but there's chilli in there too. Only eat it after the main dishes, otherwise their flavour will be spoilt.'

Isobel accepted her plate from Anna, looking at the food with appreciation. 'Would Gil have liked this kind of food?' she asked, deliberately bringing the dead man's name back into the conversation.

Berhane's face was lit with a sudden glowing smile. 'No, I don't think he would have. But he would have come and eaten it nonetheless.'

Beside Hugh Edith's restless fingers stilled suddenly, then grasped her fork. 'He'd have done anything you wanted,' she said clearly. 'Even if it meant eating poison, don't you think?'

Her words created an awkward silence. Unexpectedly it was Mike who broke it before Anna could utter the angry words that were on the tip of her tongue. He had barely followed the conversation as he looked curiously round the room, and now said abruptly, 'You've done well with this place. Not too much tarting up.'

Berhane glanced at him with a smile. 'I'll take you round it sometime, if you like.' Her attention was caught by Susannah's movement as she leaned forward. Berhane shook her head and said lightly, 'Don't worry, Aunt Susannah, Gil was far too sensible to do anything so stupid, even to encourage me. What else would you like to sample? I don't think I've tried any of this out on you yet. And I can promise it won't poison you.'

'Just the chicken and the plain beans, please,' Susannah replied. 'I'd rather not risk anything too spicy at this time of the evening. I'll probably be up all night with indigestion if I do.'

She cast a repressive look sideways at Edith. Her niece, though, was screened by Hugh, and was anyway once again fiddling with the rosemary rope in the centre of the table.

'Gil did well here, didn't he?' Isobel enquired of Susannah, who was just accepting her plate from Anna. 'Even if he didn't use his brains in the way you maybe expected.'

'He did very well for himself,' Susannah said, rather tight-lipped as she shifted her knife and fork further away from her plate. 'He owns, owned,' she corrected stiffly, 'many of the old farms. Too many for one person, I think,' she said bluntly.

'He kept them going as moor farms though, not second homes for outsiders,' Berhane said as she put Lucy's food on a plate and handed it over to Anna for delivery. 'And many of the farmers were already tenants anyway, either of a large landlord or Ravenstow Abbey.'

'That's true,' Susannah admitted as Berhane spooned out Moroccan chicken and plain beans for Edith, and looked in mute enquiry at Hugh. Susannah sniffed. 'This smells wonderful. Cardamon in the bread, isn't it? And...' She hesitated.

'Coriander' Isobel supplied. 'In this omelette sauce, I think.'

Berhane nodded, pleased, as she passed Hugh his plate. 'Very good. And there's a nice Chinon to drink with it. Sauvignon too, if anyone prefers, but the red is better with the flavours. Please help yourselves.'

'What happens to all these farms now he's dead?' Mike demanded, ignoring Berhane, who stood waiting to see what he wanted to eat. 'Many of them must be on interesting sites.'

Anna sighed ostentatiously. 'Not everywhere is riddled with archaeological remains,' she said crossly.

'This landscape is full of them,' he retorted.

Hugh nodded in agreement, watching Berhane pile a large helping of chicken and rice onto a plate. 'I was walking here years ago, in my late teens, and stopped for lunch in the shelter of some rocks. When I looked around a little later on I realised the rocks all formed a pattern, that I'd stumbled into a village of little houses built out of the local rocks. And I was fascinated to find that many had what I was sure was a little larder on the north-facing side.'

'Exactly what I mean,' Mike said, glancing pointedly at Anna, and absentmindedly accepting the plate she passed to him. 'Most people haven't the faintest idea what they're walking over or through when they're out on the moor.'

'There was a strong archaeological group here about a hundred years ago,' Susannah said, as Anna took her own plate from Berhane and sat down at the table. 'Joe Triggs inherited a collection of bits and pieces which he would probably show you.'

Mike grunted, grimly swallowing a large mouthful of food. 'The bloke wasn't exactly forthcoming when I tackled him,' he said, reaching for the bottle of red wine and pouring some into his glass. 'I saw the stones he keeps in his hall, but they aren't much use without records of where they were found.'

'Maybe Gil's diaries would say,' Edith said suddenly, stirring her fork through the food on her plate, mixing it all together.

Mike stared at her, his hand arrested in mid air with the bottle. Lucy took it from him as he spoke. 'What is this about diaries? He mentioned them in the pub, but I didn't have a chance to ask him about them, you were all talking so much.'

Anna darted an expressive glance at Lucy, who smiled as she passed her the bottle of Chinon. Ben lifted his head to watch Isobel's elderly spaniel potter stiffly towards him, slumping down near Mike's feet.

'You'd better ask Berhane,' Edith said, lifting her pale eyes to look at her sister, who had just taken her own place. 'He was telling you about them a few days ago, wasn't he?'

Berhane looked back at her, her own face expressionless. 'Yes.' She glanced at Mike on her left as he gingerly tried the Spanish beans. 'Joe and Gil's great-grandfathers were both prominent members of this archaeological group. I suppose it would be late Victorian.' She looked enquiringly at Susannah, who was watching her with sudden alertness.

'It was founded in 1892. There was a lot of interest in the discoveries in Egypt, and Baring-Gould had brought it closer to home with his excavations here in Devon. It went on strongly until the First World War,' Susannah said, 'and struggled into the 1920s, then just ceased.'

Anna was looking puzzled as she forked up some of the rice and chicken. 'I thought Baring-Gould was something to do with hymns. Didn't he write a famous one?'

'Onward Christian Soldiers,' Hugh offered.

Anna nodded gratefully, but before she could speak Mike said crossly, 'Of course he was an archaeologist. If it weren't for him we wouldn't have the plans we have of some of these early sites. If only he could have kept himself off reconstructions, but given the time he was working in…' Mike drew a breath, clearly ready to lecture for some time.

'He was a man of many parts,' Susannah said with finality. She was looking intently at Berhane. 'What's this about Gil's diaries? He mentioned them to me, but I haven't seen them.'

'Gil only found them just after Christmas,' Berhane said. 'He came across them when he was sorting out some of his father's papers.' She paused to sip at her champagne.

This time Hugh caught the last of the soft words Edith murmured into the fork of food that she was lifting to her lips. '... because of you.' When he glanced at her Edith was looking down at her plate again, chewing slowly and disinterestedly.

'What did he do with them?' Mike demanded. 'They could have important background information on what this group got up to.' He groaned, letting his cutlery clatter onto his empty plate. 'And what they destroyed.'

Susannah was looking across at him. 'They'll probably be a useful local history resource and they could fill out my research very well. I asked him if he would let me have a look at them.' She turned her gaze onto Berhane, who was eating steadily, unconcerned by the competitive undercurrent running across the table. 'Where are they now?'

'In his house, I expect,' Berhane replied. 'They'll belong to his heir.' She glanced round at the plates, all empty except for Edith's. 'Would anybody like some more?'

The older women shook their heads regretfully, but Anna said at once, 'Definitely. It's the nicest food I've had for ages.'

'That's quite a compliment,' Hugh said. 'As somebody who has dined her occasionally I can tell you that Anna has a very fine, not to say expensive, taste in food. And she is of course quite right. I can't resist having some more either.'

Anna gurgled with laughter as Berhane took her plate, but Mike snorted. 'A shame she doesn't put her talents to better use. All this wining and dining won't get her anywhere.'

Anna's amusement died. 'But I have a very good time with my friends,' she said. She added sweetly, 'Maybe you should try it.'

Mike looked at her askance as Lucy said quickly, 'Did Gil say anything about what's in the diaries?'

'He'd only flicked through them,' Berhane said, busy serving food again. 'They didn't really interest him. He wasn't much of a reader.'

Hugh said quietly, as he poured some more wine, 'I've only glanced at the one you gave me, but it's surprisingly evocative of the local area at the time, with some good titbits of earlier history, oral memories passed down through families. I'll read it through as soon as I have chance.'

'What's this?' Susannah asked quickly. 'How did you get one, Hugh?'

'I lent it to him this afternoon,' Berhane said, passing Lucy's plate back to her. 'Gil was talking about publishing them last night in the pub, and I thought Hugh would be the best person to give an opinion about that.'

'But how did you come to have one in the first place?' Susannah demanded. 'Gil was very cagey when I asked to see them.'

'You know Gil,' Berhane said. 'He always liked to keep control of his possessions.'

'At least he didn't throw them out,' Hugh commented, leaning back in his chair and sipping his wine.

Mike groaned. He leaned forward, his arms on the table and rested his head in his hands.

'Don't be so theatrical,' Anna said sharply.

Mike sat back, glowering at her as Berhane put refilled plates down in front of him and Hugh. Anna realised with a twinge of amusement through her irritation that Mike had eaten his first plateful and was preparing to attack the second very heartily. I must remember, she thought, to let Berhane know that's quite an achievement. Normally, Mike's only concession to spicy food is curry. Anything else he regards as fancy and it's usually condemned out of hand.

'So,' Mike said thickly, 'it all comes back to this. Who's the heir?'

Berhane sat down again next to him. 'He has a sister in Brussels, an economist. She's married to an Italian who works at the European Commission, but I think she works in her own name. I've told the police this, so I'm sure they'll find her.'

'But she won't keep Gil's precious pack going, will she?' Edith asked suddenly.

Berhane glanced at her. 'No.'

'He said,' Mike almost shouted, 'I remember he said at the bar last night that he'd just made sure his pack would be safe. Then he must have made a will.'

'He did,' Susannah said abruptly. 'He brought it over to my place yesterday. Joe and I signed it, so I suppose it's in the post to Gil's solicitor now.'

'Did he say what's in it?' Mike demanded.

'I wouldn't tell you if he had,' Susannah said coldly. 'That information must only be for the police.'

Mike was oblivious to the reproof. 'It doesn't sound as though it would involve his sister as far as this pack is concerned. Maybe he's left other things away from her as well.'

'Maybe he has,' Edith agreed softly. 'What do you think, Berhane?'

'That we'll soon know,' she said amiably, 'so speculation doesn't serve much purpose.'

'I must find out who to contact,' Mike pursued his own thoughts, 'before anything from that house gets dumped. Elliot in the first place, I suppose,' he added grumpily.

'I don't think there'll be any rush,' Hugh said mildly.

'Why not?' Mike asked. He did not wait for a reply. 'Oh bloody hell, of course. If it's murder this whole business could go on for months.'

The others fell silent again, even their cutlery momentarily stilled. The only sound was a loud sniff from Juno as she pottered unsteadily around the serving table, licking up a few scattered grains of rice.

'What makes you think Gil was murdered?' Susannah asked, addressing Hugh. 'You do, don't you?'

Hugh finished his last mouthful and wiped his lips carefully with his napkin. 'Yes,' he said levelly. 'I can't really discuss the details, you know. But the police must have asked you enough questions to give you an idea of what went wrong.'

'Something to do with the horse,' Susannah replied promptly. She frowned. 'I saw him down in the stables after Berhane brought him back. He didn't fall, there were no cuts, no strains or swellings, nothing wrong with him other than shock. So,' she pursued logically, 'there must have been a problem with the saddle. The girth, was that it?'

Hugh smiled but did not reply.

'The saddle came off,' Edith supplied. 'That's what Joe said.'

'Yes, I see,' Susannah agreed. 'If he's right it must have been the girth. But then why were the police interested in the horses at the hall rail? Oh, of course,' she said quickly, 'that's when the damage must have been done. Then,' she went on, 'it could have been anyone. The rail is out of sight from inside the hall, but there were a lot of people about. Somebody would surely have seen any hanky panky.' She gripped her hands together tightly. 'It's so ridiculous,' she said. 'Why on earth would anybody want to harm Gil? Surely it must be a mistake.'

Hugh lifted one shoulder noncommittally, but Mike chipped in, 'Ask Anna. She's the one with a source of information.'

Anna's eyes narrowed, but she ignored him, explaining to Susannah, 'Inspector Elliot is a friend of mine, but he never tells me anything about his work. We have better things to talk about.'

Mike snorted derisively.

'Can you think of anybody who might have had a grudge against Gil?' Lucy asked. 'Somebody who might have wanted to spoil his ride, but didn't expect the accident to be fatal.'

'No, of course not,' Susannah said impatiently. 'Any rider would know that an accident could lead to more than a few bumps and scratches.'

'But there are people,' Edith murmured dreamily, 'who might have wanted to cause trouble, to get back at Gil.'

Lucy eyed her curiously. 'Anyone in particular?' she asked.

'Nonsense,' Susannah said at the same moment.

Edith did not look at either of them; her pale eyes were considering the carved wooden owl on the wall. 'Well, Phil Avery wasn't very happy with him. I heard him talking about it to Joe when they went past here yesterday. They were talking very loudly. Joe was shouting, really.'

Lucy's attention sharpened as she remembered Edith's habit of sitting at one of the upper windows, looking out over the village green. 'Phil Avery?' she queried.

'Who's he?' Hugh asked at the same moment.

Berhane waved a hand lightly round the walls of the room. 'The man who created these carvings. He and Gil got on well enough.'

'We used to know him in our teens,' Lucy explained. 'I met him up on the moor this morning,' she added. 'It was his place that I went to with Ben to get away from the hounds. I rang the police from there.'

Hugh met her eyes for a moment. 'What was he doing when you arrived?' he asked quietly.

'He was in the middle of feeding his animals,' Lucy said, thinking back. 'Not farm animals, you know. Injured wildlife.'

'Gil wasn't going to renew the lease on Phil's smallholding,' Edith said, 'that was what Phil was telling Joe.'

'Why ever not?' Susannah demanded. 'Phil is making a good living from his work. He could easily pay the rent, or even get a mortgage to buy the place.'

Edith looked at her aunt vaguely. 'Oh, Gil wanted to use it for Berhane's training centre.'

Susannah stared. Then she turned to Berhane, demanding, 'Is this true?'

Berhane shook her head. 'Who said so, Edith?' she asked quietly.

Edith considered, her fingers playing with the feathery hem of her cotton tops. 'Joe told Phil that, after Phil said Gil wasn't going to rent him the place any more.'

Berhane glanced at Susannah. 'It sounds like Joe making

trouble,' she said.

'Why would he do that?' Hugh asked.

'He doesn't mean to,' Susannah said shortly. 'But Joe is a pessimist, always quick to see the worst possible scene.'

'So why wouldn't Gil let Phil carry on renting his small-holding?' Lucy asked.

Berhane looked puzzled. 'I don't know,' she said. 'Maybe he told Phil why.' She glanced enquiringly at her sister. 'Did he?'

Edith shrugged. 'That's all I heard. I wasn't really listening, I was watching the pigeons in the trees. I only caught that because their voices were so loud they disturbed me. And of course,' she added unexpectedly, 'Joe was angry with Gil too.'

Susannah made an exasperated sound. 'That's a long time ago. And for that matter he was angry with you and Berhane, and you're both still in one piece.' She turned to Hugh. 'Joe's sister and her husband lost their cottage when Ballamy's Farm was sold. Joe was very upset about it for a while, but they're happy enough with life where they are now and Joe got over it.'

'So,' Anna said slowly, 'is Phil Avery Joe's nephew?'

Susannah nodded.

Mike whistled. 'Quite a convenient combination. And a repeated aggravation.' He saw Anna's raised eyebrows. 'First the landlord's sister was turned out,' he explained with exag-gerated care, 'then her son gets the same treatment. Uncle and nephew could have got together to plan their revenge.'

'But then they'd want to get Berhane,' Edith said, 'not Gil.'

'This is all getting out of hand,' Susannah said. 'Phil and Joe had no real motive in either case.'

Her niece looked at her. 'But that wasn't why Joe was cross. He was telling you, wasn't he?' Edith said. 'So you know.'

'Really, Edith,' Susannah said crossly, 'you must stop sitting at that window listening to other people's conversation.'

'It is useful to know what people have said in these circum-stances,' Hugh intervened.

'But snatches of talk don't give a true picture,' Susannah

protested.

'They can give us a lead, though,' Hugh said.

'What did you hear this time?' Lucy asked Edith.

'Aunt Susannah can tell you,' Edith said, sounding bored as she lowered her eyes to the table, fiddling with the rosemary needles again.

'Joe's always getting himself into a state,' Susannah explained curtly. 'He's particularly obsessed with his great-grandfather's archaeological collections and the vague stories of hidden treasure that have grown up around them. There's always something like that,' she added dismissively 'about some ancient sites.'

Mike leaned forward. 'I hope,' he said ominously, 'that he wasn't planning any illicit digging.'

A smile touched Susannah's lips. 'No, quite the opposite. He thinks you might arrange some official excavation and find what he thinks of as his.'

'I've a fat chance of getting funding for any work right now,' Mike growled.

'But that didn't involve Gil,' Lucy pointed out.

'Joe thought Gil knew where the treasure was,' Edith contributed. 'Gil was always teasing him about it, and Joe took him seriously. And now of course he's all worked up about the diaries Gil found, in case they say where it is.'

'Joe takes everybody seriously,' Susannah said. 'That doesn't lead him to go around attacking them. For heaven's sake, he's left me alone, and he's concerned that my historical research would give me essential clues.'

Mike rolled his eyes upwards. 'A fanatic,' he grunted. 'He was damned rude when I tried to talk to him again about this collection he's got.'

'I wondered why he was shouting at you,' Edith said.

'You seem to have been around a lot at all the interesting moments, Edith,' Lucy commented.

Edith shrugged. 'I can't get mobile reception indoors. The

green's the best place, so I go out there. And then something always catches my eye, so I stand and watch for a while.'

'Or your ear,' Mike muttered.

Edith's pale eyes rested on him blankly. 'You disturbed me, you were both shouting so loudly. It wasn't difficult to hear.'

'Oh dear,' Anna said, with spurious concern, 'maybe you should be watching your back, Mike.'

'I always do,' he retorted.

Berhane looked at her watch. 'I'd better bring in the pudding,' she said, getting up to stack the plates. As Anna rose again to help her, Berhane added, 'I don't want to stop the discussion, but I thought we'd go out to listen to the bells ring in the New Year, so we haven't much time left.'

She and Anna went off to the kitchen while Lucy glanced at her own watch. 'Heavens,' she said, surprised, 'it really is late. Eleven o'clock already.'

'Time flies when you're enjoying yourself,' Mike commented morosely.

Edith raised her eyes and considered him with a spark of interest.

At that moment there was a hammering on the front door that brought Ben out from under the table, barking furiously, followed more slowly by Juno. She stood by Isobel watching the collie as he raced through the screen door into the hallway. Berhane came out of the kitchen and followed him, as the others watched, feeling strangely uneasy.

'It's too early for first footing, isn't it?' Isobel asked, as Lucy went to fetch her dog.

'I expect it's the police,' Mike muttered morosely. 'Elliot's probably come to join the feast'.

'He'll be far too busy,' Hugh said quietly. 'He won't get time off until the investigation into Hannaford's death is finished.'

Anna had brought small bottles of Beaume de Venise out of the kitchen and was putting them down on the table. She straightened up, cocking her head as she strained her ears to listen to the sound of voices beyond the screen. 'It's a man,' she said, 'but I don't recognise his voice. Lucy seems to know him though.'

As she spoke Berhane came back into the dining room. Behind her was a young man with shoulder-length black hair, who looked across at the people around the table with an embarrassed air.

He muttered something to Berhane, who said, 'Nonsense. There's more than enough pudding to go round. Just don't have too much. You know what it's like to pull bell ropes when you've eaten heavily.'

Lucy was taking her own place again, her hands cradling an oddly shaped object wrapped in newspaper. Ben slipped under the table as Berhane said generally, 'This is Phil Avery, an old friend of Gil's. He's come to tell us that the bell ringers are going to toll the mourning bell for Gil just before the New Year's rung in.'

She pulled a chair up to the table between Lucy and Edith and gestured to Phil to sit down. Hugh and Susannah shuffled their chairs sideways, but Edith was staring at him, her mouth a little open in surprise. Hugh got up and whispered in her ear, his hands on the back of her chair. She moved her head slowly, taking her gaze slowly away from Phil to look up at Hugh. Without a word, she allowed him to move her chair to create more space for the newcomer.

Phil sat down reluctantly, nodding politely to Edith, who had resumed her staring. Lucy quietly introduced Hugh and Mike, and gestured towards Anna, who smiled brilliantly down the table at him.

Phil blinked and returned the smile with a lop-sided grin. Mike watched this with a sour expression on his face, before he too stared intently at the woodcarver.

'That's a kind thought, Phil,' Susannah said briskly.

'Well,' Phil said, 'we were talking about it in the inn, and it seems the right thing to do, Gil being local, and a bell ringer

himself. Of course, we'll be doing a special peal for the funeral.'
He stopped abruptly, obviously anxious that he had said too
much.

'It must be five years since there was a mourning toll rung in
the church,' Susannah said. 'It's a nice custom.'

'Yes, it was for Gil Ballamy that time,' Phil said. 'It was the
first I ever rang. There's not been another big moor figure die
since then.'

'What is the mourning toll?' Hugh asked, looking at Lucy's
engrossed face as she carefully unwrapped her parcel.

'It's an old tradition, dating from the Middle Ages at least,'
Susannah said. 'When a person dies a single bell is rung for
each year of their age. Probably it was originally a means of
passing on the news over a wide area, when other communica-
tions were poor.'

Mike was watching Berhane cross the room from the
kitchen, a tray in her hands. His eyes skimmed quickly over the
dishes on it and his expression grew gloomy.

Berhane put it down on the serving table. She began to
unload it, describing the dishes. 'This is the main dessert,
Linzertorte. It always reminds me of a holiday in Austria soon
after I came to live with Edith's family.' She smiled across at her
sister, who was trying to see what Lucy had in her parcel.

'It's particularly good with the brandy cream,' Berhane
continued. 'Otherwise, there are the little ginger meringues, and
a whole variety of baklava. See if you can work out what's in
them.' She picked up a pudding plate, then paused and glanced
at Susannah. 'Gil was thirty, wasn't he?' she asked. 'Phil wanted
to check.'

Susannah's brows knitted as she thought. She nodded. 'Yes,
thirty last year. In September, I think.'

'That's okay, then,' Phil said. 'We want to get it right.' His
eyes were on Lucy, who was staring down at the object she held,
one finger moving gently over it.

She looked up at him with a smile that lit her pointed face.

'Thank you for bringing it.' She leaned forward. 'See, Hugh. This is what I was telling you about. Isn't he lovely?' She held out the wooden robin, rounded and cheeky, for his approval.

Anna gave an exclamation of delight. 'He's lovely,' she said. 'You'd almost expect him to hop down the table.'

Hugh had taken the carving and was examining it with care as Berhane put his plate down in front of him. 'It's beautifully done,' he said. He turned to Phil. 'I admired the others earlier, the ones on the walls here, but this is so much smaller and still very accurate in detail. It must be harder to do.'

Phil shrugged, accepting a plate laden with a selection of desserts. 'The size doesn't make much odds, really. It's what the wood lets you do that matters.' He glanced round the room, surprise on his face as he saw the woodcarvings. 'I didn't know you had these,' he said.

Berhane seated herself. 'I've collected them since I came back. You have a real knack, Phil.'

'I've Miss Ballamy to thank for helping me turn it into a trade,' Phil said. He dipped a portion of Linzertorte into the cream and took a cautious bite of it. His expression changed, pleasure obliterating the doubt. 'This is nice,' he said, his surprise very evident.

Berhane laughed. 'I've a knack for food, Phil. I hope it makes me as successful as you.'

'Successful?' he said, looking up startled. 'I make a living out of woodcarving, and I'm grateful for that.'

'Berhane thinks you'll go far,' Edith said as she cut pieces of the tart and pushed them round her plate. 'That's why she got your carvings, in case she doesn't.'

Phil glanced at her, unfazed. 'You haven't changed a bit, Edith,' he said pleasantly.

She flushed, the colour running unexpectedly up her pale face.

'Of course he's going to go a long way,' Susannah said firmly, passing the carved robin to Isobel to admire. 'And judging from the meal you've provided us with tonight, Berhane, you should too. Although,' she added more doubtfully, 'your skills may be wasted down here.'

'Yes,' Anna agreed, tucking into a ginger meringue with relish. 'I'm sure you'd have more luck further west.'

Mike snorted as he brushed pastry crumbs off his jumper. 'Closer to you, where you can eat her food more often, that's what you mean.'

'Of course I do,' Anna said gaily. 'Although it wouldn't be good for my figure.'

Susannah ignored this aside. 'What are they saying in the inn, Phil? About Gil's death?'

Phil looked down the table towards her. 'A lot of rubbish,' he said bluntly. 'Nobody could really believe it was deliberate sabotage, but without too much effort everybody could think of a possible murderer.' He laid his spoon down on his empty plate, licking a finger tip to mop up the baklava honey. 'And since I left they'll no doubt have found lots of reasons for me to have done it.' His crooked eyebrows twitched. 'But it's the hunt they're most concerned about. Still, Gil would approve of that. Joe's getting himself into a right state over it, wanting to talk to you about how they're going to keep it going. It was all I could do to stop him coming over with me.' Phil glanced at his watch and got to his feet, pushing back his chair. 'I must be off. Thanks for the pudding, Berhane.'

'Are we all going to be friends again?' Edith asked suddenly, as she crumbled her meringue into dust on her plate.

'Why not?' Phil said. 'Gil's death made me think life's too short for wasting any of it in ill will. There's not much point bearing grudges anyway. It never gets us anywhere good.' He looked across at Berhane, who had also risen to her feet. 'Next time you want to invest in one of my carvings, you come up to the smallholding and choose one. It's stupid to pay shop prices, they're for tourists.'

'If you're still at the smallholding,' Edith said. 'Maybe Gil's sister will have other plans for it.'

He shrugged. 'I'm not meeting trouble until it comes.' He raised a hand in general farewell and turned to the screen door.

'We'd better get ready too,' Berhane said. 'That is, if you want to come out onto the green to listen to the bells.'

Before Mike could voice the protest on his lips Anna was beside him, taking his arm and urging him out of his chair. 'Come on, Mike. How can you criticise us if you lurk around in here?'

'Joe Triggs usually provides very good mulled wine for the New Year,' Susannah said casually. 'We normally go on to the inn for some of his special brew with the rest of the village after the ringing ends, but this year I think everyone will want to get off home. The snow's due to start falling tonight.'

Mike got up with a show of reluctance. 'I'd better keep Hugh company. He can't get too outnumbered by you women.'

Phil had gone by the time the diners crowded into the hall, pulling on hats, coats and boots, elbows sticking into each other's ribs, tossed scarves whisking under somebody else's nose. Ben wriggled in and out of legs, his eyes bright with excitement, but Juno lingered in the screen doorway, muddled by the confusion. Susannah and Isobel hung back too, waiting for the rest to go.

'So there is some good in the start to the New Year,' Isobel remarked, watching Lucy clip Ben's lead on. 'Phil Avery seems popular with Berhane and Edith.'

Susannah shrugged. 'They all grew up together. You know what children are like, there were always spats of some kind, but they forgot them in the end. Adult disagreements are worse, and there was a lot of anger and hurt behind this one. But I've been sure Phil would get over his sense of grievance.' She shivered as the front door was opened, letting in a blast of cold air and revealing a world of whiteness outside where snow was falling heavily and silently.

'The inn landlord seems extremely generous with his drinks,'

Isobel commented idly. 'How can he be sure we pay him for drinks on the green? In fact,' she added, 'I didn't pay him for the drink I had before the hunt set out.'

'There's no need,' Susannah replied. 'The hunt committee funds that, and the village committee pays for tonight's. Both are a long-standing tradition.'

'Are you on the committees?' Isobel asked.

Susannah smiled. 'Of course. I think there's been a Ballamy on them since they were founded.' She saw Berhane was leading the way outside, and said, 'Let's get our things on quickly.'

'I'll just take Juno across to your house and leave her there. She won't want to stand about in this cold,' Isobel said. 'And then I won't have to come back here afterwards.'

The village green was transformed when they went out of the Church House. Large crisp flakes of snow were settling onto the white blanket that was already covering the grass. Under the low pink-tinged grey arch of the night sky the cottages and trees seemed like shapes in a snow globe. Cottages were covered with a pristine white thatch and each branch of the trees bore its own layer of glittering crystals.

As Berhane's party moved across the green noise and movement broke into the stillness of the winter scene. Men and women strolled out of the inn, talking loudly, many with glasses still in their gloved hands. Cottage doors opened as if synchronised and families spilt out through the brightly-lit entrances, boots on their feet, hats and scarves almost hiding their faces. Everyone moved towards the centre of the green, calling out greetings as they gathered into a loose-knit crowd, labradors and spaniels yipping in excitement.

'Ah, here comes Joe,' Susannah said. 'I'll go and give him a hand. Betsey may be a bit harassed by all the extra work.'

The landlord had come out of the inn garden bearing a wide tray. Steam rose from the tiny metal cups on it and Anna sniffed appreciatively as a spicy smell drifted around them. 'Mmm, just what I need.'

She glanced at Mike. 'I suppose I'd better get ours. Joe didn't seem very happy with you earlier so we'll probably be bottom of his list now. It's a shame you had to row with him before we leave.'

Mike scowled. 'Bloody man,' he said roughly. 'Hugh and I still bear the bruises he gave us this morning.'

'Well, darling,' Anna said with spurious sympathy, 'Joe's got quite a few too. And that spectacular black eye. Somehow I feel sure you gave it to him.'

'I bloody well hope so,' Mike snapped. 'And don't call me darling. All these arty affectations...' Words unexpectedly failed him.

'Come on then, Anna,' Lucy said, tucking her arm through Hugh's. Ben pressed against her legs, wary about the blinding whiteness and the throngs of people. 'Let's get some mull before it disappears.'

Anna clasped Hugh's other arm and they strolled purposefully into the crowd. Glancing around she saw that Berhane was talking to a group of men. Edith was not immediately obvious, but as people shifted Anna caught sight of her standing alone under a tree, gazing down towards Gil's house.

Anna hesitated, suddenly uncomfortable. Perhaps Edith really was upset about Gil's death?

Behind her Mike stumbled and bumped into her. She was only prevented from falling by tightening her grip on Hugh's arm.

'For God's sake,' Mike growled, grabbing her other arm, 'don't stop like that.'

Joe Triggs turned round at the sound of his voice. His face darkened and he deliberately turned away again, offering the last cups on his tray to people on his far side.

'Now look what you've done,' Anna said.

'It's alright,' Lucy said quickly. 'Here comes Aunt Susannah with another tray.'

Susannah paused as she drew level with the landlord and

exchanged a few words with him. She glanced around as he moved off again. Catching sight of Lucy and Hugh she wove through a few groups of people and held out her tray. 'Joe said we'd finished,' she commented, 'but he has a habit of leaving out people who've annoyed him, so I thought you might still be waiting.'

'We are,' Anna said as she took a cup. 'Thank you.'

Mike picked up one and raised it to his lips as Anna said quickly, 'Not yet, Mike. It's to toast the New Year. You almost certainly won't get another.'

'Don't worry,' Berhane said over her shoulder as Mike angrily lowered his cup, 'I've already bearded the inn for my own so I can always go back for more. I'm on Joe's blacklist too.'

'I thought you always were,' Lucy commented idly, one hand gently stroking Ben's wet head.

Berhane smiled slowly. 'Of course, but now I've added insult to injury by being alive when Gil's dead. Joe'll have realised by now that it could quite easily have been me.'

Lucy looked at her with concern, but Berhane shook her head. 'It's alright, Joe's always upfront with his feelings. And it wasn't difficult to work out that Gil might not have been the intended victim.'

Anna had not been listening. She was looking round again, peering through the knots of people, but there was no sign of Edith now. 'Where's Edith? Isn't she joining us?'

Berhane shrugged. 'Edith does her own thing. I never worry about where she is.' She dug her hand in the deep pocket of her poncho and pulled out a small parcel wrapped loosely in brown paper. 'Would you give this to Hugh? I meant to hand them over earlier. It's the other two diaries Gil gave me. I'm not going to have chance to look at them for a while, but I'd particularly like Hugh's opinion on them, as he seemed to think the first one was interesting.'

Lucy accepted the parcel, pushing it into her coat pocket

just as there was a preliminary clanging of bells. The people gathered on the green became quiet and stood waiting, faces turned towards the church tower. The spotlights that shone out from it lit the snowflakes that fell soundlessly in a heavy curtain, hiding the church itself from view.

Soon the discordant noise gave way to a single deep-toned bell that slowly and remorselessly rang out the thirty years of Gil's life. The people on the village green stood still, silent, the gaiety of the season gone from their hearts. Lucy looked round through the thickly falling snow. Faces tinged pink with cold under woolly hats were sombre, hands tightened on the arms of their loved ones.

A sudden wind blew across the green, sending the snow-flakes scurrying and dancing before it, briefly clearing a line of vision up to the inn. And there, surely, was Edith, just in front of the garden hedge. Lucy stared. Who was that with her, his arm around her? Had her bloke, what was his name, arrived at last? Taylor, that's it.

The wind dropped, the snowy screen fell again and the bell became silent as Isobel joined them. Only the sound of a motor-bike roaring into life disturbed the quietness. Nobody moved until Berhane raised her cup and drank from the warming wine. Lucy gratefully wrapped her gloved hand more tightly around her own hot cup and lifted it to her lips. Standing around in the cold was beginning to become uncomfortable. She blinked as snowflakes landed on her lashes, and as her vision cleared she heard the sudden wild joyous clamouring of all five bells, ringing out the old year with great enthusiasm. The sound reverberated around the green, through the tree trunks, reverberating off the cottages, spreading high up onto the lonely moor.

The peal stopped suddenly and a minute later a single bell rang out again, a lighter tone marking the last seconds of the old year. As it reached twelve the little metal cups were raised across the green and the sound of voices was heard again, tenta-tive at first, then stronger, more confident.

Hugh lifted his own cup, gently tapping Lucy's. 'Here's to many happy years in our new home,' he said, bending to speak into her ear.

Her eyes met his. 'Together,' she added quietly, taking another sip of the mulled wine. Her nose wrinkled. 'Wow, this is strong.'

'Just as well we're not driving anywhere tonight,' Hugh commented. 'I think there's a good dash of brandy in it.'

'I don't envy Phil,' Lucy said suddenly. 'He can't be staying down here. He's got all those animals up there on his small-holding. With the weather getting so bad he'll have to get back while he can.'

'Have some more,' Susannah's voice said at their elbow. 'Joe's excelled himself this time. Whatever his moods, his drinks are always good.' Lucy and Hugh both took another cup, and Lucy felt a twinge of concern as Susannah moved off. She's really not looking well, Lucy thought uneasily. Maybe I ought to find Berhane.

Mike reached over as Susannah passed him and took another drink as well. He stood nearby holding it, his shoulders hunched under his heavy donkey jacket, his woollen beanie pulled low over his forehead, a forbidding figure. People gave him a wide berth as they began to move away, stopping here and there to chat to friends, calling their shivering dogs to their sides, but gradually drifting back to their cottages or the 4x4s parked behind the inn.

'Well, Isobel, I think we'd better get home,' Susannah said, appearing suddenly out of the snowstorm. 'I think hot chocolate before bed would be more appealing than Joe's home-brew tonight.'

'I'm sure it will be,' Isobel said. 'And I should really let Juno out. Although she won't like all this snow.' She turned to the others. 'Berhane, it was a delicious meal, thank you very much for all the care that went into it. And goodnight, all of you. I'll look forward to seeing you later today.'

She moved off with Susannah, treading cautiously through the deepening snow on the ground. Within seconds they were lost to sight in the swirling whiteness.

'You go on back to the inn,' Berhane urged her friends. 'Betsey will make you a hot drink if Joe is busy in the bar. Although I doubt anyone is going to hang around in this weather.' She caught her breath on the unbidden thought that Gil would have been sure to be there, no matter how heavily the snow was falling. 'Come on over to the Church House tomorrow, no,' she corrected herself, 'later today, after breakfast. We can see what's happening and decide what to do.'

Calling out their thanks the four bent their heads and walked up the green to where the blurred lights of the inn were just visible through the falling snow. Ben was happier now, pulling on his lead, keen to get back to shelter.

Lucy glanced back once, concerned suddenly to see that Berhane got home safely. But it seemed Berhane was not going home. Her tall figure was visible now and then as the drifting veil of snowflakes parted briefly. As Lucy stared, trying to watch her friend, she saw that Berhane only got as far as the church gate, where she paused, pushing it open to disappear into the churchyard.

I expect she knows the bell ringers, Lucy thought practically, but then again I suppose they'll be leaving pretty quickly too. Maybe, she realised with a start, she wants time to think about Gil. An uneasy memory of that gloved hand on the curtained doorway of the chapel crept back into her mind. I wonder, Lucy thought anxiously, if she's safe there on her own.

She jerked Hugh's arm, catching his attention. He leaned over to catch her words, as she explained her sudden concern.

'Hmm,' he murmured, glancing down the green. 'Well,' he said decisively, 'there's no point going back. We'd easily miss her in this. Any assassin would be lucky to find her too.'

'Unless it's one of the bell ringers,' Lucy said, half to herself as she moved on reluctantly.

They had reached the inn, which stood quiet. When they
entered it they found all its rooms, were brightly lit. There was
no sound, though, as Lucy grabbed a towel from a stack near
the coat rack and wrapped it quickly round Ben, forestalling
his move to shake his wet coat and spray the hall with drops of
water. Not, she thought practically, that it's likely to make much
difference. I expect every dog that comes in has left traces here.

As she bent over the parcel in her pocket dug into her ribs.
'Hugh,' she said softly, keen not to disturb the dog as she rubbed
him down, 'just reach into my pocket. Berhane gave me another
couple of those diaries of Gil's for you to read.'

Hugh pulled a wry face as he fished the parcel out. 'I can't
see there's much point in reading any more,' he said. 'They'll
belong to Gil's heir now.'

'You never know, they may be a publishing coup,' Lucy said,
straightening up and releasing Ben.

Hugh raised a quizzical eyebrow, as he put the parcel down
to take off his coat and hat. 'The first one does seem more interesting than I expected,' he conceded. 'I'll glance through these
when I have time.'

'I'll go down to the kitchen and find Betsey,' Anna said,
ignoring Mike's irritable muttering as he pulled off his beanie,
exposing red curls that matched the colour of his face. 'I really
fancy some hot chocolate. Does anyone else want a mug? I'll
wait and bring it up to our rooms.'

Mike shuddered as Lucy and Hugh accepted Anna's offer.
'Disgusting,' he grunted. 'Don't bother, Anna. It doesn't sound
as though there are any customers, and I should think the
cook's gone home. I'll find the landlord. I'll even bring up your
foul drinks, but I want something better than that. Some of that
special brew Susannah was talking about sounds just right.'

He strode off through the front room into the bar, still in
his boots and donkey jacket, a trail of water dripping onto the
stone floor behind him. The women pulled off their wet coats,
hats, scarves and boots, leaving them with Hugh's as close to the

embers of the fire in the front room as they could. They went slowly upstairs and were settling into their bedrooms when they heard Mike's heavy footsteps on the stairs.

His voice called out to Anna, then he was at the neighbouring door. Hugh opened it and Mike thrust two mugs at them. A scowl darkened his face. 'The bloody man's nowhere around, and neither's the cook,' he snarled, the wet wool of his jacket mingling with the hot sweet smell of the drinks. 'I made it myself, but I'm damned if I'll drink this muck.' He stamped away and banged the door of his room shut.

Hugh looked ruefully at the clotted lumps of chocolate in the tepid milk. He met Lucy's eyes and they both laughed. 'I expect Betsey wanted to get home before the weather gets even worse,' Hugh said. 'I don't know if she lives in the village or has to go further.'

'No wonder Mike doesn't like hot chocolate, if this is how he makes it,' Lucy commented, stirring the contents of her mug with a pen before setting it down on the table beside the bed. Ben had lifted his head hopefully, but after a few deep sniffs he lowered it again, tucking it under his tail as he curled up in his own bed.

'Are you going to read them?' Lucy demanded, gesturing at the two little books with marbled paper covers, which lay in the unwrapped parcel on the bed.

'No,' he said uncompromisingly, picking them up and putting them in a drawer of the chest near the window. 'They can certainly wait. I want to finish Howse's *Pilgrim in Spain* first, but I can't even look at that tonight. It's been a hell of a day.'

A few minutes later Lucy and Hugh were snuggled down between their cold sheets. Nearby Anna lay in a tight huddle under her blankets, longing fervently for a hot water bottle. In the room beyond hers Mike sat up awkwardly against the head of the bed, the bedclothes pulled up around him as he leaned his elbows on his knees, peering at the map he had spread out across the quilt. He fell asleep quite suddenly, twisted awkwardly onto his side, as the map slithered onto the floor. The inn fell still and silent, apart from the creak of beams settling and the soft shuffling of sliding snow on the thatched roof.

Snow continued to fall during the night, and the strange quietness that it brought to the village was noticeable. Many people stirred in their sleep that night, conscious of the lack of sound, dreamily aware of the clarity of the light. But one figure lay still on a cold stone floor, oblivious to all of these things, as the lights of the inn continued to shine out through the swirling flakes.

FIVE

The sound was muffled, but in the early morning stillness it was enough to jerk Hugh awake, heart thumping, wondering for an instant where he was. It had disturbed Ben too. The collie's head was raised, his ears pricked.

The sound came again. Muffled as it was, this time there was no mistaking it. Somewhere downstairs a woman was screaming.

Hugh threw the covers aside and leaped out of bed, startling Lucy into wakefulness.

'What is it?' she demanded. She sat up, brushing hair out of her face as Hugh tripped over his shoes. Cursing, he bent over to pull them on.

'Something's wrong,' he said, running over to the door as Lucy switched on her bedside lamp. He wrenched the door open, and suddenly clearly audible was the sound of a woman sobbing hysterically.

Lucy sprang out of bed too, thrusting her feet into felt slippers and grabbing her dressing gown as she followed Hugh. Ben was beside her in an instant, the long hair in his ruff raised stiffly. She spoke to him firmly, telling him to stay, as she closed the bedroom door in his reproachful face.

Other doors were opening onto the landing as she reached the stairs. A sharp exclamation of pain and a bleary imprecation marked the collision between Anna and Mike as both tried to catch up with Lucy.

Lucy ignored the questions hurled after her. She had no attention for anything but the scene in the hall below. The thin little woman she had briefly seen in the bar last night stood there, still in her coat, her headscarf dangling from one hand. Betsey, Lucy dredged the name out of her memory, noticing that the woman's sobs were getting louder, more uncontrolled, as Hugh reached her.

She gestured wildly along the passage towards the kitchen at the back of the pub. 'Down there,' she gasped, struggling to catch her breath. 'Down in the cellar, lying there dead and cold, his eyes staring at me.' Her voice rose and Hugh looked with relief at Lucy as she appeared by his side.

'Look after her,' he ordered. 'I'll see what's wrong.'

'I'll come with you,' Mike said quickly, skirting the crying woman.

Hugh nodded curtly and walked swiftly along the corridor. The door on the right that led down to the cellar stood open, the stone steps inside faintly lit by the single bulb hanging from the ceiling.

'Wait here until I see what's happened,' Hugh said, beginning to tread carefully down the stairs.

Mike grunted, stepping to one side on the platform at the edge of the stairs. He leaned precariously past the dangling rope of the primitive hoist that brought the barrels up from the cellar below. Peering downwards Mike saw Hugh reach the ground and stoop over an oddly shaped mound on the floor.

Hugh straightened up, still staring down at the bulky heap. 'He's dead alright,' he said, his voice strained. 'And has been for some hours by the look of it.'

'Who is it?' Mike demanded.

'The landlord. Apparently squashed under one of his own barrels. It still has the loop of the hoist around it.'

'Apparently?' Mike asked quickly, stepping back as Hugh

came up the stairs.

'I can't see that well down there, the light's so poor,' Hugh said as he reached the door. 'But I think his neck is broken.' He glanced at the winding gear beside the platform. 'It's a bloody lethal way of moving barrels, and it looks as though he or the barrel slipped and both went over the edge.'

'But you don't think it's that straightforward,' Mike growled. 'Do you?'

Hugh shrugged. 'It's difficult to tell,' he said slowly. 'The body seems to be at an odd angle if Triggs fell from the platform. And I wouldn't have expected the barrel to fall on top of him if they went over together.'

'Maybe it bounced,' Mike suggested hopefully.

'Maybe,' Hugh agreed, 'but I'd expect it to shatter a stave or two if it hit the floor. The floor should show signs too, at least marks in the beaten earth. And,' he added reluctantly, 'it looks from the bloodstain on the floor as though he may have a wound on the back of his head.'

Mike groaned loudly, stopping abruptly as Hugh waved a hand irritably, hushing him.

Hugh continued in a low voice, 'He could have got it by striking the shelf. But another death in this village must instantly be suspicious. Particularly when the man was closely connected with the first victim.'

'What the hell do we do about it?' Mike asked, running his hands through his untidy hair. 'I don't know how bad the weather is, but the police and ambulance are going to have a hell of a job getting through.'

'I know,' Hugh said. 'And I wonder if somebody has taken advantage of that. But the police and ambulance crews must have experience of situations like this. We'll probably have to clear space for a helicopter to land on the green.'

Mike's expression darkened. 'Just how I want to spend New Year, doing more digging. God,' he suddenly clutched his head, 'let's get at it. Or we'll have bloody Elliot skiing in heroically, no doubt with a pair of St Bernard's lolloping along behind. How the hell do I always get drawn into these situations?'

'There's no time for that now,' Hugh said sharply. 'Where's the woman who found him? I presume she works here.'

'She's the cook, she was around the place last night. I think they've taken her through the bar into the kitchen,' Mike said. 'I heard them banging around in there just now. You'd have thought they'd have stayed in the bar and started on the brandy.' His gloomy expression lightened. 'Now that's an idea. Purely medicinal, of course. I know I'm suffering from shock.'

'For God's sake, Mike,' Hugh said with unusual force, 'give it a rest. Go in with the others if you like, while I try to call the police, but please don't needle Anna. We've got enough trouble without you two having a spat.'

Mike scowled, but Hugh strode back to the hall. He cast a quick look over the clutter that filled it before running upstairs to fetch his mobile phone.

The kitchen was small, but well-equipped and spotlessly clean, white and chrome surfaces both immaculate in the bright light from the fluorescent strip that lit the room. Mike, though, had no attention for anything other than the women sitting at a small table by the inn yard window. Anna and Lucy sat on either side of the table, Betsey between them, her back against the small window, blocking most of the view outside. He was relieved to notice that she had stopped crying.

The two friends were quiet, their eyes on Betsey, who was talking feverishly, seemingly unable to stop. '... all night. That must be why the lights were on when I got here. I knew it was strange as soon as I saw them. I felt sure there'd be trouble. Joe's that careful about money, you wouldn't believe the fuss he makes about having lights on. Especially now when he might have to use the emergency generator if the weather stays bad.' Her soft voice droned on, and Anna cast Mike a despairing glance.

'What's that you're drinking?' he demanded abruptly, glaring at the mugs on the table. 'I could do with something myself.'

Anna's eyes flashed but Betsey's monologue stopped as if it had been a cut recording. She stared at Mike, aware of him for the first time.

'Yes, of course you could,' she said, suddenly calm as she pushed her chair back and stood up. 'You come and sit down with the ladies, and I'll make us all a fresh pot of tea.'

Mike scowled and Lucy said quickly, 'It's good for shock, better than alcohol. Especially this early in the day.'

Anna stared at him, taking in his appearance for the first time. A bubble of laughter rose in her chest. Mike was in a nightshirt, garishly vivid in purple and gold stripes, his hairy legs protruding under its hem. If only she'd known, she thought wildly, she'd have bought him a nightcap for Christmas.

As she stared he began to hop up and down and she realised he was barefoot on the cold floor. She swallowed hard. 'Do sit down, Mike, and get your feet off the floor,' she said fairly steadily. 'Or get some slippers.'

He pulled out the chair nearest to him, glowering at her as he sat down heavily, quite oblivious to the sartorial elegance of her own nightwear, scarlet pyjamas edged in cream, the slender feet in suede pumps tucked up on the seat, and the raffish disorder of her tumbled black curls.

'Where's Hugh?' Lucy asked, the white lace collar of her nightdress protruding crookedly over the turquoise Jacquard dressing gown her grandmother had given her for Christmas.

'Ringing the police on his mobile.'

'He won't get no reception here, my lover,' Betsey said at his shoulder as she plonked a mug of tea down in front of him. 'He'll need to use Joe's phone. It's to be hoped the lines aren't down.'

'Where is the phone?' Lucy asked, getting up.

'Across the yard. He took out the old one from here, said folks always wanted to use it for free calls once the call box was taken off the village green,' Betsey replied, stretching up to fetch down a frying pan from the rack above the Aga. 'He's got a nice little place of his own over there, in what were the stables. Miss Ballamy persuaded him to change them over. Weren't no real use him keeping his horse there, when Gil was doing livery. That was when Joe made the inn bedrooms ensuites. Miss Ballamy's idea again, that was. Said as how nobody's going to want to stay without them.'

Lucy hesitated uncertainly and Betsey carried on, 'Joe's place won't be locked, dear, there's no need round here. You go and get your husband to ring from there. I'll make us all some breakfast. We'll need setting up for when the police come. And poor Joe'll not be fussing about what I'm using now.'

'I'll come with you, Lucy,' Anna said, following her friend into the passageway. 'I suppose we'd better get dressed, although I guess it'll be some time before anyone can get here. I wonder how deep the snow is.'

They had just reached the hall when the front door opened, startling them both. Hugh came in on a burst of icy air, stamping his feet on the threshold to loosen the snow clotted under his boots. He had pulled his coat over his pyjamas, but his face was pink with cold and his mobile was clutched in one gloved hand.

He banged the door shut and shook the mobile irritably when he saw them. 'No reception anywhere,' he said. 'I'll have to find a landline. Surely he'd have had one.'

Anna went up the stairs as Lucy nodded. 'He lived out in the old stables across the yard,' she said quickly. 'Betsey said the place won't be locked, and there's a landline there.'

'How is she?'

'Fine.' A smile touched Lucy's pale lips. 'All our fussing over her was nowhere near as useful as Mike's demands to be looked after. She snapped right out of the state she was in when he needed his tea.'

'I'll go round the outside,' Hugh said. 'I don't want to get caught up with her. I suppose Mike'll be there for a while if there's food in the offing, but make sure one of you stays with her at all times.'

He was turning away when Lucy said his name. Hugh looked back at her questioningly.

'Is it suspicious too?' she asked quietly.

'I'm pretty sure it is,' he answered grimly. 'And I don't want to leave him down there any longer than we have to. This damned weather,' he added, 'is going to make things difficult.'

'Well, Betsey was making breakfast when we left her,' Lucy said. 'Come and have something to eat before Mike finishes it all. Goodness knows when we'll have chance to get anything else.'

Hugh lifted an impatient shoulder and walked quickly back out through the front door. Moving over the hall to shut it behind him Lucy glanced across the inn garden to the green. In front of her was a picture postcard image of a country village in the winter. The snow lay so deeply that it was impossible to see where the lane began and the green ended, although the lines of oaks showed where the demarcation should be. There was no movement anywhere and Lucy realised with a shock that it must still be very early. She glanced at her wrist, but her watch was upstairs beside the bed. The enamelled clock face on the hall wall had been permanently stilled at half past two since they had arrived, so Lucy went up to her room.

Ben was ecstatically happy to see her, his whole body wriggling as she opened the bedroom door. He followed her closely as she went across to the bed to collect her watch from the side table. Just after seven, she noted, as she sat down in the armchair by the window to make a fuss of the collie. Part of her attention was on the view she had of the green outside, where there was still no sign of any movement.

She started as Anna spoke from the open doorway, making Ben spring up with a warning bark. Turning, she saw Ben rushing apologetically over to Anna, who was now fully dressed in black jeans and a thick scarlet jumper, her curls tied up in a loose knot on top of her head.

'What's happening?' Anna asked, coming further into the room. She reassured the collie, before kicking off her shoes and sinking cross-legged onto the dishevelled bed.

'Hugh's over the yard in Joe's apartment, ringing the police, I hope. Mike is probably being fed copiously by Betsey.'

Anna's eyes narrowed, but she said mildly, 'It seems to make her happy, so I suppose you could say Mike is being useful. Although I can't say I've got much appetite for eating breakfast while the landlord lies below in the cellar weltering in his gore.'

Lucy looked surprised, one hand outstretched to the collie as he pressed against the armchair. 'I wonder if he is.' Seeing Anna's confused expression, Lucy explained, 'Weltering in his gore. Hugh didn't say how he died.'

'Just that he was murdered, I suppose?'

Lucy nodded. 'More or less. I've been wondering what we ought to do before the police get here. I know we shouldn't broadcast what's happened, but I feel we should let Berhane know. After all, she's expecting us to go round this morning.'

'Umm, that is awkward,' Anna agreed. 'I suppose the police won't be here for ages, if they can get here at all.' She shivered. 'I can't believe they'll leave us indefinitely with the corpse.'

'I'm sure they won't, although I expect there's somewhere it could be put,' Lucy said practically. 'After all, the weather is so cold it won't be a problem for a bit.'

Anna looked taken aback. 'I suppose not,' she said.

'But,' Lucy pursued her own thoughts, 'they won't want the scene disturbed. I'm sure they'll get here, but goodness knows when.'

'What about Aunt Susannah?' Anna demanded. 'Surely she's going to expect to know what's going on? I get the impression that she pretty much runs things here.'

'Or at least has a finger on the village's pulse,' Lucy said. 'Well, let's not worry about it. We'll see what Hugh thinks, and what the police tell him to do.'

The collie's head lifted at the sound of feet on the stairs and he pattered to the door in time to greet his master.

Hugh had left his sodden coat downstairs with his boots and was unconsciously rubbing his hands together, trying to restore the circulation as he came into the room. 'I couldn't get through to Elliot, but I managed to raise the local station,' he said, frowning. 'They seemed to think there'd be no trouble getting Elliot over here. It seems he stayed nearby overnight. The sergeant I spoke to wouldn't say how he'd get here, only muttered vaguely about a local's hobby coming in useful. At least we won't have to clear landing space for a helicopter, which I'd rather expected.'

He glanced at Anna. 'Go on down to keep Betsey company while we dress. Mike's just come up too, and I don't want her left on her own.'

'She's much better now,' Anna said as she got to her feet, 'but I hear and obey. At least I can make sure Mike doesn't get started on his seconds before we've had a go at the food too. And I'll make sure there's coffee on the go. You look frozen.'

Her feet pattered on the wooden stairs as Hugh headed for the shower room, the wet ends of his pyjama trousers leaving damp marks on the carpet. 'This is a hell of a business,' he said over his shoulder. 'However Elliot gets here it looks as though we're stuck with the locals for the time being. With a murderer among us. So for God's sake, Lucy, be careful.'

In the kitchen Mike was squeezed in with the others at the table, having hastily scrambled into the clothes he had been wearing last night. His chin was bristling with stubble darker than his red hair, which stood up in uncombed ridges as he bent over his second helping of eggs and bacon. Anna was fiddling with an uneaten piece of toast and staring at him in disbelief when they heard Berhane's husky voice. She called again from the yard as she rattled the back door.

Ben leaped up, barking. Hugh got to his feet nearly as quickly as the dog. He held on to Ben's collar as he unlocked the door, barring the way in with his body.

'Sorry,' Berhane said, staring at him in surprise, 'but the front door seems to be stuck. I expect it's swollen in the damp.'

'I've locked it,' Hugh said bluntly, 'and this one. I'm afraid you can't come in, Berhane.'

Betsey was at his elbow, wiping her hands down her apron. 'Berhane, my lover, it's Joe, lying down there dead all night, poor soul. Found him there, I did, when I come in this morning. I went to close the door to the cellar, and saw the light was on. My blood ran cold, it did, I knew something was wrong. I called out, in case he was there, though what he'd want down there at that time I couldn't imagine. Then I thought I'd best have a look, it wouldn't have done to shut him in, and there he was, lying under one of his own barrels, his eyes staring up at me. Oooh, awful it was.' She shuddered dramatically. 'Such a turn as it gave me. I screamed, and I screamed.'

Berhane's horrified gaze moved to Hugh. He nodded. 'I'm afraid it's true. Look,' he said quickly, forestalling any further comments from Betsey, 'why don't you take Lucy and Anna back with you until the police get here? Betsey, I'm afraid you'll have to stay. The police will need to talk to you as soon as possible.'

She nodded complacently. 'With my finding him, and all. I'll clear up the breakfast things, then I've my knitting to be getting on with. My Eli will only wear jumpers I make. Can't get on with these scratchy modern things, he can't.'

'We'll go over to the Schoolhouse,' Berhane said, watching Anna gulp down her coffee and push away the plate with the untouched toast. 'We're all in the habit of taking matters to Aunt Susannah, you know, and she'll be getting ready for the morning service. I suppose,' she asked, 'it's alright to tell her?'

'Word will get round fast enough, especially if there's a church service. And once the police get here the rumours will be flying,' Hugh said grimly.

'How on earth…' she began, breaking off to say apologetically, 'no, don't worry, I won't start asking questions. Lucy and Anna can tell us about it when we're all together. I'm sure they won't want to repeat it more than they have to.'

'We'll just get our coats,' Lucy said as she and Anna pushed back their chairs and got up. 'We'll see you round the front.'

Berhane nodded, smiling sympathetically at Betsey, who was now folding her apron into narrow pleats, her work-roughened hands trembling again. 'You're doing really well, Betsey,' she said gently, as her friends went out through the bar to the hall, Ben keeping close to Lucy's side. 'I expect Mike and Hugh will be too busy to eat once the police arrive, so do keep them well stoked up while there's chance. I'm sure the police will need feeding too, they're going to have hard work getting here.'

The cook brightened. 'Yes, of course, that's what I'll do. I'll make some soup, there's plenty of turkey left, and vegetables. And I'll get more bread out of the freezer.' She faltered suddenly. 'I was just thinking that I ought to let my Eli know, him and Joe being brothers, even if they've not spoken for all these years. Though my Eli wemt up to see him on the green last night, and I hoped they'd come together again. But all Eli wanted was to tease him about the hunt ending.' She sighed, twisting her roughened hands together. 'And there's Phil, too, and his Mum. She'll be coming for the service. Always was keen on God, was Millie. Much closer to Joe too, she and Phil were, but then...' She broke off, and in the hall the front door banged behind Lucy and Anna.

'I'll go and lock that after them,' Mike said. 'We don't want punters coming in for an early pint.' He scowled as he strode to the door, muttering half-audibly, 'Snowed into a pub for God knows how long, and the bloody landlord has to get himself killed.'

'It's better to let the police inform your husband,' Hugh said to Betsey. 'They've got their procedures to follow.'

She nodded, relieved to have the issue taken out of her hands, and turned to the dishwasher, starting to load the breakfast plates into it. She picked up a pan from the worktop, tutting as she saw the dried milk encrusted on its interior.

Berhane turned away, but Hugh put a hand on her arm. 'Make sure the news doesn't go any further than Susannah and Isobel just yet,' he said quietly. 'And try to get Lucy and Anna to eat something. The police won't be here for some time, so we'll soon need to stop any more people trying to come into the inn. We'll need to stand at the gates in pairs, and one of us will have to stay with Betsey. We'd probably better take it in turns, giving everyone chance to warm up.' He smiled bleakly at her. 'I'll send Mike out there immediately, but come back here with Anna and Lucy as soon as you can.'

She considered him gravely. 'I see,' she said calmly, her face tightening above the purple folds of the shawl she had pushed back from her head. 'Yes, we'll do what we must.'

She turned away, pulling the shawl up more closely over her face, and Hugh shut the door behind her, turning the key in the lock again. He had just sat down at the table, his hands clasped in front of him on the worn wood, when Mike came back.

'All this to-ing and fro-ing,' he grumbled. 'Elliot's going to crucify us.' He glanced across at Betsey, who had her back towards them as she slotted the cutlery into the dishwasher tray. 'What about footprints outside? The women'll be trampling all over them.'

Hugh raised his eyes from his hands, shaking his head. 'There was nothing to trample. I checked the approaches to both doors, and the only trail I saw was Betsey's.' He lifted a shoulder in a partial shrug. 'And in here we've kept the corridor clear as far as possible. Everybody knows not to touch anything in the bar, just to walk straight through. Betsey had already been in here, so there wasn't much point closing off the kitchen.' He smiled suddenly as Mike slumped into his chair. 'And as Berhane so rightly said, we need to eat while we can. This is going to be a difficult day.'

'Another one,' Mike grunted. 'No trails leading away from

the inn. That's bloody difficult, isn't it? Makes it look as though it was one of us.'

'Yes,' Hugh agreed. 'But a lot will depend on the time he died.' His mouth thinned. 'I guess it was before we got back here last night. You couldn't find him then, which is odd, when you think about it. And a lot of snow fell after that, and would obliterate any footsteps in the earlier layer. Even,' he said in exasperation, 'if it would have been possible to distinguish any particular ones from the tracks left by the crowds.' He shrugged. 'No point speculating until we have some more facts.' He ignored Mike's muttered expostulation and continued, 'We're going to be too busy anyway. We need to stand guard at the entrances, making sure nobody else gets in. We'll do it in pairs at the drive and garden gates, with one of us in here in turn with Betsey.'

'What a bloody brilliant way to start the New Year,' Mike said. 'Just make sure I'm not on guard duty with Anna.'

'You can't imagine I'd be that stupid,' Hugh said dryly. 'But it would be a good idea if you went out there now. Berhane will bring the others back as soon as they've eaten, and I'll come out and swop places with you then. I imagine families with children will soon be out in the snow and it won't be long before people come to church, so we should be in place as fast as possible.'

Mike stamped out, muttering profanely, and after a couple of minutes Hugh heard the front door bang.

As they reached the foot of the terrace of cottages Lucy looked across the village green. The only tracks she could see were the ones they had made themselves, above the buried lane to the Schoolhouse. Three narrow troughs ran parallel behind them, and a more diagonal one cut across from the Church House. Presumably that marked Berhane's route when she had made her way up to the inn. Ben was floundering through the thick snow, leaving a wavering line under the trees and occasionally disappearing altogether into a deeper drift.

Berhane had walked them down the green past the terrace without a word being spoken. The snow was deep enough to make walking difficult, but looking around Lucy wondered how long it would be before children were out playing in it. She bent to pick up a handful, letting it drop again as she felt its consistency. It was just right for building a snowman and making snowballs. She tucked a stray strand of chestnut hair under her woollen hat, her eyes sombre. Somehow, it seemed odd to think of all that gaiety about to happen when Gil was dead, and now Joe was too.

Lucy and Anna were both pink in the face and puffing when they reached the Schoolhouse, but Berhane's longer legs had given her an easier walk. Ben's tummy and sides were plastered with snow and he limped slightly, favouring his front left paw.

'He isn't used to such thick snow,' Lucy said, as she lifted the paw and prized out an icy lump of compacted snow.

The collie put his paw down gratefully. He wagged his tail as the door opened and Susannah appeared. She was dressed for the weather in thick tweed trousers and a dark jumper. Her round face wore an expression of surprise. 'You're all about early,' she commented. 'We're only just having breakfast.' She looked at them more closely. 'What's the matter?' she demanded, her eyes running over them. 'Where's Edith?'

'Still asleep, I hope,' Berhane said. 'We've more bad news, I'm afraid. Can we join you? The inn is out of bounds right now, and Lucy and Anna could probably do with something to eat.'

Susannah's gaze flickered up the green towards the inn, where lights still blazed from all the windows as they had done throughout the night. She looked back at Berhane, then Lucy. 'How's that dog of yours with cats?'

'He's fine,' Lucy promised, crossing her fingers behind her back.

'If you're not sure, keep hold of him,' Susannah said briskly, stepping back to let them into the kitchen. 'Otherwise Solomon will teach him his place.'

Solomon was already aware of the intrusion. He stood on the worktop between the kitchen and dining area, creamy fur puffed out, doubling his size, bristling eyebrows arched over staring amber eyes.

Ben took one look, then glanced nonchalantly away, sidling round to Lucy's far side. Juno ambled over to greet him and he sniffed her in a friendly fashion, still ostentatiously keeping his head turned away from the cat.

Isobel appeared behind the cat, a green chequered napkin grasped in one hand. Berhane had pulled off her shawl and poncho as the heat of the kitchen hit her, and hung them on the dark oak coat stand in the corner. Lucy and Anna were hurriedly taking off their own coats. Isobel's gaze lingered with relief on her granddaughter, rather sombre, but rosy from the cold and obviously in one piece.

'Here,' Susannah said, handing Lucy an old towel she had taken out of a cupboard, 'you'd better dry him. Well,' she turned abruptly to Berhane, 'what's wrong at the inn?'

'There's no easy way to tell you,' Berhane said gently. 'Joe's dead. I went up as soon as I saw the lights were still on this morning. You know what Joe's like about them burning money, so it seemed strange. That was sometime after seven o'clock. I don't know any more than that, except that Hugh has called the police.'

'A stroke, I suppose,' Susannah said. Her voice was level, although her face had gone very white and she leaned back against the worktop for support. 'He was getting more and more over-excited about things that were bothering him. I wanted him to get his blood pressure checked, and have his heart looked at, but he wouldn't hear of it. Stubborn old fool.'

Tears glimmered in her eyes and she turned away abruptly, picking up the kettle and taking it to the sink. 'Well, go and sit down at the table then. I'll make us some coffee, and some toast too. There are my cranberry muffins as well if you're really hungry. I can't run to the sort of breakfast Betsey produces.'

Lucy glanced at Anna who nodded, her eyes brightening. 'Yes please,' Lucy said gratefully, straightening up from drying the dog. 'I could certainly manage both. The muffins sound lovely.' She pulled a grimace of distaste as she folded the soggy towel and draped it over the nearby radiator. 'We didn't feel like eating at the inn, not even to give Betsey something more to occupy her mind.'

Susannah paused as she switched the kettle on, one hand resting on the handle as she glanced at Lucy. 'Betsey,' she repeated. 'Do you tell me Betsey is up there?'

'She came in early, I suppose to get things ready for our breakfasts,' Lucy said, walking into the dining area. Ben carefully kept between her and the wall as Solomon swivelled around, keeping his arrogant gaze fixed on the dog. As Lucy squeezed round the table and sat down with her back to the French windows Ben scrambled underneath the tablecloth and lay across her feet.

Anna sat next to her and Isobel resumed her own place, Juno sinking down beside her with a little thump. Berhane hooked out a stool under the far end of the worktop and perched on it, her long legs tucked around its rails. Solomon sat down near her, his eyes fixed on the table above the spot where the collie lay.

'It was Betsey who found him,' Anna said, accepting a piece of rather soft toast when Isobel passed a basket to her. 'The first I knew of it was when she was screaming the place down. I thought I was having a nightmare at first.' She cast a sideways look at Lucy. 'And I was sure of it when I burst out onto the landing and ran into Mike.' She rubbed one ankle. 'He kicked me so hard I'm surprised I can walk.'

Lucy's smile was perfunctory. 'That's what woke us too. The sound of Betsey screaming. Hugh was out of the room before I realised where we were, let alone what was happening.'

'And what was happening?' Isobel enquired, taking a plate

of fresh toast from Susannah and tipping the slices carefully into the empty basket.

The aroma of freshly made coffee filled the room, making Anna sniff appreciatively. She pushed the stale toast to one side and reached over for another new slice. Lucy pushed the butter dish towards her, but did not take any toast when her grandmother proffered the basket.

'Betsey found all the lights on when she arrived,' Lucy said, shifting her feet awkwardly under Ben's damp body. 'She went looking for Joe and found him dead in the cellar.' Lucy felt the bald sentence hung in the air, but could not think how to soften it.

At the kitchen counter Berhane took the coffee pot from Susannah, noticing with concern that the older woman's hands were shaking. Berhane slipped off her stool and put the pot down on the table.

Lucy watched as she walked round the counter into the kitchen, where Susannah had begun to put muffins onto a plate. She murmured something to Susannah, who shook her head. Berhane waited for a moment, then returned to her stool, watching as Susannah went back into the dining room.

'Here we are,' Susannah said, leaning forward to put the plate down. Isobel stretched out a hand quickly, straightening the plate as it reached the table, just preventing the muffins from sliding off.

'Come and sit down,' she said firmly. 'You've had a terrible shock. You knew Joe very well, didn't you?'

Susannah sank heavily into her seat. 'Yes,' she said, lifting a mottled hand to shield her eyes. 'All his life.' She mustered a smile, lowering her hand to let it fall on the table. 'I didn't teach him, of course, he wasn't that much younger than I am. He was an awkward, stubborn boy, and just as bad when he was a man. Silly old fool,' she said gruffly, 'this wouldn't have happened if he'd listened to me.'

'You always did all you could for him,' Berhane said guiltily. 'And Joe generally did listen to you. But even you couldn't help him when he worked himself up into a lather over something. He didn't want to think of being ill, you know.'

'Who takes over the inn?' Anna asked. 'Do you know?'

Berhane's eyes widened. 'Oh dear, I expect it'll be his brother, Betsey's husband. That probably means the end of the inn. Unless,' she added thoughtfully, 'Joe left it to Phil. But then Phil won't want to run it.'

'No, of course not,' Susannah said, her voice strengthening. She hesitated, then said, 'I suppose it doesn't matter if I tell you. Joe meant to leave it to Betsey, to make sure it kept going.'

'That was your doing, of course,' Berhane said appreciatively. 'Brilliant.'

Anna leaned forward to take a muffin. It was no good letting them go to waste, she thought philosophically.

Isobel smiled encouragingly at her and picked up the plate. 'Have one, Lucy,' she encouraged her granddaughter, noticing with concern how pale her pointed face was.

Lucy shook her head. 'Thanks, Gran, but I'm not really hungry after all. Though I'll have some of the coffee, please.'

'They're delicious,' Anna said. 'You should try one.' She held out the plate coaxingly.

Berhane leaned over and took one. 'One of Aunt Susannah's specials, made to an old family recipe. I've always associated them with winter here.' She glanced at Lucy. 'You should eat, Lucy. Hugh's relying on us to repel invaders at the inn until the police get here.'

Susannah looked up. 'The police?' she queried. She sighed. 'Of course, I suppose they have to come in the case of another death. As if we haven't got enough on our plates with Gil's death.'

'At least Rob hadn't gone too far away,' Anna commented, wiping butter from her chin.

Isobel looked at her sharply, her dark eyes suddenly alert. 'Inspector Elliot?' she queried.

Anna nodded, her mouth full.

'Why has he stayed around?' Isobel asked.

Lucy stared at her grandmother in surprise. Isobel rarely asked personal questions, and she must know that Anna and Rob Elliot were friends.

'He's staying with his sister for Christmas,' Anna explained. 'I forget where exactly, but somewhere on the edge of the moor. I wonder how he'll get here.'

Lucy started to nibble a muffin, frowning as she listened to Anna with an uneasy feeling that her friend was concealing something. Perhaps she knew more about Rob Elliot than Lucy had realised. It came as a shock to Lucy, the thought that Anna might be serious about the relationship.

Berhane stood up abruptly and walked quickly through the kitchen into the sitting room. Isobel started to her feet in concern too, seeing the blue tinge that had crept into Susannah's face.

Susannah waved Isobel away, pressing her hand against her chest. 'Pills,' she said with an effort.

'Here they are,' Berhane said from her side. She put a small silver box on the table and lifted its lid to take out a pill. She put it to Susannah's mouth and the older woman parted her lips to take it.

On the far side of the table Anna put her next muffin back on her plate, her appetite suddenly gone. Lucy's hands were clasped around her mug, as she anxiously watched Berhane hold a glass of water for Susannah to sip.

'Better,' Susannah said after a few minutes, pushing Berhane's hand away. Her skin had lost the blueness, although she was now very pale.

Solomon leaped suddenly onto her lap, turning round and round before settling heavily across her knees. Susannah's fingers stroked his fur and gradually the tight lines in her face relaxed. 'I'm sorry to frighten you,' she said. 'I normally have the pills within reach.' She looked across at Isobel. 'I suppose the inn will be out of bounds, so I shall have to open the village hall if the police are coming. They're sure to need refreshments. Perhaps you wouldn't mind helping me.'

'Of course I'll help,' Isobel said. 'But surely there's somebody else who could do it, so you can rest.'

Susannah shook her head. 'Betsey would manage, but I suppose she'll be tied up with the police for a bit.' She gathered her thoughts visibly. 'It's all quite straightforward really. Just putting the urns on for hot water. There's plenty of tea and coffee, and biscuits.' Her voice strengthened, and she sat up straighter. 'I'll have to take out milk from the freezer, and perhaps I should make some soup.'

'Betsey's doing that,' Berhane said, perched again on her stool. 'She's using up all the seasonal extras with the left-over turkey. I expect she froze plenty after Christmas. I hope we'll get some of her sprout soup.'

'Betsey?' Susannah said, a note of surprise in her voice.

'I thought it would be good for her to have something to do,' Berhane explained. 'Hugh's staying with her, but he can't keep eating to occupy her.'

'I'm sure Mike could,' Anna said scornfully.

'But he'll be outside on guard,' Berhane pointed out. She glanced round. 'If you've both finished, perhaps we should go to join him. Hugh wants us to take turns at the gates to keep people out of the inn.'

Anna stood up and edged towards the kitchen. Ben slithered out cautiously under Lucy's seat, avoiding Solomon's glare. His mistress got to her feet and slid out from behind the table, following Anna.

'How are the police getting here?' Isobel asked, beginning to stack the plates. She pressed Susannah back into her chair. 'At least you should rest for a while now, if you really must go to the village hall later. We surely don't need to hurry.'

Susannah subsided reluctantly. 'I suppose not.'

Isobel looked enquiringly at her granddaughter.

'I don't think Hugh knows when or how the police are

coming,' Lucy said cautiously. 'Obviously they'll get here as fast as they can. He thought it would be by helicopter, but they said not. So all he knows is that they'll be here.'

'Come on, Lucy,' Anna urged from the door, where she was holding both their coats. 'Berhane's out there already. Let's go and give Mike a hand.'

Isobel crossed to them, buttoning Lucy into her coat, and saying quietly to her, 'Tell Berhane I'll keep an eye on Susannah. I won't let her do too much, but I think it's perhaps better to keep her thoughts occupied.'

Lucy nodded, kissed her grandmother's cheek lightly and followed Anna outside. Berhane was waiting for them, her patterned poncho belted around her waist, her purple shawl pulled over her head. As they joined her the clock in the church tower chimed the half hour. Immediately afterwards the bells began to ring.

Lucy glanced at her watch. Eight thirty. I can't believe it's so early, she thought. I feel as though this has been going on for hours. She gave herself a mental shake. Come on, she castigated herself. Pull yourself together. We've been in much worse situations than this, and really we're not actually involved with this. She tried to blot out the mental image that was at the front of her mind, of the moment not so long ago when a madman stood in front of her telling her Hugh was dead.

The excited cries of children and the yapping of a small dog brought her attention back to the village green. An animated group of youngsters was digging a black spaniel out of a drift over by the Church House. The spaniel was getting more and more hysterical, flinging himself again and again into the deep snow. Beside Lucy, Ben watched with interest and she suddenly became aware of the discussion between her friends.

'Plenty of people will get here for the service, it's always special on New Year's Day,' Berhane said, obviously in answer to something Anna had asked. 'A surprising number are within walking distance, and a lot of those further out will come on quad bikes. Most of the farmers have them.' She smiled ruefully at Lucy, aware that her thoughts had been elsewhere. 'And many of those from further afield will be expecting one of Betsey's lunches. We are going to have our hands full keeping them out of the inn.'

She began to walk back up the lane beneath the fringe of trees, and the others followed her. On the far side of the village green people on foot were approaching the church, calling gaily to each other.

Lucy watched Ben, who was still uncertain of the snow, floundering now and again when he found a deeper patch. As they approached the terrace she saw a thickset man hunched in a thick fleece jacket, leaning over the gate of the central cottage, staring towards the inn.

He turned as they reached him, revealing a large flabby face, stubbly with several days' growth of beard. He looked vaguely familiar, but it was only as he scowled at Berhane that Lucy recognised the resemblance to Joe Triggs.

'Right strange, that is,' he said truculently to Berhane, jerking his head towards the inn. 'All them lights on. And what's that bloke doing, standing out there? He's just been stood there for near an hour. It's right strange, I reckon.'

'I'm sure we'll find out fast enough, Eli,' Berhane said, without slowing her pace.

The man turned his head to one side and spat. 'I'll do that right enough,' he said. 'If my Betsey don't get over here and tell me, young Phil will be coming with his mother. He'll fetch me the news.'

Berhane raised a hand, but Eli was not watching her. His bloodshot blue eyes had turned back to Mike, who was stamping his feet and banging his mittened hands together, a cloud of white breath surrounding his head in a nebulous halo as he muttered to himself.

Ben reached Mike first, throwing himself against the man's legs and sending him staggering backwards against the yard gate. 'Bloody dog,' Mike growled, fending the excited collie off. 'What kept you?' he demanded, glowering at Anna.

'Hello, Mike,' she replied sweetly. 'Here we are, come to rescue you again.'

Mike's expression darkened ominously. Lucy intervened quickly, 'Do you want to go in for a while, Mike? You must have got very cold.'

He grunted. 'I'll wait for a bit, then change with Hugh. He wants us in pairs at each gate. Lucy, you can stay with me.' He grinned unpleasantly at Anna. 'You and Berhane can stand at the garden gate. I'm sure your charm will deal with the rude local yokels when they find you're depriving them of their pints.'

A loud rumble drowned Anna's reply, and they all looked down the green to where a cavalcade of quad bikes had come roaring up the snow-covered lanes that edged Gil's house to converge by the green. Most of them went on past the Church House and into the parking space in front of the village hall, the bikes bearing at least two or three people, clinging tightly together. One quad bike peeled off from the others, bouncing on up towards the inn with a solitary rider as pedestrians stood aside to allow him to pass.

As it approached the inn, Mike straightened and stepped forward. 'Here we go,' he said. 'I didn't think anyone would come this early.'

'It's Phil,' Berhane said quietly, 'I expect he's come to see his uncles, Joe here at the inn and Eli over there at the cottage.' She gestured faintly towards the man leaning on his cottage gate.

'I thought Eli looked familiar,' Lucy exclaimed, 'but I'd forgotten the landlord had a brother.'

Anna was peering uncertainly at the driver of the quad bike, wondering how Berhane knew who it was. It definitely was a man, but so well wrapped in fleece, scarf and Russian-style sheepskin hat that she could not recognise him.

He pulled the quad bike up at a distance from them and

scrambled off, his booted legs sinking into the snow as he came towards them. He pulled his scarf away from his face as he approached, and undid the flaps of his hat, allowing them to hang loose, and Anna saw that Berhane was quite right.

'Happy New Year,' he called. 'I didn't expect to see you all out so early.'

Berhane laid a hand on Mike's rigid arm. 'Let me speak to him,' she said, stepping forward.

'Hello, Phil,' she said as he came to a stop in front of her.

He was leaning to kiss her cheek when he saw her expression and froze. 'What is it?' he demanded, straightening up slowly. 'You've not had more trouble?'

'Not me.' She took a deep breath. 'It's Joe, I'm afraid. He died last night.'

'What?' Phil stared at her. 'Are you sure?' He passed a hand over his face. 'Sorry, stupid of me. Of course you're sure.' He turned to look at the inn. 'Was it his heart?'

'We're not sure,' Berhane said. 'But we've got to stay out of the way and keep everyone else out until the doctor and the police get here.'

'What?' he said again. 'Why the police?'

'They always come for an unexpected death,' Berhane replied. 'Oh dear, Eli's on his way here. He must have realised it's you.'

Phil looked over his shoulder. 'I'll head him off.' He turned and waded through the snow towards the other man, passing Anna who had moved to stand in front of the garden gate. The men met at the end of the terrace and after a brief discussion Eli began to plough on towards the inn. Phil put out a hand, swinging his uncle round and supporting him as he staggered off balance. Eli's raised voice was angry and hectoring as he pulled away from Phil's grasp.

The older man's face was red with effort and rage as he reached the inn, where Mike had moved to bar the garden gate, standing in front of Anna. 'What's this then?' Eli demanded, as

Phil came up behind him. ''Tis my brother what's died, according to young Phil here. I've a right to be told.'

'It's for the police to do that,' Mike said. 'As soon as they get here.'

'And I'm not leaving my Betsey in there with a corpse, police or not,' Eli bellowed, putting out a brawny arm to push Mike aside.

Phil grabbed at his uncle, seizing his arm. Eli swung round, his other fist raised. 'For God's sake, Eli,' Phil said urgently. 'Do you want the police to find you making trouble again?'

'Listen!' Anna said sharply. 'What's that?'

Eli stood stock still, his head cocked, a fierce frown on his face. The faint tinkling sound grew louder.

'Bells!' Lucy said in surprise. 'It's sleigh bells.'

By now the sound was louder, attracting the attention of the children playing in the snow and the families on their way towards the church. Every face was turned towards the main lane leading into the top north-eastern end of the village.

Seconds later a team of huskies swept into view, pulling a long low sleigh. Behind it came a second team of dogs with a covered wagon on runners. They came smoothly up the snow-filled lane, and sharp commands brought both teams to a jangling halt, side by side in front of the inn before a staring audience.

After a quick glance, Lucy caught Ben's collar and pulled him up the path to the front door. She pushed the letterbox open and called urgently through it for Hugh.

Almost immediately there was the sound of the lock turning and Hugh opened the door. He stood in the doorway, one finger holding his place in the pages of the small book he carried, that Lucy recognised as one of Gil's diaries by its marbled paper cover. 'What is it?' Hugh demanded. 'More trouble?'

'I don't think so,' she said, a note of amusement in her voice. 'But you ought to see this. And can you pass me the lead.'

Hugh put the diary down unceremoniously on one of the

shelves littered with carved stones, and held out the narrow leather lead. Lucy clipped it onto Ben's collar and turned to face the lane, Hugh coming to stand beside her, pulling the door shut behind them.

Mike's eyes were bulging as he stared at the panting dogs, whose pink tongues were hanging out, clouds of steamy breath obscuring their furry heads. His gaze moved on to the four men riding in the first sleigh, their faces scarlet under their hats, their bodies wrapped in layers of bright blankets and sheepskin rugs. It lingered on one man. 'No,' Mike muttered, 'no, I don't believe this.'

Anna glanced at him in surprise, and choked with laughter at his expression of horrified disbelief. Forewarned by this, she turned back to look at the nearer sleigh as one of the men threw aside the covers and stepped out.

He was a tall man, bulky in several layers of jumpers and fleeces. Anna recognised him at once in spite of the fur hat pulled low over his head, concealing most of his face. He pushed the hat back a little as he reached the stunned group outside the inn.

Inspector Rob Elliot's cool grey eyes surveyed them, resting with a brief flash of humour on Mike's congested expression of incredulity. 'Good morning,' he said pleasantly. 'I'm sure you were expecting me again.'

Anna gurgled with laughter. 'Yes, but not like this.' She gestured gracefully at the huskies, then turned the movement into a wave as she saw Isobel and Susannah.

The older women were half way across the village green. They both waved back, but continued their laborious progress over to the village hall. Children, though, were already running up the green, cries of excitement preceding them. The team handler spoke to the inspector as he went to the lead dog.

Elliot nodded. 'This is all courtesy of John Bowen here, who has four husky teams in training. He often puts them at the service of the local police in weather like this. I thought,' he said, looking enquiringly at Berhane, 'that the huskies could rest in the yard at Hannaford's house. Unless you think they'd disturb the hounds or the horses.'

'You can put them in the yard here,' Eli broke in, jerking his head towards the inn. 'It's my say what happens to the place now, and I say you can put them in there.'

'That's very kind of you, Mr...?' Elliot replied.

'Triggs, Elijah Triggs, brother to him in there,' Eli said, his chest swelling with importance.

'Well, Mr Triggs, it's best that we don't disturb things around here just yet,' Elliot said, casting a wry glance over the lines of footsteps leading up the path and across the yard.

'You can certainly take the huskies down to Gil's yard,' Berhane intervened, 'but I'll go down with them, just to keep an eye on the horses. If they are unsettled, we'd probably better move the huskies to the village hall car park.' She frowned at the sound of more engines. 'Although there'll be quite a few quad bikes coming for the service, there's no reason they can't be left out on the green if necessary.'

'That's fine,' Elliot said, 'but can you come back when you're satisfied the horses are okay. I've a few things to go over with you.'

Berhane looked at him consideringly. 'Of course,' she said. 'I won't be long. Why don't I meet you in the village hall? Susannah Ballamy is over there, turning up the heating and getting some drinks and food together. It's free today, so it'll probably suit you better as a base than my house did.'

'I don't know quite when I'll get there, but that will be fine,' the inspector said. 'It sounds as though we're going to be well looked after.'

Berhane was looking at the covered wagon, whose huskies had been unhitched. They swarmed around two uniformed constables, whose dark blue overcoats were pulled tightly up to their chins. 'Is that staying here?'

'Yes, but the huskies can go down to the yard too. Bowen

says they're okay with children, so I suppose you can let them visit if they want to. I don't know how long it will be before we're able to leave.' He cast a look at the sky, now high and clear blue, but with a faint line of pale towering cloud castles on the western horizon. 'The forecast is for more snow this evening.'

'Then you'd better not hang around,' Hugh said from the front door. 'Come in. Betsey's got soup on the go here, and coffee too. I expect you're freezing.'

'Actually we're not,' Elliot replied. 'It's surprisingly warm under all those layers. Albeit a bit smelly behind the dogs.'

Mike snorted.

The inspector looked at him thoughtfully, his gaze passing on smoothly to include Anna and Lucy. 'I expect you're colder than we are, but I'm glad to see you're here in force to keep people out. If you can manage for a while longer,' his eyes rested briefly on Eli, who was shifting irritably from foot to foot, 'I'll have you relieved as soon as I can spare my constables.'

Behind him Berhane had finished speaking to the driver of the wagon, who was leading his huskies beside one of the older boys from the crowd, down the green towards Gil's house. The remaining children fell in behind the team as Berhane climbed into the sleigh and John Bowen swung his own team round to join the tail of the procession.

Elliot moved in the other direction, past Mike into the inn. He was followed closely by the other two men from the sleigh, who were awkwardly unfastening their outer fleece jackets with gloved fingers. Sergeant Tom Peters' already square figure seemed to have expanded massively, forcing him into an unusual rolling gait. He nodded at Lucy and Anna, a twinkle in his blue eyes, as he walked by them. The other man clutched a bag, and muttered something to Phil as he passed him.

'Dr Harford,' Phil murmured to the others. 'He's local, not the police doctor.'

'What's all this?' Eli demanded belligerently, his eyes

narrowed as he watched the procession filing through the front door of the inn. 'Are you telling me somebody's done the old bugger in? Well,' he uttered a harsh croak of laughter, 'I'll be damned.'

'Very probably,' Mike muttered as he moved grimly back to stand in front of the gate, gesturing impatiently for Anna and Lucy to go down to the yard entrance.

SIX

Lucy looked appraisingly around the village hall. From the outside it was just a standard prefabricated building, but inside it had been cleverly personalised. The plasterboard walls were painted a deep pink, complementing the diamond-patterned curtains in green and gold. Altogether it felt warm and inviting, which was just as well, Lucy thought wryly, glancing through the window at the thick snow that crowned the hedge.

She glanced at her watch. Ten thirty. She felt as though she'd been sitting at this table for hours, nursing yet another cup of tea, but it had not really been that long. She studied the large picture on the wall nearest to her, although she had already closely scrutinised it and the others. Still, at least it was interesting, a beautifully drawn charcoal sketch of a walker on the high moor. Ben shifted impatiently at her feet and Lucy glanced down to see his golden eyes watching her hopefully. He clearly felt they had been here for too long as well.

Anna stood at the window, one foot tapping gently on the floor. From here she could see over the car park and round its screening hedge to a narrow view across the top of the village green and up to the inn and the terrace of cottages beyond. The church service seemed to have ended, for more people had gathered in small knots in front of the pub, where one of the constables was repelling enquiries. Some of the onlookers lingered, but the groups shifted, growing and shrinking as newcomers came up and others wandered off. Anna watched a bulky figure making its way stolidly across the green. When it stopped in the open, well away from any of the groups, Anna recognised it and pulled a disgusted face. Edith. What on earth was she doing out there? Still, Anna thought grimly, I'd rather she was out there than in here. She'd be the one thing we need to make things worse.

Anna wiped the steamed-up glass in front of her. She sighed with relief as she saw Edith ploughing on towards the inn. Edith came to a halt before she got there as somebody came out of the middle terraced cottage and approached her. I bet that's Phil, Anna thought, although she was unable to see the figure. Getting away from his dear uncle Eli and falling straight into Edith's clutches, poor man.

A movement in the crowd in front of the inn caught Anna's eye. 'Here they come,' she exclaimed, turning round and breaking the silence that had fallen heavily over the room some time ago.

Behind her the others were sitting round one of the small tables they had taken out from the stack along the back wall. They were as close to one of the radiators as they could comfortably get, and although Susannah had turned up the heat Isobel was still firmly wrapped in her coat.

Berhane was next to Lucy, her poncho hanging over her the chair, the purple shawl around her shoulders. She had been silently gazing in front of her, but now Anna'a words brought her attention back to the room.

Isobel gestured to Susannah to stay in her own seat and got up stiffly herself. She lifted the flap in the nearby counter and went into the tiny kitchen to switch on the kettle. Everything else was ready. Cups and saucers laid out, milk and sugar to hand, a plate of chocolate biscuits ready to be eaten. None of them had felt like eating or drinking, but Susannah had been adamant that they should prepare things for the police.

The hall door banged open and Mike entered on a burst of cold air. Ben leaped to his feet and rushed across to him, hugely pleased that something was happening at last. Mike bent over the collie, patting him absently as Hugh came in, followed closely by Inspector Elliot and Sergeant Peters.

Susannah got up, her face very drawn, and held herself awkwardly erect. 'Was it his heart?' she asked at once.

Hugh was pulling the free chairs closer to the radiator, shifting the table that had been put out for them. 'Let's sit down and warm up,' he suggested. 'I'm sure the inspector is going to be here for some time.'

'There are hot drinks,' Susannah began, waving a hand towards the counter.

'Not right now, thank you, Miss Ballamy,' Elliot said. 'We've just had soup at the inn.' He saw the slightest flicker of annoyance cross her face, and added smoothly, 'But I'm sure we'll be glad of them after we've finished talking to you all.'

Isobel had returned to the table. Touching Susannah on the elbow, she encouraged her to sit down again. Relieved, Hugh and Mike followed suit, still wearing their coats, which had started to drip water onto the floor around their feet. Ben sat between them, his excitement fading as everyone settled down.

'Well?' Susannah demanded, her fierce eyes on the inspector, who was adjusting a chair so that he faced the others.

'We're not sure,' Elliot said, sitting down as his sergeant shrugged out of his coat and moved a chair out of direct sight of the group. 'I can't say very much until the doctor sends in his report.'

Susannah put a hand up to her eyes for a moment, then let it drop into her lap, straightening her shoulders. 'It really must have been his heart,' she insisted, 'but I suppose you have to do things by the book.'

'I do,' he agreed. 'So I should interview you all individually, but in the circumstances if everyone's happy to do so I can just run through your movements last night now.'

'Last night!' Susannah exclaimed. 'Oh,' she wrinkled her nose, annoyed with herself, 'of course, that's why the lights were still on this morning.'

'Did you see them?' Elliot asked quickly, as Sergeant Peters began to make notes.

'They were on when I left the inn,' Susannah said, frowning. 'But Joe would still have been about then.'

'What time was that?'

She hesitated, frowning. 'Well, I'm not exactly sure,' she admitted. 'After the bell ringing of course, but not much after.' She glanced at Isobel. 'We were back here by half past twelve, weren't we?'

'Yes,' Isobel agreed. 'I glanced at my watch when I was trying to persuade my dog to go outside. It was a few minutes after half past then.'

'Thank you,' Elliot said. 'We may need to narrow the time later on, but that will do for now.' He looked at Susannah again, asking, 'Did you see the landlord when you left the inn?'

Her frown deepened. 'Not to say goodbye. I saw him earlier on, when I was fetching one of the trays of drinks to take outside.' She glanced at the inspector. 'I suppose by now you know most of the village was out on the green, waiting to hear the New Year rung in, and,' she added grimly, 'to hear the bell toll for Gil Hannaford.'

Elliot nodded. 'Yes, and that the landlord was out serving drinks. They normally include his home-brew in the inn afterwards, don't they?'

Susannah looked surprised. 'Yes, that's right. He decided not to offer it this year.' She hesitated. 'He said it was because most people wouldn't want to hang around in the bad weather, and he wasn't going to waste it on just a few scroungers.'

'But you think there was more to it than that?' Elliot asked softly.

'Well,' Susannah said reluctantly, 'he can, could,' she corrected herself painfully, 'get himself into a terrible state when he was anxious about something.'

'What was he anxious about?'

She smiled sadly. 'Rather a lot of things, Inspector, but chiefly I think his biggest worry last night was what would become of Gil's pack of hounds.'

Berhane stirred in her chair, loosening the shawl around her shoulders.

Elliot turned his attention to her. 'Were you aware of the landlord's anxieties too?'

Berhane smiled calmly. 'You can't have heard all the village news, Inspector. Joe wouldn't confide in me. I'm one of his worries.'

'Oh?'

'Nonsense, Berhane,' Susannah said gruffly. 'You make too much of it.'

Elliot kept his attention on Berhane, waiting for her to speak again.

Berhane's expression warmed as she glanced at Susannah, but she said coolly, 'Joe thought I was taking his business away with my dining club, which put me on his blacklist. So I only saw him briefly last night among the crowds, as he was keen to keep away from me.'

'I'm afraid that's true for us as well,' Anna said. 'As Berhane's friends we were tarred with the same brush, and he didn't want to serve us. He especially...' she broke off, coughing.

'He especially?' Elliot repeated, making it a question.

'Oh, he especially went out of his way to avoid us,' Anna said.

The inspector considered her thoughtfully for a moment. Anna met his eyes, a bright smile on her lips, unusually pale without their normal vivid lipstick.

'Don't bother,' Mike grunted. 'Elliot already knows that the bloody man hated my guts. And I was the mug who went looking for him when we got back to the inn last night. So naturally,' he continued sarcastically, 'it has to have been me who...'

'Mike!' Hugh said sharply, leaning forward on his chair. 'Don't be more stupid than you can help. We don't yet know how Triggs died.'

'True,' Elliot said blandly. 'Did any of you go into the inn during the bell ringing?'

They looked at each other, consideringly. 'No,' Anna said slowly, 'I don't think so.'

'I did,' Berhane said, 'quite early on, before the mourning bell, to get our drinks. Otherwise,' her smile flickered again, 'we may have waited for a long time.'

'Did you see the landlord?'

She shook her head. 'I got the drinks from Betsey.'

'Were you deliberately avoiding him?'

'No. He wasn't in sight in the inn, so I supposed he was out in the crowd. But,' she added, 'I didn't see him there either.'

'What is this all about, Inspector?' Susannah demanded. 'You're behaving as if,' she swallowed hard, 'as if there's something wrong about Joe's death.'

'It's better to ask questions straight away,' Elliot replied imperturbably, 'while you can all remember what you were doing and what you saw.'

Susannah opened her mouth again, but Berhane said quietly, 'He's right. And I'm sure you have more questions, don't you, Inspector?'

'Several,' he agreed. 'But I'd like to go back to Gil Hannaford.' He was looking at Susannah. 'You and Joe Triggs signed Mr Hannaford's will on Friday. Do you know what the main provisions were?'

Susannah sat quite still, staring at him. 'Why are you asking me?' she queried. 'I've no doubt Gil's solicitor will be able to tell you what you need to know.'

'I hope so, when the signed copy arrives,' Elliot replied. 'But we've already checked with the Post Office to see if we could obtain the envelope that Mr Hannaford may have posted on Friday evening.'

'I hadn't realised it was that urgent for you to know what's in Gil's will,' Susannah said, surprised.

'This is a murder enquiry,' Elliot pointed out. He watched her stricken face as he added, 'Mr Hannaford didn't post anything from the village on Friday evening or Saturday morning.'

Susannah looked surprised. 'Then it must be in his house,' she said, with the careful air of a teacher pointing out something simple.

'We can't find it there,' Elliot said. 'And we've been through the place thoroughly.'

Berhane sat up, leaning forward across the table. 'Have you spoken to his sister?'

Elliot regarded her approvingly. 'Yes; he talked to her on Friday night. I mentioned he was himself taking in the will to his solicitor next week. She also solved the question of what he intended to do. Her account tallies with the solicitor's.'

'Well then,' Susannah said, relieved, 'there's no problem.'

'Without a signed copy of his will, whatever his wishes may have been there's no guarantee that they'll be carried out,' Elliot explained.

Susannah's eyes widened. 'I suppose not,' she said slowly.

'I ask you again, Miss Ballamy, did you and Mr Triggs know what was in the will?'

Susannah hesitated, then made up her mind. 'I don't really feel comfortable repeating this, but if you already know I suppose it doesn't make much difference.' She looked directly at the inspector. 'When we were discussing bringing forward the hunt, Gil, Joe and I, Gil asked us to sign his will. He told us then that he was leaving a legacy to his sister, and the rest of his estate to Berhane.' Susannah sniffed disapprovingly. 'He wanted to make sure that his horses and his pack of hounds were taken care of, and he knew he could rely on her to do it.' Susannah's lips twisted in a difficult smile. 'She's as crazy about them as he was.'

The surprise was palpable in the room as Susannah finished

speaking. Several eyes turned to Berhane, who was contemplating the inspector.

'Did you know that was what he intended?' he asked her.

'He had mentioned it,' she said tranquilly, 'but I didn't know whether he was serious about it or not.'

'What did Mr Triggs think about it?'

Elliot's question surprised her. She shrugged, glancing at Susannah. 'I don't expect he liked it.'

'He didn't,' Susannah confirmed. 'But then there was nothing unusual about that, Joe never liked anything to change. Well, Inspector, is that what you've heard from Gil's sister?'

'Yes,' Elliot replied. 'It's what she was expecting. And the solicitor confirms that was how he drew up the will.'

'I don't approve of leaving family property away from the family,' Susannah said stiffly, 'but Gil had to do what he wanted.'

'And surely,' Isobel interposed, 'a lot of what he must have left he acquired himself.'

Susannah's lips tightened. 'That's true, of course.'

'Anyway,' Hugh said, 'if you'll forgive me, that is irrelevant now. The question must be where the will has got to.'

The inspector nodded. 'Did he leave it with you?' he asked Berhane.

'No,' she answered, 'there's no reason why he should.' Her brow furrowed. 'Gil didn't like to leave important things lying around. He must have put it somewhere safe until he could hand it over.'

Watching her curiously Lucy thought that for an instant Berhane's eyes widened slightly. Before Lucy had chance to speak the door opened again, allowing a blast of cold air to rush across the room. Ben sprang up, barking, and dashed forward.

Edith drifted in, a bulky shape in a heavy cotton skirt and layers of woollen tops, a thick scarf wrapped around her neck and head. Her matt white skin was barely tinged with pink and as she hovered in the open doorway, ignoring the collie, Lucy wondered if Edith actually felt the cold.

'Shut the door,' Anna snapped, straightening up from the windowsill, where she had been leaning against a radiator. 'We've just got lovely and warm in here.'

'Really, Edith,' Susannah said crossly, 'whatever are you doing out without a coat?'

Edith shut the door with exaggerated care and took a few steps into the room, her protuberant eyes staring at them as Ben returned to his post by Lucy. 'I never wear them,' she said. 'They're so restrictive.'

Mike snorted in disbelief. Edith turned her gaze on him. 'I thought it would be you in danger,' she said dreamily. 'I never expected it would be Joe.'

'Why should Professor Shannon be in danger?' Inspector Elliot demanded as Mike's face grew scarlet with annoyance.

'Well,' Edith said as she reached the group at the table and sat down gracelessly in a vacant chair, 'Joe was very suspicious of him, and Joe really had a bad temper.'

'We've been over all this,' Susannah said abruptly. 'That was yesterday.'

'But Joe was still mad,' Edith insisted, one finger idly tracing a pattern on the table top. 'He was talking about it on the green last night.'

'Really, Edith,' Anna said curtly, 'anyone would think you were trying to distract attention from yourself.'

Edith looked up from the table, a flicker of surprise in her eyes. 'Would they? Why?'

'All this pointing of fingers at other people,' Anna said.

Edith stared at her. 'I was just saying what happened.'

'Leave it, Anna,' Mike snarled. 'You're just making it worse.' He turned to Elliot, who was listening to the exchange with a spark of amusement lighting his grey eyes. 'I should think the bloody man spent his time shouting at people who asked him about his precious collection.'

'Oh no,' Edith said. 'And he never shouted at Berhane, and

he dislikes her too.'

'Not many people asked him about his collection,' Susannah pointed out. 'Except me. But he was always anxious that it would give somebody a clue to the treasure he was sure lay out on the moors waiting for him.' She looked at the inspector. 'Joe was brought up on a diet of tales about his great-grandfather's wonderful discoveries on the moor. Sheer fantasy, of course, but he wouldn't believe that. And he'd see an archaeologist as a very definite threat. That was why he was so awkward with Professor Shannon.'

Lucy saw Elliot lean back, the fingers of one hand tapping the table gently as he contemplated Mike. With a sinking feeling, Lucy recalled what Mike had just said. He had been the one looking for the landlord when they returned to the inn last night. She pursed her lips. That was going to be awkward for Mike.

It was a silent group in Berhane's sitting room on the upper floor of the Church House. It was a striking room, taking up the bulk of the apartment. Berhane had used the burnt umber that was so effective on the walls downstairs. Here it seemed brighter, more lit with the snow glow that came through the two sets of arched windows that overlooked the green. The pair of sofas were black, significant features in the sparsely furnished room, and the cushions scattered over them were green silk, embroidered with animals. The rugs on the stripped floorboards were a deeper green, thick and soft underfoot. The few decorations were mainly ceramic and glass, bowls and jugs of glowing primary colours. But the figure that took pride of place was wooden, an elongated bust of a woman in pale wood that made the shape stand out from its position on the shelf against the wall at the top of the stairs.

Hugh and Anna were the most active people in the room, their heads bent over a chessboard. Hugh had pulled a low stool up to the coffee table, while Anna was curled comfortably on a large beanbag, her eyes fixed on the stylised wooden chess pieces.

Hugh had laid aside on one of the sofas the small book with a marbled paper cover that he had been reading. Glancing at it, Lucy recognised one of Gil's diaries, and remembered that he had been reading it in the inn that morning while they were waiting for Rob Elliot to arrive. She wondered what Hugh was making of it.

Her gaze moved on, over Hugh and Anna, resting briefly on the black and white landscape photographs on the walls. She felt a stirring of interest, wondering where the places were and whether Berhane had taken the pictures herself. She must remember to ask her.

With a small sigh Lucy tucked her legs under her, settling more comfortably on the sofa, and tried again to concentrate on the book that Berhane had lent her about seed banks. Her thoughts kept wandering and looking up from the page she had now read twice, Lucy's eyes fell on Edith, sitting hunched up on a chair beside one of the set of arched diamond-paned windows that overlooked the village green. Last time that Lucy had seen her, perhaps only a few moments ago, Edith had been looking dreamily through the glass, one hand playing with the lower edges of the layers of jumpers she still wore. Really, Lucy thought, she seems to be impervious to the temperature, whether it's hot or cold.

Lucy's gaze sharpened as she realised that Edith was actually focused on something in her hand. Lucy stretched a little, trying to see what it was. Then she saw. It was only Edith's mobile. It hadn't rung, surely they'd all have heard it. Oh, of course, Lucy recalled, Edith had said she couldn't get reception in the house.

Edith looked up suddenly, straight at Lucy. Lucy was startled, faintly guilty at being caught staring, but she noticed with a jolt of surprise the faint flush in the matt white skin of the other woman's face. Just for an instant Edith's pale eyes seemed to hold a spark of life, before her usual vague expression descended.

'I expect Taylor's trying to get in touch,' she said, standing up heavily, letting her thick skirt fall awkwardly around her legs. 'I'll just go out onto the green. The reception is better there.'

'Look out for Mike and Berhane,' Anna said lightly. She glanced at her watch. 'They've been gone with Ben for a couple of hours. If Mike's managed to cope with snowshoes I expect he'll be back for tea any time now. His meal clock is infallible.'

Edith was drifting to the top of the stairs and gave no sign of hearing this.

Lucy moved to the window and looked out. A minute or so later Edith emerged, having only wrapped her thick scarf around her neck and head. She ploughed slowly and purposefully across to the open heart of the green.

This was quieter now, with only a couple of people walking past on the far side, intent on reaching their goal quickly. The opalescent light reflected from the snow made the scene quite bright, but pinkish-grey clouds lay low above the trees, like a cotton wool coverlet descending on the earth.

As Lucy watched Edith's distant figure, head bent over her mobile phone, a few tentative flakes of snow fell, floating down in lazy spirals. A flurry at the bottom of the green heralded Mike's arrival. He moved quite competently on the snowshoes strapped to his feet, but Lucy noticed with amusement that Ben was keeping his distance and wondered how many times Mike had fallen. Quite a few, judging from the snow caked onto the front of his donkey jacket.

Lucy got up with a sigh. Ben would be soaking wet too. She glanced at her watch and pursed her lips. She would be able to dry him a bit before they took him over to the Schoolhouse for tea. He would get damp again just crossing the village green, of course, but at least she could deal with the worst of it now.

'Checkmate,' Anna said triumphantly. 'That's the first time I've ever beaten anyone.'

Hugh smiled. 'Well done. Your game has improved a lot.' He quirked an eyebrow at his wife as Lucy moved to the stairs.

'Mike and Ben are just about here,' she said. 'They both look as wet as each other, so I'd better deal with Ben. I wonder how he took to snowshoeing. It was Edith's dad, Gil Ballamy, who made it popular locally. He used to go to Austria or Switzerland as often as he could for the winter sports, long before they became such a generally fashionable thing to do.'

Anna strolled to the window as Hugh carefully packed away the chessmen. 'Mike's met Edith. That was careless.' She leaned forward, craning to look down the green. 'I wonder where Berhane's got to.' She uttered an exasperated exclamation. 'For goodness' sake, that stupid woman's wandering off.'

'Maybe Edith's going straight across to the Schoolhouse,' Hugh said mildly. 'We must be due there soon.'

Anna shook her head, her long curls dancing around her shoulders. 'No, she's going down to the bottom of the green.' Anna's face was pressed awkwardly against the glass now. 'She's not even going to Gil's house, she's going along the lane out of the village, the little one on the right, not the one we took up to the moor.'

'Ah well,' Hugh said, not really interested, 'she's local after all. Perhaps there's somewhere she likes seeing in the snow.'

They heard the sound of the front door opening, followed by Mike's loud voice saying crossly, 'Come back here.'

Lucy's exclamation indicated that it was too late, and Hugh grinned, picturing the scene, sure that Ben had rushed up to his mistress, leaving a trail of wetness across the floor. Anna pattered down the stairs, taking care to stay some distance from the hall where she could see what was going on.

Mike grabbed the collie by the collar and Ben turned his head, licking Mike's face enthusiastically.

'Urrgh,' Mike growled, lifting an arm to fend the dog off. 'Lucy, have you got a towel yet?'

As he spoke Lucy enveloped the dog in a thick towel,

catching him before he could shake himself. Mike let go of the collar and stood up. 'You should have come,' he said. 'Snowshoeing's a wonderful experience. Completely silent. I can see why Edith's dad got so hooked on it.'

Anna's eyes ran over his flushed face as he pulled his sodden coat off and dropped it carelessly on the floor. 'Mike,' she called sharply, 'pick that up, or you'll ruin the rug. You'd better take it out to the kitchen. Here,' she added, as he stood holding the coat, glowering up at her, 'give it to me. I'll take it.'

'Just hang on to it for a couple of minutes,' Lucy said, her words muffled as she bent over Ben, rubbing him vigorously. 'I'll have to take the towel out when I've finished here, so I'll take that too.' She glanced up at Mike, who was unlacing his boots. 'Where's Berhane got to?'

'I haven't left her in a snowdrift,' he said shortly. 'She went into Gil's house, said she'd remembered something.'

Lucy paused in her work, looking at him uneasily. 'Did she say what?'

Mike shook his head, whose unruly red hair had been flattened by the beanie he had just pulled off. 'I didn't ask.'

Lucy glanced at Anna, whose face mirrored her own uncertainty. 'I just wondered if it was safe for her to be on her own.'

'Who?' Hugh asked.

The others all looked up at him as he walked down the stairs to join Anna, who was now sitting on one of the steps, with Mike's coat draped over the banister.

'Berhane's gone to Gil's house,' Lucy said, restraining Ben's sudden lunge as he attempted to greet Hugh.

'Surely it's locked?' Anna said. 'The police wouldn't leave it open.'

'She had a key,' Mike said. 'A Yale. On her own key ring.'

'Did she now?' Hugh said slowly. His eyes met Lucy's worried gaze. 'Well, we're sure to see her at Susannah's tea.'

'Mike can't go like that,' Anna protested. 'His trousers are soaking.'

'No point changing,' he said smugly. 'They'll only get wet again.'

Anna opened her mouth to retort, but Hugh spoke first. 'Did Edith say where she's going?'

Mike snorted. 'That woman's plain crazy.' He shook his head disbelievingly. 'She was out on the green without as much as a coat. When I met her she just said she was going for a walk. She had a fancy to see the old place, or something. Crazy.'

'The old place,' Lucy repeated. 'Surely,' she looked questioningly at Anna, 'surely she can't mean Ballamy's Farm? It's miles away.'

'Maybe there's a viewpoint,' Anna suggested. 'Berhane will know.'

'Then let's go and speak to her,' Hugh said briskly. 'Susannah won't want to be kept waiting anyway.'

'Oh, she's out and about too,' Mike said. 'She was coming across the green, but I managed to dodge her.'

'We seem to have missed the action,' Hugh commented.

Lucy looked at him, her hazel eyes clouded. 'I hope there isn't any,' she said, pulling on her fleece. 'Somehow I don't like the feel of this.'

Berhane stood in the small room at the back of Gil's house. Pictures and photographs covered two of the walls, almost obscuring the faded green paint on them. They had been that colour for as long as Berhane could remember. Overcrowded stacks of shelves lined the other two walls, crammed with books on horses and dogs. The pictures and books normally spilled over into heaps on the floor, half obscuring the old riding boots and moth-eaten hats Gil could never bring himself to throw away.

He had always called this room his office, and for Berhane it was the place that brought his image back as if he were still alive. There was Gil looking up from his chair behind the desk in the centre of the room, a look of pleasure on his face when she called in unexpectedly. Gil leaning over the stud book, his expression intent as he discussed the hounds. Gil falling back in his seat, his face alight with laughter as he described Joe's latest comment.

Berhane glanced around, her eyes lingering on the neat piles of papers, the stacked towers of books, the ordered ranks of boots. There was nothing of Gil's usual comfortable mess there. The police must have tidied up as they examined the place. Even the pictures on the walls had been straightened. Berhane's gaze ran over them. There was Gil on a variety of horses, from the time he first rode when he was five years old, to the time this summer when they had gone out riding on her return to the moor. As she looked at his smiling face staring back at her, Berhane's hands tightened at her side.

She turned her head, consciously uncurling her fingers, and moved over to the worn leather wing chair in the far corner beyond the window. The picture in her mind was very clear. Gil full of mischief pushing the chair aside as she was now, lifting the corner of the moth-eaten carpet just as she was, exposing the small safe built into the floor.

Berhane stared down at it, remembering his words. 'I've never had much of a memory for numbers and codes.' She had laughed, knowing how much he had enjoyed murder mysteries and thrillers. 'So,' he continued, 'I kept it simple. Not my birthday, of course, that's asking for trouble. I used yours.' He had grinned at her, and she had smiled back, although his words had startled her.

Now she stared down at the safe, reluctant to touch it. Abruptly she crouched and reached out to push the buttons. The door swung open soundlessly and she looked down into the cavity it revealed.

There wasn't much there. A few papers, which looked to Berhane like deeds. A dozen or so little books with marbled paper covers that she recognised as more of the diaries Gil had shown her. A small packet tied with ribbon. She could not stop herself reaching out a hand to pick it up. Her breath caught as she saw what it was. Not letters, no, she had always emailed her friends, but the cards she had sent him from wherever she went. There were very few words on any of them, just brief comments, knowing Gil would get the point, enjoy the humour, understand why she had chosen that image.

Berhane put the packet back carefully, wishing she had not looked. But there beside it was what she had come for. The long envelope was unmistakably the size of a will, and it was addressed to a solicitor in the nearby town.

'I never like to leave anything important lying around,' Gil had said once. Her brow furrowed painfully as she remembered how he had continued. 'You never know what you can be killed for these days.'

A slight movement in the doorway made Berhane spin round.

'Very clever,' Susannah said approvingly. 'I was sure you'd remembered something when the inspector was talking this morning. You never give much away, Berhane, but I know you very well.'

Berhane faced her, holding the long envelope loosely at her side. 'Did you know about the safe too?' she asked curiously. 'Everyone normally confides in you. I was surprised you didn't mention it.'

'Gil didn't tell me,' Susannah said stiffly. 'He didn't tell me everything.' She fell silent, breathing rather harshly, leaning against the back of a chair.

'Why did you come?' Berhane enquired, eyeing her anxiously. 'The weather's getting worse, much too bad to come out unnecessarily.'

'I saw the light on,' Susannah explained, 'and wondered who was here. With all that's been happening, I thought I should check.'

'That was brave of you,' Berhane said, 'but why were you out in the first place?'

Susannah swayed and her free hand went to her chest.

'Aunt Susannah,' Berhane exclaimed, dropping the envelope onto the desk. She moved forward quickly, supporting the older woman and helping her into the chair. 'I expect the cold's bothering you. Where are your pills?'

Susannah was fumbling in the pocket of her woollen trousers and succeeded in pulling out the little silver box. Her fingers could not open it, so Berhane took it from her, extracting a pill and popping it into the older woman's mouth.

Berhane put the box down on the desk and leaned back against the wooden surface that had been swept clear of its usual litter of papers, watching the blue tinge fade from Susannah's face and her tensed posture relax. When Susannah's breathing had returned to normal Berhane straightened up. 'Let's get you back to the Schoolhouse. And that's your last pill. We'd better make sure you top up the box when you get back. You've been taking rather a lot recently. I really think Dr Harford should have another look at you as soon as possible.'

'No,' Susannah said strongly, her fingers clenching round the arms of her chair. She levered herself more upright in the seat. 'Edith, she's being stupid, I must go after her, find her.'

'What's she doing now?' Berhane demanded, watching closely as Susannah clung to the arms of the chair.

'She went off down the lane towards the farm.' Berhane stared at her in surprise. Susannah shook her head, a grim smile on her lips. 'With not even a coat on. I was going after her when I saw the light on here. She's gone to meet Phil Avery, I'm sure of it.' She groaned, sagging a little. 'She was always a bit sweet on him.'

'I never noticed,' Berhane said incredulously. 'Well,' she added, 'it's crazy to be out now, but Phil will make sure she doesn't come to any harm.'

Susannah sank back into the chair and put her hands up to her face.

'Aunt Susannah, what is it?' Berhane asked, alarmed.

'I couldn't bring myself to believe it,' Susannah said faintly. 'I thought Phil had got over all his hatred about the farm, but I'm afraid that this business about losing the smallholding has triggered it off again.'

'Surely not,' Berhane expostulated. 'Phil is a gentle soul at heart.'

'But he cares so much about his animals. Probably about them more than anything else. I'm afraid,' Susannah forced the words out reluctantly, 'that he may have convinced himself that he's protecting them.'

'You surely can't think he'd hurt Edith after all this time?' Berhane asked. 'Why should he?' She stiffened suddenly. 'Aunt Susannah, you think he killed Gil, don't you? He can't have done.'

'The police think he did, because Gil wouldn't renew Phil's lease,' Susannah said quietly. 'And I'm sure Phil knows that. And you know Edith, she's always hearing things that aren't intended for her. I'm sure she picked up something, and she's bound to say so.' She pushed herself out of the chair with difficulty. 'I can't let Edith just drift into danger. She's never been very aware of other people's feelings.'

Berhane frowned. 'Now, I thought she was,' she said slowly. She put a hand on Susannah's arm. 'No, you rest for a bit. I'll go after Edith. You get back to the Schoolhouse when you feel better and tell the others what's happening.'

Susannah fell back into the chair, relief on her face. She watched Berhane pull off her patterned poncho and purple shawl and drop them on the desk, half concealing the long envelope that lay in solitary splendour on its surface.

'I'll borrow some of Gil's things,' Berhane said. 'They'll be more useful in this weather. It's not that far to the farm, although it'll seem like it now the wind's getting up.' She glanced out of the window, her lips tightening as she saw how heavily the snow was still falling.

'She wasn't going there,' Susannah murmured. 'She went

along the farm lane towards the stile. I saw that much before I came in here. I'm sure she'll go up over the fields to Phil.'

Berhane's face was grim. 'She must be mad to even try. The snow's lying nearly two feet deep already, and there's no sign that it's going to stop falling soon. I'll cut down the lane here and go over the bridge. I should be able to cut her off before she gets far.' Berhane had reached the door as she spoke and was gone from Susannah's sight.

Susannah turned round awkwardly, peering out of the window, watching to see Berhane enter the yard. It was only a few minutes before she left the house, muffled in a thick coat that was obviously too large. Her head was covered by a sheepskin hat, the flaps pulled tightly over her ears, while a scarf swathed her neck and lower face. She had strapped her snowshoes on again and moved noiselessly over the immediate yard, out of sight of Susannah's straining eyes as soon as she had taken a couple of steps. Susannah's body sagged heavily again into the chair and her eyes closed.

It was some time later that Susannah sat up slowly and looked round the room. A clock chimed the half hour tinnily and she peered at it, her vision oddly blurred. It was a strange clock, she thought irrelevantly, blue and green with black blobs. As she peered more intently the black blobs formed into shapes, and Susannah saw horses and hounds capering madly over a hillside. She had seen that clock before, she thought confusedly. Somehow it mattered that she should remember where she had seen it.

Susannah straightened a little in the chair, her mind clearing. Of course, that was the silly present Berhane had given Gil at Christmas. A child's toy really, and yet he'd put it on the wall in his own private room. A child's toy, she repeated, and the image that was clear in her memory was from fifteen years ago. Gil was running eagerly up the slope of a heather-covered hillside, Berhane not far behind him, her legs already nearly as long as his. And there was Edith, meandering dreamily along behind. Even then she had never seemed part of the life around her.

Susannah shook her head, trying to clear her mind. Edith, there was something about Edith she ought to remember. And Berhane. What was it? She must get home, there was a reason why she must get home, but she could not seem to remember that either.

Susannah struggled awkwardly out of the chair. She leaned on the desk, supporting herself along its edge on her way across the room. It was there she saw the long envelope sticking out from under Berhane's purple shawl. Susannah focused on it and the scene with Berhane in this room rushed back to her, almost making her stagger. This was Gil's will, this was what she must take care of. She pushed the shawl aside to pick up the envelope and stared at the small mobile that it had concealed. She took it in her hand. A picture flashed into her mind of Berhane leaning against the desk. The mobile must have fallen from Berhane's pocket then. Well, there probably was no reception where Berhane was going anyway. She slipped it into her own pocket and tucked the envelope carefully under her coat.

Outside the house, she paused again, confused. Darkness had come down, but the whole view in front of her was filled with swirling snow, flakes dancing hypnotically before her eyes, settling on her face and melting, leaving drops of water running down her grey skin. It was fortunate that Susannah knew the way to the Schoolhouse. She moved like an automaton, stumbling and slipping, bumping into trees, scratching her face on low hanging branches. She had often said she would be able to find her way to the Schoolhouse in her sleep and tonight it was as if she had.

It was only as Isobel opened the front door and hurried out that Susannah realised where she was. She had come home.

'My dear,' Isobel exclaimed in horror, 'we've been so worried about you. Whatever's happened?'

Susannah stared at her. 'Isobel,' she said, but her voice

sounded like a croak. 'Isobel.' This time the name came out more strongly.

'Yes. Come in and let's get you warm,' Isobel said practically. She put her arm around Susannah's shoulders and steered her indoors, through the kitchen and into the long sitting room.

Susannah looked around her beloved room, her eyes passing over the windows, where the drawn curtains hid her views. Her gaze lingered on all her many treasures, all those things that other Ballamys had brought into the family. Those dark oak bookcases her great-grandfather had made. And the cabbage leaf plates she had played with as a child, a special treat to handle her grandmother's collection. Even here, away from the farm, she had kept them safe. A trust to be handed on. Perhaps now Edith ... Susannah's thoughts broke off, unwilling to take that route.

But who were these people in her room? Isobel, yes, she knew Isobel. But these people, standing in her room, staring at her. Why were they looking so shocked? They had been having tea. Somehow that surprised her. The women were attractive, especially the well-shaped one with the long black curls. And the woman with the chestnut hair that fell in a long bob around her pale pointed face. Susannah was sure she was familiar. But the men. No, she shook her head. She was sure she did not know them. Why were they having tea in her house? Sitting in front of her stove, where the flames flickered silently, gold and yellow. The one with the untidy red hair looked alarmed. But the other, the one coming towards her, was very ordinary until you looked at his face. Such strength of character, such concern there. Edith could do with somebody like that.

Susannah felt sure she should make an effort, say something. 'I am so sorry,' she began, but her voice wavered and stopped. There was a dog, a collie there with the chestnut-haired woman. The woman who looked a little like Isobel, that was why she was familiar. But the dog was not, there had not been any dogs on the farm at the end. And that was a spaniel too, an old one, lying in front of the hearth, lifting its head to peer myopically at her.

Now there was a cat coming towards her, a large cat with thick creamy fur tipped with mink, and bristling eyebrows over big amber eyes. 'Solomon,' Susannah murmured as she fell forward into Hugh's arms.

He supported her, looking at her grey face with concern, as he lowered her onto the sofa that Lucy had hastily pushed forward.

'Do you know what's wrong with her?' he asked Isobel urgently.

'It could be her heart,' Isobel said doubtfully. 'I know she takes pills for it, but,' she studied Susannah's face carefully, 'I'm not sure. When I saw her take a pill she was rather blue in the face and short of breath.'

'This looks more as though she's had a shock,' Anna said. 'Mike's gone to ring the doctor. I expect there's a number by the phone. I'll go and put the kettle on for more tea, and a hot water bottle.' She hurried out of the room.

'Maybe we should get her pills anyway,' Lucy said.

'They're probably in one of her pockets,' her grandmother said. 'I don't think she goes anywhere without them.'

'Let's get her out of this coat,' Hugh suggested. 'It's very wet. I'll hold her shoulders if you can ease it off her.'

Susannah hung limply in his hold, so it was an awkward business for Lucy, easing first one arm out of its sleeve, then the other. But at last it was done and Hugh lowered Susannah back on the cushions, where she lay with her eyes shut.

Lucy bent to pick up the coat, feeling carefully in its pockets to see if the pillbox was there. She only found a mobile, but as she moved the coat a long stiff envelope fell to the floor.

Hugh stooped quickly, recognising it at once.

'What is it?' Isobel demanded, her hands clenched on the back of one of the armchairs.

'It looks like the missing will,' Hugh said slowly. He turned to look thoughtfully at Susannah. 'Now I wonder where she came across this.'

His eyes turned to Isobel. 'Do you know where she went when she left the house?'

'No,' Isobel said slowly. 'She had been sitting by the window ever since we came back from the village hall. I wanted her to rest, she was very upset this morning, on top of everything that's happened since we got here. She was quite willing to do so, which worried me. It was so unlike her.' She put one hand up to her lips for a moment. 'That was why I was sure she wasn't feeling well. She only had a bowl of soup for lunch, and she had that by the window too.'

'Wasn't that strange?' Hugh asked. 'Why did she sit there for so long?'

'She once said she enjoyed watching the variety of life that passed by on the village green,' Isobel answered. 'I think it soothed her. But then, I suppose it was about three thirty, she suddenly got up and went out, putting her coat on as she went.' Isobel looked rueful. 'I'm afraid I must have been dozing. It was so cosy by the stove. I didn't quite realise what was going on until she was going into the kitchen.'

'Did she say anything?' Hugh asked.

'She mentioned Edith,' Isobel replied. 'But I didn't really catch what she said.'

'That must have been about the time Edith went out of the Church House onto the green,' Anna said, returning to the room with a cup of tea in one hand. Mike trailed sheepishly behind her, awkwardly clutching a hot water bottle wrapped in a knitted cover.

'Yes, of course,' Hugh agreed as Lucy lifted Susannah gently up. 'I remember her going out. Do you know why she did?'

Anna suppressed an acid response as she held the cup to Susannah's pale lips. The older woman sipped automatically and her eyelids flickered.

'Put the hot water bottle on her far side, Mike,' Anna

instructed. 'No,' she added sharply, 'not on her tummy. Put it between her and the back of the sofa.'

'Anna,' Hugh's tone was insistent, 'why did Edith go out? I wasn't listening to what she said to you and Lucy.'

'She said she was looking for a text message from her bloke,' Anna said shortly. 'She wanted to ring him, I think. She's always trying to get in touch with him. Although I thought he'd been over a couple of times. I've seen her with a bloke in motorcycle gear. In fact, I thought he was here last night, but he's surely not going to try to get out again in this weather.'

'That doesn't explain why she went wandering off,' Hugh said.

'She mumbled something about looking at the farm,' Mike blurted out, suddenly remembering that he had met Edith as he came back to the Church House.

'Why are you talking about me?'

The voice startled them all. Lucy's hands tightened on Susannah's shoulders, while Anna's hold on the cup wavered and a little tea spilt onto Susannah's jumper.

They knew the voice, but it was different. And the woman who stood in the doorway was obviously Edith, her long skirt draggled and her jumpers and scarf bedewed with drops of water. Her frizzy brown hair hung wet and limp on both sides of her round face, as it so often did. But her pale eyes were bright, her expression was unusually alert and oddly happy.

Nobody had noticed that Susannah's eyes had opened, focusing on her niece. 'Edith,' she said feebly, her arm twitching as she tried to move it.

Edith looked past the men to where her aunt lay on the sofa. A look of alarm clouded her face. 'Aunt Su,' she said, lumbering forward, 'whatever's wrong?'

She knelt heavily next to the sofa, and Susannah reached out to her. 'You went to the farm. I saw you go,' Susannah murmured, as Edith took her searching hand. 'I knew you'd come back to it.'

Anna bit her lip. Surely Edith would be bright enough to play along.

'No, I only went to see it, you know, from the stile on Fourways Corner.'

Beside her Anna shifted, wondering if she should kick Edith, just a little kick, a tap really.

'But I am coming back to it, Aunt Susannah. Me and Taylor. He got home this morning to find a letter from a publisher in the States about our book. You know, I told you about the fantasy we wrote together. Well, they want it, want it a lot, and you wouldn't believe how much they're paying as an advance. They want a whole series, too.' The words were spilling out of Edith, and even Anna knew that she was not just comforting her aunt. 'So Taylor and me, we're going to set up our own commune, out at the farm. We'll have someone farm the land, of course, but any spare buildings we'll convert for artists, and we can keep the house for ourselves.' She looked anxiously at her aunt, who was staring at her in disbelief. 'I don't know if Gil would have sold it back to us, but Ballamy's Farm will belong to Berhane now, and I'm sure she will.'

Susannah struggled to sit up, waving away the anxious hands that tried to help her. 'Berhane,' she said, struggling over the words. 'She's gone. To find you, to stop you. I told her you were meeting Phil Avery. God forgive me, she thinks he means to harm you.'

Edith rocked back on her heels, staring at her aunt.

'Why on earth would he?' she asked. 'Phil would never hurt anyone.' Her eyes bulged with alarm as Susannah began to gasp for breath, her hands scrabbling feebly at her chest.

Anna took one look at Susannah's face, noting the blue tinge that had crept into it. 'Heart,' she said sharply. 'Did someone mention her pills?'

Isobel came forward quickly. 'Yes. She carries them in a little silver box, but we haven't found it.' Isobel picked up Susannah's wet coat from the floor where Lucy had dropped it and plunged a hand in one pocket.

'I'm sure it's not in there,' Lucy said. 'There was only the mobile.'

Edith turned her head to stare at Lucy, a puzzled expression crossing her face. But Lucy ignored her, bending over Susannah and carefully inserting a hand into first one trouser pocket, then the other. 'Nothing,' she said tersely.

Edith stood up awkwardly. 'Aunt Su tops up the box from the big pot of pills in her room,' she said. 'I'll get that.' She moved to the corner of the room where a spiral staircase twirled upwards, its elegant beech treads edged with cast-iron spindles.

'Well, get a move on,' Anna snapped, watching the blueness deepen in Susannah's face.

As Edith's deliberate step reverberated on the staircase her aunt lay back against the cushions of the sofa, her eyes shut, the lids looking bruised and purple against her tired face. Her hands had moved from her chest and were on Solomon, who had sprung onto the sofa to lie across the top of her legs.

Hugh moved towards him, intent on lifting him away. The cat's amber eyes flicked away from Susannah's face to glare at Hugh with distinct menace.

'Leave him there,' Isobel said, as she lowered herself cautiously onto the floor beside the sofa. 'Look.'

Hugh followed her gaze and saw Susannah's fingers were entwined in the cat's creamy fur. Solomon looked away from Hugh, back towards the woman on the sofa and a hoarse rusty purr rolled out of him.

Heavy footsteps and panting breath heralded Edith's return. Hugh looked round in time to see the delicate staircase shaking under her clumsy descent.

She shook her head as soon as she reached the floor, her wet straggling hair swinging backwards and forwards across her face. 'I found it in the bin,' she gasped. 'Empty. And I can't find another one.'

Hugh swung round to Mike. 'When does the doctor expect

to get here?'

Mike pulled a face. 'I couldn't get through,' he said. 'The lines are down.'

'Try a mobile,' Anna said impatiently. 'Even if there's no reception here there is out on the green.'

He glowered at her. 'I've already tried, remember. While you were getting the tea. Nothing doing.' He looked at Hugh. 'Elliot's gone off with the huskies too. No chance of using them.'

'What about Berhane?' Lucy said. 'She's out in the storm on her own.'

'Won't she go to the house we passed, at the foot of the moor?' Anna demanded suddenly. 'She's going that way, isn't she?'

'Yes, I expect she is,' Edith agreed, 'but there won't be anyone there. The Simmonds have gone to their daughter's for January. They're always worried about being cut off at their own house. I saw Jean Simmonds on the green last night. She told me they were going straight off after the bell ringing, while they could still do the drive, rather than wait to go this morning.'

'We can't even get through to Phil to warn him about Berhane if none of the phones are working,' Lucy said. Her face lit up. 'But surely we can try to get her on her mobile, and tell her to come back. She just might be somewhere with reception and surely we can find some here.'

Edith was standing by the table, holding the mobile that Lucy had taken out of Susannah's coat pocket. 'It won't do any good. This is hers.'

'Are you sure, Edith?' Anna asked suspiciously. 'Why would your aunt have it?'

'There's no time for this,' Hugh said. 'We'll have to split up. Edith, do you know anyone who can go for the doctor?' He glanced at Susannah, whose harsh breathing was now drowning the cat's rhythmic purring.

'I can do better than that,' Edith said, letting the phone drop back onto the table. 'If we can get hold of Phil he'll be able to contact the doctor, and go out to look for Berhane. He knows the route up to the moor like the back of his hand. If anyone can find her, he will.'

'And how,' Anna asked crossly, 'are you planning to get hold of Phil? I presume he's gone back up to his smallholding. Even if he didn't want to get away from his family gathering, he'll have to feed his animals.'

'The radio,' Edith said simply.

Lucy looked at her with sudden understanding, but the others were staring blankly at Edith. 'Of course,' Lucy exclaimed. She turned to the others, saying quickly, 'Phil is an amateur radio buff. Surely that won't be affected by the weather.' She swung back to Edith. 'Is there a radio down here?'

Edith nodded. 'Joe has one. It was him who got Phil interested, years ago.'

'Do you know how to operate it?' Mike demanded disbelievingly.

'I'm not sure,' Edith admitted. 'I've done it once or twice, when Phil was still living at the farm. I expect it'll come back to me. And I only have to get him, he can contact everyone we need.'

Mike snorted.

Edith's eyes moved to him. 'But the police will have locked up at the inn, won't they? Even Joe's rooms, where the radio is?'

'Yes,' Hugh said shortly. 'Are there any other radio operators in the village?'

Edith looked vague. 'I don't know. I suppose we can ask around.'

'No time,' Hugh said. He glanced at Mike. 'Take an axe to the door, if you have to.'

'Me?' Mike demanded, alarmed. 'What about you?'

'I've had more practice on snowshoes than you, so I'll go off after Berhane,' he said, turning as he spoke and walking swiftly into the kitchen. 'She may not have got very far. The snowshoes will help me for the first part of the way, along the lane. She could even have turned back. Thank God we went out that way yesterday. I may recognise the route.'

He had put his coat on, and was fumbling with the buttons as Lucy reached out for hers. 'What do you think you're doing?' he asked quickly.

'You can't go alone,' she said, taking her own coat off the coat stand. 'I'm coming too.'

'Don't be ridiculous.' He caught her by the shoulders and swung her around. Behind them Ben stood uncertainly, his face moving unhappily from one of them to the other.

'You can both take snowshoes from the Church House,' Edith chipped in. 'Mike used my dad's, so I expect they're out in the hall already. Mine are in the cupboard under the stairs. Lucy can use those.'

Lucy stared at Hugh, her face very white, her pointed chin jutting out. 'Mike's going with Edith, Anna's the best person to stay here with Gran as she's got some first aid experience. That leaves me to go with you.'

'Lucy,' Hugh struggled to sound reasonable. 'Look at the weather.' He jerked his head at the window beside the door. The outside light illuminated a pristine white coverlet almost two feet deep, with a heavy fall of snow still coming down unendingly in a steady curtain, unmoved now by any wind. 'One person out there is too many. But we can't leave Berhane, so I must go. There's no need for you to risk it as well.'

'I'm coming too,' Lucy repeated. 'She's my friend.' She looked at him steadily. 'If you don't let me come with you I'll follow anyway.'

'For God's sake,' Mike snarled, forcing his donkey jacket on over his thick jumper. 'Let's not stand around arguing.'

Lucy flickered a smile at him before turning round to Anna. 'Hang on to Ben. He'll try to follow, and I couldn't bear him to get lost.'

Anna nodded wordlessly, hooking a hand through Ben's

collar. She stood watching as Hugh opened the front door, allowing a huge blast of cold to enter. A second later the four of them had gone out into the blizzard. Her view of them, grey shapes in a whirling white world, was cut off abruptly as Hugh swung the door shut.

SEVEN

Berhane struggled to a stop under a tree, its wide branches burdened with a thick crust of snow. Beyond the tree's shelter, minimal but definitely appreciated, she looked out on a surreal world. She was not going to ferret under her jacket cuffs to look at her watch, but she was sure that it was still early evening, no later perhaps than five o'clock. She should be surrounded by the soft blackness of night, pierced perhaps by the calls of the tawny owls from the lime avenue in the nearby cottage garden. Instead all around her there was swirling whiteness and complete eerie silence.

Berhane had not had time or spare energy to think about the situation as she had made her way along the lane that the hunt had taken yesterday morning. She had just kept her head bent against the storm of whirling flakes, the scarf pulled up over her mouth and nose and the borrowed hat low over her head, but the area round her eyes was red and sore from the stinging flakes.

She had moved expertly over the thick snow on her snow-shoes, finding the first part of the route almost easy, compared to the later section. The high stone walls edging the lane had kept her on track, although she had barged into them pain-fully more than once. Her face was scratches by the brambles that had caught her by surprise, and heavy clumps of snow thumping onto her head and shoulders when she stumbled into overhanging bushes had left damp seeping down her neck. She had soon learned to drop her pace to a painfully slow speed, but at least she was sure she was on the right track.

The going was much harder once she had branched off onto the footpath, finding the entrance by pure luck, simply by bumping into the signpost. Out in the open meadow there was no shelter from the wind and the snowfall seemed heavier. Worst of all was the uncertainty about direction. There were no guiding walls here, and if she went off route she had no way of knowing if she was going round in circles, the nightmare that haunted anyone out in bad weather. There was not even any hope of seeing or smelling woodsmoke from the house nearby, for she knew that the owners had gone away that morning, keen to get to their family before they were snowed in.

It was sheer luck, Berhane felt, as she stood under the tree, that she had got as far as she had. She hunched her shoulders, knowing as she felt the cold penetrate Gil's coat and her own thick jumper that she must decide quickly whether to go on or to return. Now only her long engrained knowledge of the route would keep her safe, and she was not sure it would be enough. She knew that just a little way ahead was the brook, because from time to time she could hear the roar of water rushing along.

Once she crossed that she would be on the high open moor. The weather would be worse there, the drifts definitely deeper. And what landmarks there were would not be visible. There would be no way of checking her path, no way of spotting hazards, and above all no way to be sure she would not get lost.

Surely, surely, she thought, Edith must have turned back before this. But the whole situation was bizarre. Was Phil Avery truly out in this weather searching for Edith, planning to harm her? Really, Berhane thought, it was mad. Maybe, she wondered suddenly, Susannah was ill, having hallucinations. That would certainly make sense. The older woman had certainly looked very unwell at Gil's house, and she hadn't seemed her usual self ever since Gil's death.

I'll go back, Berhane decided. I can't believe Edith's still trying to get up on the moor. If Edith isn't at home we'll have to call out the rescue services. But if I go on they'll certainly have to come out for me.

The decision made, she shifted the scarf over her face, securing it more tightly inside the collar of her coat, shivering as the coldness penetrated deeper into her body. She certainly could not stand here any longer.

As she turned back a sound in the distance made her freeze. She undid the flaps of her hat, exposing her ears to the biting cold, straining to hear. Nothing was audible now, but surely that had been a voice, its words blown eerily across the distance.

Berhane bit her lip irresolutely. Was her mind playing tricks? No, she did not think it was. So then who was up there on the moor, calling out? Edith, in need of help, or Phil, for who knows what reason?

I have to check, she realised, tying the hat flaps under her chin, but I won't go far. Just over the bridge onto the slope. If I don't hear anything more I'll come straight back.

She stepped out of the tree's shelter, full into the snowstorm. Head bent she plodded carefully on, keeping close to the line of trees on her left. She knew the house must be nearby, but there would be no welcome glint of yellow light through uncurtained windows, no opportunity to go in out of the storm and summon help.

Berhane did not even know she had passed the house until she noticed the constant noise of rushing water that warned her she was approaching the brook. The sound came suddenly through the silence, loud and strangely menacing, and she realised that the water level must have risen dramatically. Not surprising given the amount of snow that had fallen.

She stepped forward slowly, testing each step, unable to see a handspan ahead, brushing cautiously through the sallows and alders that she knew edged the line of the brook. Her hands were stretched out in front of her, her feet moved forward inch by inch until one bumped into something solid. She felt it cautiously, aware that there were no branches poking into her face or catching at her coat. This was it, the bridge post, she realised with amazement. She always believed in luck, good or bad, and for a second wondered what she was experiencing this evening.

The noise was now all enveloping, a terrific sound that seemed to shake the rail itself, and Berhane hesitated. She was unusually daunted by the thought of crossing the fragile bridge, with its slender rails between her and the torrent below.

Gritting her teeth, she edged forward onto the planks. The layer of snow here was not as deep as it was on the surrounding land, but nonetheless she had to bend down slightly to keep her hands on the rails.

She shuffled forward a few paces and paused. She really could not do this. But how could she turn round? She would have to move backwards, or take the snowshoes off.

In the moment that she stood there running over her options the heavy snowfall around her parted, as if a curtain had been pulled back. She glimpsed the brook below her, a yellow foaming roll of water, surging past at terrific speed, tossing big boulders and huge logs like toys on its heaving surface.

She had only a second to realise her danger as the height of the brook seemed to grow, until it seemed that a huge wall of water was bearing down on her as she stood frozen on the bridge. The veil of whiteness came down again, concealing the threat, but nothing disguised the crack as the water hit the upper struts supporting the bridge.

The planks on which Berhane stood sagged and dipped inwards. She slipped, a scream torn from her as she grabbed at the rails. They snapped under her fingers and she felt herself sliding downwards into the roiling waters below.

The man on the high moor above was retracing his steps, sure that he was on a wild goose chase. There had been no response to his calls and he was convinced now that he was the only person out here in the storm. It had been a mad story that Edith had blurted out. He would not have believed it if it had not been for the bloke, that archaeologist, supporting what she said.

He struggled up the slope, the snow blowing into his face, making his eyes water, blurring his vision even more. But in the valley beyond he would be marginally more sheltered. And on the far slope was his house, whose lights he had left blazing, hoping the generator power would last, to provide him with a welcome beacon. Although he knew the land like the back of his hand this was the worst weather he had ever known, and he would take no more chances of getting lost and caught out in it.

He crested the ridge and had no intention of stopping again when noises behind him made him pause, turning back slightly, one arm raised to protect his face from the driving wind. There was no mistaking the sounds. The bridge over the brook had come down with a terrific cracking, audible above the roar of the water that had hit it. But there had been a scream too. Not a shout for help, but a woman's scream of terror. It had to be Berhane, he thought as he turned, plunging back down the steep slope. There were no other thoughts in his mind as he struggled desperately down the steep slope. Only when he floundered into a deep drift, fighting against the softness that covered him, pulling him further down as he struggled, did he gather his wits.

Slowly, carefully, he worked his way out of the drift and stood, plastered with snow, but unaware of the damp working its way insidiously through his coat and jumper. His mind was clear, calm, now as he picked his way down the rest of the slope, the roar of water loud in his ears, drowning out anything else. He could not see where he was, but he knew where he was going. Down. Once he reached the brook he could work his way along the bank to find the bridge, or what was left of it.

It seemed to take hours, but he knew that time was deceptive in these circumstances. Anyway, it did not matter. If that was Berhane down there he had to take this opportunity to find her and see if she was still alive.

Edging cautiously forward he stopped in mid movement. The ground fell away under his foot. He pulled it back and began to move carefully to his left. At last he edged into a hard post. The bridge. Or, his hand felt upwards, to where the rail hung loose, all that remained of the bridge.

He stood still for a moment, wondering what to do. The storm lantern slung over one shoulder had been useless in the driving snow. But now, looking around, he was sure the storm was easing. He stared around more carefully. Yes, although the flakes were still falling he could see much further. There were the dim outlines of trees around him. He had not been aware of passing through them, but now he could see them.

His eyes fell on the bridge, also now visible in the uncanny snow light. Planks at either side sagged but were still anchored in place by the bank posts, but the centre of the bridge had gone completely. He pulled the lantern round into his hand and switched it on, his heart beating loud enough to drown out the roaring of the flood below.

He pointed it down into the void, his breathing harsh and shallow as he turned the beam this way and that. The light shone on the thundering yellow water, flashing off a boulder bouncing by. The narrow beam moved over the far bank, its thick covering of snow littered with the darker shape of fallen planks right down to the edge of the water.

His heart leaped into his mouth. There she was. He leaned precariously forward. She hung awkwardly, three quarters of the way down the precipitous bank. She was very still. As he watched he could see no movement. Was she still alive? He waited, his eyes straining. There was still no movement. But he had to be sure. He must get closer to see properly.

He stood up straight, the light of the lantern swinging away from the motionless body and flickering over the water below it. His lips tightened. There was no way through that. Too deep and too many obstacles in the water.

He swung the light onto the end of the bridge on the far side of the brook, then back onto the end beside him. This was the only way. He bent to test the planks. Firm enough to hold him, at least for a few seconds.

Without another thought he laid the lantern down on the bank, shining towards the far end of the bridge, shedding a faint light on the planks that hung suspended there. He took a few paces back, before running forward awkwardly over the thick snow.

Straight onto the bridge he went, not thinking of the risks. He leaped out over the void, landing heavily on the planks beyond. They sagged instantly under the sudden weight and he threw himself forward, grabbing at the far post. He seemed to hang for an eternity, feeling the planks sliding away below him, hearing them thudding on the ground below. Would they hit Berhane, perhaps knock her into the water? He could not look down, there was no time to do more than drag himself up onto the bank before the post gave way.

He lay still, deep in the snow, trying to get his breath back. listening to the post bouncing down the slope. It was the cold on his face, the wetness against his body, that made him move. And the need to see whether she was still alive.

The lamp still shone its light across the brook, the very edge of its beam falling on Berhane's body on the bank below him. There was only the snow light to help him find his way down, and he went with extreme care, skirting round splintered planks, testing the ground before he trusted his weight to it. The slightest mis-step here and he would be in the water.

At last he was there, close enough to see that Berhane was held precariously against the bank, one snowshoe wedged against a rock, her body supported by the scarf that had snagged on the sharp end of an old tree stump. A fraction of an inch further and that pointed shard would have gone through her throat, he thought, and that would be the end of her. But perhaps she was dead anyway.

He edged a trifle closer and her eyes flickered open. She could only glance out of the corner of them, any movement of her head might dislodge the scarf and then surely the snowshoe would not be enough to save her from falling.

'Phil.' Her voice was quite calm.

'Yes.' So was his as he reached out towards her.

Mike perched uncomfortably on the stool at the end of the kitchen counter in the Schoolhouse. He was absentmindedly watching Anna as she poured boiling water into the coffee pot.

'Are you sure Phil understood?' Anna asked, her head bent over her task.

'Of course I'm not,' Mike growled. As she looked up quickly, lifting the kettle, he added, 'I'm sure he understood about Berhane being out in the storm in his direction. I told him myself, when it was clear Edith's ramblings were confusing him. The rest of it, no, I'm not sure he understood that. It didn't seem worth trying to explain.' He jerked his head towards the sitting room. 'She was going on for ever without making the story any clearer, but then,' he snorted, 'I don't understand what's going on either.'

'Neither do I,' Anna admitted, putting the coffee pot down on the counter in front of him. She took three mugs off a shelf nearby and pulled up a stool for herself beside Mike.

She was about to sit down when she hesitated.

'What now?' Mike demanded. 'Not enough mugs, are there? What about Isobel?'

'She drinks tea, so I'll see if she wants some more, but she's already had quite a bit. It just that I think Edith likes coffee really weak,' she said. 'I'd better pour hers now.'

'She would,' Mike mumbled. 'Is it safe to leave her alone

in there with her aunt? And Isobel. After all,' he added more loudly, 'we know none of us killed the landlord. She could be IT.'

'Don't be silly,' Anna said. She glanced quickly at the closed door. 'And do keep your voice down. I think there's nobody Susannah would rather have with her now. And,' she added practically, 'Isobel will call us if she needs us. I don't really think there's anything we can do for Susannah, except wait for the doctor and pray she doesn't get worse.'

She added a lot of milk to the mug of coffee she had poured out. Glancing across at Mike as he poured coffee into his mug, she said, 'Edith didn't sound confident about using the radio, so I'm surprised she managed to get through to the police as well as Phil. I suppose they didn't give you any idea of how soon the doctor could get here?'

'I've already told you,' Mike snapped, banging the pot down on the counter, slopping the coffee out of its spout. 'They've got to find him, get the husky team sorted out again and then make their way here. Nobody knew how long that will take.'

Anna nodded, and walked across the room, leaving him to mop up the coffee with a piece of kitchen roll. She glanced at Ben as he lay morosely across the mat by the front door. Although his eyes followed her as she went into the sitting room, the collie did not even lift his head from where it lay on his paws.

'I know just how you feel, mate,' Mike muttered, his eyes resting on the collie. 'Just sitting here waiting makes me feel bloody useless.'

'Me too,' Anna said as she came back into the kitchen. 'I'm not good at this. But,' she pinned a smile on her lips, 'let's make the best of it. Hugh was right, there's no point us all being out in the snow. Pour me some coffee, please, and remember I like mine black.' She looked round the room, considering. 'I suppose we can see if we can make soup or stew. Once they all get back they'll need feeding and warming up. Let's see what Susannah's got in the place,' she said with more enthusiasm, accepting the mug Mike pushed towards her. 'I'll check out the fridge, you see what's in that cupboard over there. It's like a larder, with a rack for fruit and vegetables.' Anna pointed to the far corner beyond the front door.

'Cooking!' Mike expostulated, banging the coffee pot down again. 'Is that all I'm good for?'

Anna shrugged. 'Please yourself,' she said shortly, sorting through the contents of the fridge. 'Go and dig snow off the front path if it'll make you feel more macho, but I can't see it'll be much use. Ah, this beef will do nicely. It's already diced too. Susannah obviously stocked up in case of bad weather, I was sure she would.'

Mike pushed his stool back, scraping it along the floor.

Anna glanced over at him, frowning. 'Don't make so much noise, Mike. We don't want to disturb her.'

He scowled, tiptoeing across the room with deliberate caution, and placing his mug down with exaggerated care. 'I thought she was completely out of it.'

'We can't be sure,' Anna said, putting the meat in a bowl. 'Unusual sounds may bother her, and it's much better she doesn't wake up and start to fret.' She glanced at Ben. 'Do you think I should give him some beef? It might cheer him up.'

'You can try,' Mike said, his voice muffled by the cupboard door.

Anna took a good-sized chunk and bent down beside the dog, offering it to him on the palm of her hand. Ben lifted his head a little, turning towards Anna, his nostrils whiffling. Then he lowered his head again and lay still, his nose pressed against the bottom of the door.

Anna stood up and put the meat on one side. 'Maybe later,' she said to the collie. 'Mike, do be careful if you open the front door for any reason. I'm sure Ben will be off if he gets a chance.'

'So will I,' Mike said glumly, piling carrots and leeks next to the heap of potatoes he had already put on the worktop.

'You know the risks,' Anna said forcefully. 'Ben doesn't.'

'Alright, alright,' Mike said. 'I wouldn't want him to get lost in the snow either.'

He wandered over to the window, peering out across the village green. 'No sign of it letting up,' he reported, his breath steaming up the window so that he had to wipe it with his sleeve.

Anna came to stand beside him, her face pale. She stared outside, biting her lip hard to keep it from trembling. 'Why don't they come back?' she burst out. 'Surely they can't see anything out there.'

Mike shrugged. 'They've got to try. We can't just leave Berhane to freeze to...' He broke off, realising too late that his comment was injudicious.

Anna turned towards him, her dark blue eyes dilated with fear. 'You think she's lost out there, don't you?'

He looked at her set face. 'Well, what do you think?' he demanded roughly. 'In weather like this? What possessed her to listen to the old woman?'

'The same thing that possessed Hugh and Lucy,' Anna said tightly. 'Wanting to help somebody they care about.' She gave a great sniff, determined not to cry. 'I thought we'd lost Lucy last Easter, I can't bear to think of her in danger again.'

Mike watched her uneasily, and saw her chin wobble. Awkwardly he reached out a hand and patted her shoulder. 'It'll be alright, you'll see. We've got through worse than this.'

'No we haven't,' she said desperately, her voice wavering up and down. 'However bad things have been, none of us has ever been at the mercy of the weather like this. We can't sort that out.' Tears trickled out of the corners of her eyes, running unheeded down her smooth skin.

'Come on, Anna,' Mike said, pulling a crumpled and stained handkerchief out of his pocket. 'You never cry.'

'I'm not,' she gasped, ignoring the handkerchief he held out, and brushing her face with both hands. 'If only we could go out and look for them.'

'Don't be stupid,' he said sharply. 'We can't help them by doing that.'

'You'd have gone with Hugh,' she said, lifting her head to glare at him.

'Of course I would,' he retorted. 'And so would you. You've never thought before you act. Come on, Anna,' he added hastily, 'you know Hugh was right. And so were you. We need to get on with something here.'

'Look,' he reached out a long arm, collecting her mug, 'you sit down and drink your coffee.'

She was stunned with surprise, limply taking the mug he pressed into her hands, and letting him steer her gingerly to a stool. He stood over her, watching as she sipped at the tepid drink.

'Sorry, Mike,' she said after a few moments. 'I feel better now. When do you think the rescue team will get here? They'll probably need feeding too, so I'll look in the freezer to see what else there is once we've got the stew on.'

'I don't know when they'll get here,' he said grimly. 'Elliot's bound to get over here as soon as there's any chance. The local team has search dogs and handlers, and quad bikers, with a rescue helicopter on call. But,' he ground the words out, 'with the snow coming down so heavily there's virtually no visibility. However well they know the terrain they still can't operate, so they'll have to wait for the weather to improve. But they're ready to move as soon as possible.' Mike shrugged. 'For what that's worth.'

'It's better than nothing,' Anna replied, her hands cradling her coffee mug. 'Mike, which of these vegetables do you want to do? Potatoes, or the carrots and leeks?'

He turned round slowly, staring at her in disbelief. She met his gaze steadily and his mouth twisted in a muted snarl. 'Oh alright. I'll do the potatoes. I've had plenty of practice with those.'

She lifted her beautifully marked eyebrows enquiringly as she put her mug down and slid off the stool.

'Punishment rota at boarding school,' he said succinctly. 'Designed by sadists.'

'I see.'

There was silence for a while, other than the scrape of knife and peeler on vegetables, and the occasional slither and plop of snow sliding off the roof.

'Have you any idea what's going on around here?' Mike demanded suddenly.

Anna was chopping the leeks into chunks. 'I'm not sure,' she said thoughtfully, pausing with the knife in mid air. 'Let's start from the beginning and see if we can work it out.'

Mike snorted. 'And where the hell is the beginning?'

Anna glanced at him and away again, horrified at the potato peel he was scattering over the wall and floor. 'The evening when we arrived,' she said, putting down her knife, 'Berhane told us her plans for this dining club and the international training centre. We all concentrated on that, partly because Berhane is interesting and partly because they're such unusual ideas. And we know there was opposition to her plans.'

'But the landlord is dead,' Mike pointed out impatiently, 'and Gil supported her.'

'I know,' Anna agreed. 'It doesn't make sense. I'm just trying to get straight in my mind the things that happened, perhaps ones we didn't think much of at the time. For instance, Edith,' she added ruefully, turning on a cooker ring to heat oil in a large terracotta casserole dish, 'told us about her book, but nobody really paid any attention to her.'

'That's a point,' Mike said. 'I shouldn't think anybody ever has paid any attention to her.'

'You're probably right,' Anna admitted. 'I know we all tended to write off her and her ideas at school. Although she often had an uncanny knack of saying what everyone was thinking. But,' Anna added, 'Susannah always noticed her.'

'She's her aunt,' Mike said. 'It comes with the role.'

'And presumably her bloke does. What's his name? Ah,' Anna remembered triumphantly, 'Taylor.'

'Perhaps,' Mike said cynically. 'But I think we should notice that nobody generally does notice what she says or does.'

'Okay,' Anna agreed, slipping the beef chunks into the casserole dish. 'Mike, slice those potatoes thickly and then put them in here. I'll find some wine if you cut up the carrots and put them in too, then we can leave the dish in the oven until we need it.'

Mike looked up from his job, considering the casserole. 'That looks as though it'll feed at least ten strong men. Have you used all the meat you found?'

'Yes,' Anna said. 'Susannah must have been expecting to have us all over for a meal. I don't know how many people we'll need to feed. And anything we don't eat today can be frozen for another time.'

'Hmmph.' He took a carving knife out of a wooden stack and began to chop the potatoes into ungainly pieces on a large plastic board. 'What about Edith's bloke? I haven't met him. Have I?' he asked uncertainly.

Anna glanced at what he was doing and looked quickly away again, determined not to criticise. 'No, none of us have. But,' she said slowly, 'I do wonder if he's been over here. I've seen Edith talking to a bloke in motorcycle leathers a couple of times, and thought it might have been him. But what could he have to do with what's going on?'

'Edith might have a reason,' Mike said, 'and he could be involved.'

'What reason?' she asked dubiously.

'How the devil should I know?' Mike demanded crossly. 'Perhaps Edith doesn't want her here, perhaps she hates the sight of her. Or,' he added more seriously, 'perhaps she inherits the Church House if something happens to Berhane.'

'That doesn't seem very likely,' Anna said uncertainly. Her eyes widened. 'But,' she exclaimed, 'there were all those little incidents that happened to Berhane. Maybe somebody does want to drive Berhane away.'

'What incidents? I don't know about them.'

'Silly things, but there seem to have been quite a few.' Anna began to tick them off on her fingers. 'There was the oil stolen from her tank, and just enough spilt on the outside steps for her to slip on. You were there, Mike,' she pointed out, 'at the inn, when she told Gil about it, and the burglar who knocked Susannah down. And,' Anna added with increasing excitement,' we were locked in the church with her that evening when we arrived. I think,' she frowned slightly, trying to remember, 'there was some odd bother earlier in the day about her food orders being cancelled as well.'

'It doesn't sound like much,' Mike said dismissively. 'Just people being stupid or greedy. Now,' he put down the knife and gathered the potato slices in his hands, dumping them into the huge dish, 'that landlord, I reckon he was up to something.'

'But he's dead,' Anna pointed out.

'Still,' Mike insisted, 'why should he have been so shirty with me about his collection of bloody stones?'

Anna bit her lip, wondering whether to point out that Mike often upset people, but for once not wanting to get into this discussion. She stirred the potatoes further into the casserole, covered the pot and lifted it up. 'Open the oven door, please.'

Mike yanked it open, muttering under his breath. Anna lowered the pot and pushed it in, closing the door with the pan holder nearby.

She stood up with relief. 'Well, that's done. Maybe,' she added cautiously, 'we ought to sort out a pudding. Stewed apples would be easy.'

'Not bloody likely,' Mike said. 'I'm having some more coffee.' He seized his mug and strode round to the far side of the kitchen counter.

'I suppose there'll be plenty of time,' Anna said, going to join him. 'I'll make some more. And you might as well read that diary Hugh brought over with him.'

'What!' Mike spun round, almost dropping the coffee pot he was holding.

'Really, Mike, do be more careful,' Anna said, leaning over to tear off a piece of kitchen towel and mop up the puddle.

'Do you mean he brought one of those old diaries here?' Mike persisted.

'Mmm. You weren't listening when we were having tea with Isobel. He wanted to talk to Susannah about something in it.'

'Bloody hell! Where is it?' Mike demanded, looking wildly round the kitchen and dining room.

'He put it on one of the little tables in the sitting room,' Anna said. 'Mike! You can't go in there now.'

He had reached the door into the sitting room when it opened. Edith stood there, clutching the handle, her eyes bulging fearfully.

'Anna,' she said thickly, 'can you come? I think, oh, I think Aunt Su's dying.'

Lucy's one fixed thought was to keep Hugh in sight. Both of them were thickly encrusted with snow, from their hats down to the trousers tucked into their boots. Around them all was whiteness, the landscape's features hidden under the snow.

The whirling flakes stung her face and blurred her vision, but she kept on steadily, her attention fixed on the figure ahead as she moved one foot after another. She could only just see him, a more solid shape in the opaqueness of the blizzard, and was staying so close that she had several times bumped into him.

She was immensely grateful for the snowshoes. If she had been without them she knew she would not have been able to get through the snow, which was several feet deep where it had drifted against stone walls and bushes. Or at least against the places where she thought walls and bushes were.

Lucy had not the faintest idea of how far they had come, or how far they had to go. She knew they would have to cross the brook, and surely they could not be far from it. They seemed to have been out in the storm for hours. Already part of her mind wondered how Berhane could have come so far. Another part worried about whether they might have missed her if she had fallen.

Her head came up at the sound of a muffled shout ahead of them. Hugh stopped abruptly too, and Lucy almost cannoned into him again before she came unsteadily to a halt.

He put out an arm to help her keep her balance, but he was not looking at her. Instead he was peering ahead through the falling snow, in the direction the shout had come from.

Lucy strained her eyes and her ears too, but her heart was pounding with effort and anxiety, and she could barely see a foot in front of her. For a second she thought she saw a light glimmering on her right. Her heart leaped. There was a house at the foot of the moor, she remembered passing it on yesterday's walk. Surely Berhane would be sheltering there. Then her hopes plummeted, as she remembered Edith's voice, commenting on the absence of the people who lived in the house near the brook.

Suddenly a figure was almost upon them, looming up out of the storm. Lucy would have staggered back, if Hugh's arm had not held her upright.

'Berhane!' she called in relief. Hugh's arm tightened just as Lucy hesitated uncertainly. The figure was even more covered in snow than she and Hugh were. Its body was thickly wrapped, disguising its shape, and its face was all but hidden by hat and scarf.

It was not Berhane. Lucy knew that, however much she willed herself to be wrong. But she did not recognise the man, even when he spoke.

'The bridge is down,' he shouted, grasping Hugh's shoulder. He was bellowing into Hugh's ear to make himself heard above the storm, and the words floated faintly to Lucy.

'Berhane?' Hugh yelled.

'On it when it came down,' the man shouted back.

Lucy's free arm lifted, pressing a cold wet gloved hand to her face. 'No, oh no,' she whispered, her lips stiff with cold and shock.

'She's okay,' the man shouted, and now Lucy knew that he was Phil Avery. 'Well, pretty much. I've taken her into the Simmonds' place. Come on, let's all get in there. Thank God I caught you before you went any further.'

He took each of them by an arm, turning them to the right. Again there was that brief flicker of yellow light ahead through the swirling flakes. It encouraged Lucy to move again, now that she knew it was real and that Berhane was almost within reach, safe in the house.

Within minutes Lucy and Hugh were awkwardly unstrapping their snowshoes in a porch that gave them a little shelter from the storm. Phil pushed open the door into the house and they all stumbled into warmth and glowing light.

Phil pulled off his sodden scarf and sheepskin hat, releasing his wet black hair to fall limply to his shoulders. 'Is there anybody else coming?' he demanded urgently. 'Edith is manning Joe's radio, and she said you were on the way. I hoped you'd turned back. She thought nobody else was coming until the storm abates.'

'How long ago were you in touch?' Hugh demanded, pulling off his own hat.

'Half an hour ago, when we got here,' Phil said, checking the grandfather clock that stood behind him, ticking steadily. 'Sam Simmonds, the woman who lives here, belongs to the radio network.'

'Has Edith been sitting at the radio all this time?' Hugh asked, finally managing to undo his coat and pull it off with fingers that had started to tingle painfully.

Phil shook his head, glancing over his shoulder. 'No,' he

said quietly. 'We'd arranged to be in touch on the hour every hour if we could. But I've been out on the moor for some time and she's been with her aunt Susannah until she died.'

Lucy caught her breath, shocked by the news, even though she knew how unwell Susannah had been when they left her.

Phil glanced at her quickly as he continued, 'Edith went back to the radio as soon as she could to see if there was any news or weather updates. She was waiting there, even though it's well past the hour, hoping I'd get through.'

'Does Berhane know about Susannah?' Lucy asked.

'No, I don't want to tell her yet,' Phil replied firmly. 'She took a bit of a beating from the bridge planks as she fell.' He closed his eyes for a moment, before he added, 'She was precariously wedged under the far end when I got to her, so altogether I reckon she's pretty uncomfortable. And wet through.' His lips twitched in the travesty of a smile as he looked at Lucy. 'But you know Berhane. She would never admit to feeling bad.'

'Where is she?' Lucy demanded, handing her sodden coat to Hugh.

Phil jerked his head to the closed door at the left end of the hall. 'In the sitting room, well wrapped in blankets beside the fire. I've lit it, there are plenty of logs. It'll take a bit of time for the warmth to come through, so I've put on the heating too. She's out of her wet clothes and wrapped in Sam's dressing gown, but when the water's hot she should have a bath.' He stopped, considering his words. 'If she's asleep though, don't wake her up,' he warned. 'I dosed her with brandy, although she doesn't like it. But she was fair worn out by the time we got here. Managed on her own feet all the way in spite of everything,' he ended with grudging pride.

'You're wet through too, Lucy,' Hugh expostulated. 'At least change first.'

'I'll just look in on Berhane,' Lucy said, 'but I won't stay. Then I'll come back and get dry.'

'What do we do about changing clothes?' Hugh asked as

Lucy opened the sitting-room door quietly and went in, shutting it soundlessly behind her.

'Strip the beds, I suppose,' Hugh answered his own question.

Phil shook his head, spraying water drops from his long hair like a wet dog. 'No, we'll raid the Simmonds' clothes again.' He grinned unexpectedly. 'We'll be okay with Doug's things, and Sam's clothes fit Berhane well, but they'll swamp Lucy.'

Hugh was looking round the hall, his hands clutching his own coat as well as Lucy's, as well as soaking hats, scarves and gloves. His gaze roamed over the beautifully polished kneehole desk and the Georgian console table, the delicate carved chairs, without finding somewhere to drop his burden.

'Here,' Phil said, realising his dilemma, 'bring them through to the kitchen. I've got Berhane's things out there in front of the Aga, and we can add yours and mine.'

'How did you get in here?' Hugh asked, following him through an archway beyond the stairs into a wide kitchen that ran the full width of the house. He blinked in surprise at the glittering array of cherry red kitchen equipment on the spotless marble worktops, almost dazzled by the spotlights reflecting off the gleaming white cupboard doors.

'I've got the key. I usually keep an eye on the place when Sam and Doug are away,' Phil answered, pulling up kitchen chairs in front of the Aga. 'Here, hang your things over these. I'll get out of mine then we can have some of Doug's brandy too.'

'How are you going to explain all this to the owners when they get back?' Hugh enquired curiously.

Phil looked over his shoulder in surprise as he prised off his sodden coat. 'It's an emergency; they would have helped if they were here. They came from London some years back, but they've fitted in right well. He's a clever chap, a professor of something or other, and she's something to do with design, but they know the moor ways. They won't mind us using the place.' He turned away, glancing quickly at the long expanse of window. Snow was still falling heavily, sparkling in the outside lights.

'It's the worst weather I can ever remember,' Phil said grimly, turning back to Hugh. 'I couldn't believe Berhane was out in it. What the hell is going on? I couldn't make head nor tail of what Edith was saying. Not,' he added wryly, 'that I often can, of course.'

'Can we make tea too?' Hugh asked, avoiding an answer as he looked round for something as simple as a kettle. 'Lucy's not really keen on spirits.'

Phil pointed towards the sink. 'Over there, that triangular kettle. The tea's in the cupboard above. Help yourself.'

Hugh filled the cherry-red kettle from the tap and plugged it in. He turned back to face Phil, who had pulled up a chair and straddled it, his arms crossed over its back as he watched Hugh's movements.

Hugh sank gratefully onto another chair and stretched his legs out. 'We'd better go through the story out here,' he said. 'I don't want to bother Berhane with it yet.'

'Fine.' Phil waited as Hugh sorted his thoughts.

'I'm beginning, I'm very much afraid, to get an idea of what's been going on. Lucy has a fine instinct for something wrong in the order of things. So when she expressed unease I paid attention, although I never really had much doubt that the deaths were not accidents. I don't want to go into that until I've had chance to order my thoughts a bit more. But,' he raised his voice as Phil made an abrupt movement, 'as far as this evening goes, Susannah had a strange idea that Edith had gone off to meet you, and that you meant her harm, serious harm. Susannah was sure you still wanted revenge for the loss of your home when Ballamy's Farm was sold.'

Phil stared at him disbelievingly. 'Berhane knew better than that,' he said gruffly.

'Yes, I think she did,' Hugh agreed mildly. 'But Edith had really gone wandering off, and there have been two suspicious deaths in the last forty-eight hours. Berhane had no more real choice in the matter than we did. She went to look for Edith, just as we all went to look for her.'

'So where the hell had Edith gone, starting all this with the storm coming on?' Phil demanded. 'She's not stupid, even if she seems to be when it suits her, and she'd know the weather was getting real bad.'

'It seems,' Hugh said, a quiver of laughter in his voice, 'that she'd had such good news that she had to go and look once again on the old homestead.'

'What?' Phil was taken aback.

'She and her bloke, the one with the odd name that I forget, have written a science fiction novel that some American publisher seems to think is going to be a roaring bestseller.'

'Edith has?' Phil sounded stunned. He rallied. 'What's that got to do with Ballamy's Farm?'

'Edith hopes to get it back.'

'Well, that would have pleased Susannah. But it sounds like one of Edith's fantasies to me,' Phil said dubiously. 'I hope it doesn't turn out to be a mare's nest. Still,' he sighed, 'Susannah died happy if she believed there was going to be a Ballamy back down on the farm.'

Hugh had his doubts about Susannah's state of mind, but he had no chance to voice them.

Phil was frowning now. 'But what was Susannah up to, to say such a thing about me and Edith? She's always been so good to me. She must know I wouldn't do such a thing. Or,' he went on thoughtfully, 'somebody put the idea into her mind.'

'Susannah was afraid,' Hugh said carefully, 'that the loss of your smallholding had brought all the original distress back to you.'

'But I'm not losing it,' Phil almost shouted, remembering at once to lower his voice. 'I'm buying it. Gil didn't want to go on renting it out, and he gave me first chance to purchase it. At a damned good price too.' He was frowning. 'Although

I suppose that's gone by the board now that Gil's dead.' His frown deepened. 'You know, I can't see that Gil would have sold or let Ballamy's to Edith if she wasn't going to farm the land. He was a businessman through and through, but he had certain sticking points. Using the land was one of them. He just about accepted what I do on the smallholding, partly because I do have stock. Even,' he added wryly, 'if it's only a few cows and ponies grazing on the moor.'

The kitchen door opened and Lucy came in. 'Berhane's awake, and wants you to join us.' She glanced at the steaming kettle. 'Brilliant. Just what I need. You go on in to her and I'll make some tea.' She glanced at Hugh, who was about to expostulate. 'I'm alright, I've virtually steamed dry by the fire.' She looked at the puddles the men had left around their chair legs and on their seats. 'Why don't you both try it too?'

Phil was already on his way hastily out of the kitchen into the hall, his wet socked feet slipping a little on the quarry tiles. Hugh caught up with him, taking his arm and holding him back.

'How do we get back to the village from here?' he asked quietly. 'There must already be at least three feet of snow out there. Are we going to be snowed in here?'

'When the storm ends the rescue team will come out for us,' Phil said. 'It's not too far, and I want Berhane checked over by the doctor. Either the quad bikes or a couple of husky teams will get down here to take us away.' He grimaced. 'I expect the police will be coming too. Edith said they were on their way.'

'Won't it be best to wait until the morning before we leave?' Hugh queried. 'We've intruded so much here, that sleeping in their beds doesn't seem too awful.'

Phil shook his head emphatically. 'No. We need to get out as soon as there's a break in the weather. The forecast is just as bad for tomorrow.'

Lucy appeared behind them, balancing a tray. 'Look, I've found chocolate biscuits too. Don't hang around here, go in by the fire. It's amazingly cosy in there, in spite of all the big windows.'

Hugh moved ahead, opening the door into the sitting room, trying not to think of an enforced stay in the village. At least, he supposed, he should be grateful that they were all alive and well. There had been more than one moment in the last hour when he had doubted that he and Lucy would pull through.

Unbidden, another thought reared up in his head, growing out of Phil's comments. What if his own thoughts were completely out of kilter? What if Edith, Edith whom no one took seriously, was after all the person behind all this? Behind the deaths.

EIGHT

Mike shifted awkwardly on one of the black sofas in the Church House, one of his feet knocking against the table in front of him. The china cups tinkled musically as they joggled on their saucers, drowning Hugh's quiet tones.

'Sssh,' Anna said in a low voice, looking up from the beanbag where she sat in effortless comfort listening to Hugh. 'We don't know if she's awake yet.'

'I'll go downstairs,' Mike muttered. 'Call me when we get to Hugh's punchline.'

Hugh grinned as he looked up from the small diary in its marbled paper covers that he was flicking through. 'You might see where Lucy's got to with the coffee,' he suggested.

'That sounds like a good idea,' said a husky voice from behind them.

They all turned quickly as Berhane came out of one of the small bedrooms at the far end of the room. An expression of concern crossed Hugh's face at the sight of her, but Mike sat up straighter on the sofa, his scowl easing as he saw her.

Anna got up lithely from the beanbag, asking anxiously, 'Are you sure you should be up yet?' She shot a reproachful look at Mike as she added, 'We didn't mean to disturb you.'

'You didn't,' Berhane assured her. 'I've been awake for some time.' She wore a long straight dress in cream wool, cinched round the waist with a woven belt, and looked her normal calm self. But she moved more stiffly than usual as she sat down in a chair, pushing the embroidered cushions around her into a more comfortable place against her back. Her eyes were strained, but her expression tranquil. She had made no attempt to conceal the network of scratches that marred one side of her face.

Berhane glanced around the room, past the trio sitting by the coffee table. Edith stirred on the window seat, swinging clumsily round from the view over the village green to stare at her sister. Isobel sat in one of the wide chairs beside the fireplace, where flames flickered noiselessly behind the doors of an egg-shaped stove that hung from the ceiling. In spite of the warmth she seemed to huddle into the shelter of her chair as if she was cold all the way through. Her little spaniel was sprawled across her feet, and with one hand Isobel was lightly stroking the large creamy-furred cat that lay on her lap.

Berhane's eyes rested on Solomon, before lifting to meet Isobel's steady gaze.

'He misses Susannah,' Isobel said. 'I couldn't leave him behind.'

'No, of course not,' Berhane said. 'This will probably be his home now anyway.' She looked at Edith. 'Unless you'd like to have him.'

Edith shook her head, the frizzy brown curls swinging over her round face. 'He'll be better here,' she said. She fixed her eyes on Berhane. 'He knows Aunt Susannah died. He stayed with her, right until the end.'

Isobel's fingers tightened on the cat's fur, and he unveiled his huge amber eyes, glaring at her reproachfully as he flexed his claws against her trousers. She relaxed her grip, thinking that she would never forget his feline vigil, that continuous rumbling purr that seemed to stop abruptly the minute his mistress died.

'Ah,' Anna said with relief, hearing the sound of footsteps on the stair. 'Here's Lucy with the coffee.'

Lucy appeared, a large cafetiere in each hand, trailed closely by Ben, his claws clicking on the wooden floor. She moved purposefully over to the table to put them down, her face lighting up as she saw Berhane.

'Hello,' she said. 'We didn't think you'd be up until later. That's why I made the coffee in the downstairs kitchen.'

'I couldn't sleep any longer,' Berhane replied, one hand resting on the collie's head as he came to greet her. 'There must be things to get sorted out.'

Silence fell as Anna settled herself back on the beanbag while Lucy poured coffee into the cups that were already on the table. Anna nudged Mike as he seized the cup she pushed towards him.

'What?' he growled. 'I was going to.' He passed the cup and saucer to Berhane.

'Thanks, Mike,' she said, her fingers lingering with familiar pleasure on the raised leaf pattern that rioted around the pale green china. 'Are we all here? What about Phil, is he coming?'

'No,' Edith replied. 'It's all those animals he's got. He had to go back last night, after...' Her voice tailed away into a mumble, re-emerging more strongly to say, 'I shouldn't think he'll get down again today. There was a lot more snow during the night and the forecast is still bad.'

An unusual frown scored Berhane's forehead. 'I hope he got back alright,' she said.

'Oh yes,' Edith replied, 'I stayed by Joe's radio until he called.'

Mike was staring at her, looking rather bemused, remembering how the vagueness that cloaked her again now had fallen away in the long hours of waiting last night. He looked round, scowling suddenly. 'I suppose we're waiting for Elliot.'

Hugh shook his head. 'No, he won't be coming back either until the weather improves.'

'Unless there's another death,' Mike said bluntly.

'There won't be,' Hugh said with conviction, watching Lucy sit down next to him, turning to rest her back against the arm of the sofa as Ben lay beside it.

Everyone, including his wife, looked at Hugh expectantly, without surprise.

Mike wore an expression of a man whose suspicions had been confirmed. 'I thought you'd worked out what's been going on. Well,' he ordered, 'don't keep us waiting. Tell us who did it. You can always,' he glanced at Anna out of the corner of his eye, 'repeat it for Elliot later. I'm sure he'll be back here as soon as he can.'

'Whether I repeat it, or leave Elliot to pursue his own line, depends on how well you think I make my case now,' Hugh replied. 'I should make it clear immediately that I'm only making an educated guess. I have no proof to support the picture I've pieced together. Although I'm sure it fits all the facts.' He looked from Berhane to Edith. 'It will involve you both very nearly. Do you want me to go on?'

The sisters looked briefly at each other, and it was Berhane who deferred the decision. 'I think,' she said, 'that it's up to you, Edith.'

Edith's bulbous eyes were fixed on a spot on the floor. 'It's better to know,' she said, her fingers pulling at a fold in her long skirt. 'After all, we might carry on wondering whether one of us is a murderer.'

Hugh quirked an eyebrow in surprise, regarding Edith with sudden respect. He sipped his coffee slowly, before pushing the cup and saucer away and sitting back on the sofa, steepling his fingers together.

Before he could speak Anna said impulsively, 'Just a minute, Hugh. Surely Berhane should have something to eat before you start.' She glanced at her friend. 'You must be hungry.'

Berhane shook her head, a wry smile on her lips. 'Not really. Perhaps later, Anna. I'd rather hear what Hugh has to say first.'

Mike gave an impatient snort. 'Let him get on with it then. Anna can get to the food afterwards.'

Anna's expressive face darkened, but she relaxed back

into the beanbag as Hugh said firmly, 'Berhane's return to the moor, as you've probably all guessed, was the catalyst. For all the people who were glad to see her come back, there were a few others who found her a threat, who didn't want her here. Joe Triggs, the inn landlord, was the most obvious. Phil Avery emerged as a possible enemy, if he still bore a grudge from years past. That grudge could involve Edith too, but she seemed unaffected by the incidents that dogged Berhane.'

'People always thought it was Berhane's decision to sell the farm,' Edith said unexpectedly. 'But Phil knew I wouldn't have kept the place. I never wanted to farm. Phil watches a lot and knows things that other people don't notice.'

Hugh nodded. 'A useful skill.'

Lucy looked at him sharply. Mike grunted and poured himself more coffee, banging the cafetiere down again.

'There was one more person who regretted Berhane's return to some degree.' He lifted his eyes apologetically to Berhane.

'Susannah,' she said quietly.

'Yes.'

'But what the hell for?' Mike demanded. 'I can't see why she did it.'

Hugh sat up straighter and leaned across the table to the diary he had put down. 'I had an advantage over you all,' he said. 'I'd read this.'

'Don't tell me.' Mike ran both his hands through his tousled red curls. 'Not the bloody treasure Triggs was on about.'

'Not exactly,' Hugh replied carefully. 'Although the writer does keep a detailed account of excavations carried out by the local archaeological group. You'll certainly find it useful.'

Mike bent forward, one hand outstretched to take the diary, but Hugh retained his clasp, moving the book out of reach.

'Not yet, Mike. The excavations only have an indirect bearing on events here.'

Mike sat back, swearing under his breath.

Anna glanced at him forbiddingly. 'Ssh, Mike. Let's hear the rest.'

Hugh looked at Berhane questioningly. 'Do you know what else is in here?'

She was puzzled. 'No. Gil lent me three of the diaries, but I haven't had chance to read any of them. I didn't even glance through that first one before I passed it on to you. Then when you sounded interested in it I gave you the other two without looking at them.' She sounded apologetic.

'Gil's great-grandfather recorded everything in meticulous detail.' Hugh ignored Mike's sharp intake of breath. 'This diary includes every scrap of news or gossip that the old man heard.'

'How do you know he was old?' Lucy asked quickly.

Hugh grinned at her. 'He mentions his birthday quite early on, and expounds on how his interests have kept him active at the great age of 75.' He frowned at his wife. 'But that is a digression. One of his throwaway descriptions is an account from an old woman in the village, reputed to be over a hundred years old, who grew up on Ballamy's Farm.'

Edith's hands were entwined in her long skirt, and she sat motionless on the window seat, her eyes fixed on Hugh. She showed no sign of interest or distress when Hugh glanced at her, so he continued his story.

'This old lady passed on a piece of folklore, speculation, whatever you want to call it, that she had learned at her grand-mother's knee.' He looked round at his audience, who were waiting in rapt expectation.

'If you calculate the dates, given that old man Hannaford was 75 in 1885, the year he wrote this diary, and given that the old lady came from a long line of women who lived to a ripe old age, it could take us back to the late seventeenth, early eighteenth century. A repeated tale was handed down through this woman's family of something that happened before then, something in the Ballamy family.'

Lucy stirred, looking at Hugh with an arrested expression as she remembered the tomb she had looked at in the church only a few days ago.

'This involved another Susannah Ballamy,' Hugh continued. Lucy's exclamation was muted, so he only cast her an enquiring look but did not stop talking. 'The name has to be a coincidence, a family one that was used down the generations. But there was a similarity between the women. I think there's no doubt that family mattered more than anything else to our latter day Susannah. The tale in this diary shows that it did to her namesake ancestress too. The tale also reveals what that overwhelming obsession led that earlier Susannah to do in the cause of family.'

Edith was watching Hugh curiously, but said nothing. Berhane said quietly, 'It probably influenced everything Susannah did. It was part of her, bred into her.'

'She was so proud,' Isobel said regretfully, 'of keeping so many of her family belongings in her own home. She knew them so intimately, it was as if they connected her to her ancestors.'

'And it was that sense of pride, of belonging to the family and its history, that motivated the first Susannah. And the latest one.'

'What was said in the diary about the first Susannah?' Anna asked, leaning forward, her dark curls falling about her intent face.

'Old Man Hannaford reported in detail that Mistress Susannah Ballamy was a skilled herbalist, much respected in the neighbourhood, even though it was widely believed that she had poisoned her daughter-in-law. The account, which reads much as Hannaford must have heard it from the old woman, rather implies that locals felt she was justified. The daughter-in-law was Spanish, a Catholic, married to a Ballamy who had sailed in the Elizabethan navy and reputedly fought with Drake. The woman couldn't settle here, and persuaded her husband to go with her and their son, not to Spain, but to the West Indies, where her family held estates. She died before they could leave, and Susannah's son stayed here with his own son, presumably working his own ancestral lands and passing them on down the Ballamy line.'

'She was called Catalina,' Lucy said suddenly, blinking hard, her hazel eyes bright with unshed tears. 'She died when her son was only a little boy. He probably never even remembered her.'

The others looked at her in amazement, except for Berhane. And Edith, Lucy realised. So Edith knew the tomb too. They really had all underestimated Edith.

Lucy gathered her wits to explain, 'In the church there's a tomb in the Ballamy chapel to Susannah and her husband.' Lucy hesitated, trying to remember his name.

'Daniel,' Edith supplied. 'Aunt Susannah wanted me to give his name to Dixon when he was born. She said it was time for the name to be used again and my son should have it.' Edith shrugged without further comment.

'There's a memorial to Susannah's son and his wife, with interesting images of them,' Lucy said regretfully, remembering the entwined hands.

'They probably wouldn't be accurate anyway,' Mike said. 'They'd have been idealised. Less than the real amount of warts, double chins, middle-aged spread.'

Lucy shook her head. 'Not for Susannah and Daniel. They looked far too realistic.'

Mike was about to argue the point, but Anna cut across him. 'Why do you think this old story is relevant today?' she asked Hugh.

'I'm not sure that it is particularly,' he replied. 'But it gave me a different perspective on what was happening here.'

He looked at Edith, who was staring at him unblinkingly. 'I think the root cause of all the trouble was getting you back on Ballamy's Farm. I wondered for a time if you wanted to go back more than we might have thought, whether family mattered to you more than first appeared.' He waited for a comment from Edith, but none came.

'Obviously you did harbour feelings for the family place, but were they strong enough for you to kill for? Or to collaborate with Taylor to do it?' Hugh asked rhetorically. Nobody stirred, but all eyes were on Edith, who was watching him blankly. 'I didn't know. But the timescale fitted your arrival to stay at the Church House. Both deaths happened while you were here. Against this is the fact that by then you already knew that you stood a good chance of returning to the farm if your novel was accepted. So I had to think, what had you to gain by Gil's death at that moment?'

He spread his hands slightly. His audience was waiting. Mike leaned forward, his hands clenched on his knees. Anna had her arms around her legs, her chin resting on her knees, her face intent. In the background Isobel waited, her face looking for once elderly, and very sad.

'Nothing,' Hugh said. 'You gained nothing.'

Anna released a pent up breath, appreciating the drama of the moment. Mike shot Hugh an irritable look.

'I don't think,' Hugh continued, 'that you wanted to go back enough to make all this trouble and effort anyway. And the timing was wrong. Without the novel's success you couldn't hope to persuade Gil to sell you the farm. And I doubt you'd have wanted it then, without being able to put your ideas into action. Should the novel be accepted on good terms, as it was, you could hope to buy the place.'

Lucy had been listening carefully, a frown gathering on her forehead, as one hand absentmindedly stroked the collie who lay beside her. 'And, Hugh, what would Edith have to gain by driving Berhane away? Surely all the little incidents that plagued her are relevant?'

'Mmm,' Hugh said with appreciation, 'that brings us back to the crux of the matter. Yes, I think they were connected to the deaths. In fact they are a strong indicator of the reason. Which brings us back to Susannah. What she definitely wanted above all else was a Ballamy back on Ballamy's Farm.' He glanced at Berhane. 'I think that desire grew to be such an obsession that it overwhelmed everything else, even her very genuine affection for you, Berhane, and for Phil Avery. She was very proud of him and what he had achieved.'

Edith's gaze fell to her lap, where her hands still lay hidden in her skirt. Berhane clasped her cup more tightly, uninterested in the cooling coffee it held.

Hugh's eyes swept around the rest of the people listening to him. 'As I've already said, Berhane's return was the catalyst. Susannah had hopes, quite unfounded hopes, that Gil Hannaford would marry Edith and the farm would return naturally to her family. It must have become evident soon after Berhane came back that Gil's interests lay elsewhere. Susannah tried to persuade herself that this was merely friendship, but she was secretly afraid that her last hopes were crumbling about her.'

Mike snorted. 'You should go in for romantic novels,' he muttered. 'Cut the suspense, Hugh.'

Hugh grinned, but sobered again quickly. 'Remember, Mike, this is just a story I've pieced together. One I think is true, but one I can't prove.'

'Don't keep interrupting, Mike,' Anna suggested sweetly. 'The rest of us want to hear Hugh.'

'She suborned Joe Triggs, didn't she?' Lucy asked quietly.

Hugh shot her an approving glance. He nodded. 'I think so. Joe was, so to speak, ripe for mischief. He resented Berhane's plans for the dining club, as Susannah knew very well. And he was used to doing what Susannah suggested, she'd been manipulating him for years, generally for his own good. She encouraged Joe in those petty incidents that surrounded Berhane and the Church House. She hoped to drive Berhane away from the area, no more than that, I think.'

'But Susannah was knocked over when she disturbed an intruder in the apartment,' Berhane objected suddenly. 'I found her on the floor, remember, and heard somebody running down the back stairs. Surely Joe wouldn't have hurt her?'

'Hmm, but there were two complicating factors,' Hugh said, his face intent now. He picked up the diary from the table and held it out for them all to see. 'The first was these diaries that Gil found. Gil wound Joe up with little hints on his second favourite topic, ancient treasures in the earlier sites on the moor. I think,' Hugh added slowly, 'that Gil may have done the same thing with Susannah.'

'She wasn't that interested in village history, unless it impinged on the family,' Berhane said doubtfully.

'No, but I guess Gil had found the earlier Susannah story, and he hinted about that. I suspect that's why he gave you this particular copy, to see what you thought about it before he decided whether to show it to her. After all, I believe he said there were several diaries.'

'There are,' Berhane said quietly. 'I found the rest in Gil's safe, along with his will.'

Mike's attention moved quickly from the diary in Hugh's grasp to Berhane's face. 'How many are there?' he demanded.

'Not now, Mike,' Anna said repressively.

'I'll show you later,' Berhane promised. She looked back at Hugh. 'It sounds right, what you're saying. Gil wouldn't have been able to resist dropping hints. He'd never dream of causing trouble though.' She closed her eyes for a second, then fixed them on Hugh. 'Is that why he died?'

Hugh shook his head. 'No, I don't think so. Joe wanted to see what was in the diaries, and so did Susannah. But it was Joe's obsession that drove him to search the Church House, looking for the ones he knew Berhane had. I think Mike's interest in the Victorian digs probably helped to drive him on.' Hugh stopped as Mike uttered a grunt of disbelief.

'Oh yes,' Hugh said. 'Once somebody gets to that level of paranoia anything and anybody can be seen as a threat. He didn't want you to find his treasure. And having got away so easily with Berhane's oil, perhaps he couldn't resist trying his luck a bit further. After all, he'd know that people don't lock their doors around here.'

Berhane shrugged, leaning forward to put down the cup of congealing coffee. 'Yes, I leave the doors unlocked. He'd have known that.'

'Well,' Hugh continued, 'I think Susannah went over with maybe the same aim, who knows, but found Joe in the apartment and had an argument with him. Joe heard you return through the front door and pushed past her to get out before you came upstairs. No doubt he pushed harder than he meant to, because I'm sure he was then still too much under Susannah's control to assault her deliberately. But that was the first indicator.'

The others were totally silent now. Even Mike was watching him with interest, forgetting briefly about the diaries.

'That must have been an indication to Susannah that her mastery of the situation was slipping, and I think she recognised it as such. The second indicator,' Hugh's face hardened, 'was when Gil died.'

Isobel spoke, her voice harsh as though the words hurt her throat. 'Susannah can't have been involved in that. She was in the village hall with me all the time.' The cat on her lap lifted his head again, and Isobel resumed her rhythmic stroking.

'Susannah didn't even know Joe planned to damage the saddle girth,' Hugh said. 'He was beginning to act on his own initative.'

'How can you be sure?' Anna asked dubiously.

'Neither Susannah nor Joe had any reason to harm Gil. Susannah still had hopes of getting him and Edith together, but even if that failed Gil was a better owner of Ballamy's Farm than some outsider who might make it a holiday home and take it forever beyond Edith's reach. And Joe, well, Joe's first and overriding obsession was the hunt. Gil was essential for the hunt to continue. Not many pack owners will want to run drag hunts, but Gil was just concerned with getting a good ride with his horses and hounds.'

'So why did Gil die?' Anna asked.

Lucy had been studying her fingers. 'That's how you know it wasn't Susannah who damaged the girth, isn't it?' she asked her husband.

'Yes,' he said grimly. 'Susannah knew about the horse exchange between Berhane and Gil. You'd told her, hadn't you, Berhane?'

'Yes,' she said slowly. 'So are you saying Joe tried to kill me?'

'I don't think it was that deliberate,' Hugh said. 'I think it was a spur of the moment action. He saw your horse when he was down in the stables, perhaps for a moment everybody was busy elsewhere. I'm sure,' he added, 'we'll find he carried one of those knives riders always seem to have, for picking stones out of hooves, or cutting tangled reins.'

'That's generalising,' Lucy pointed out.

'I know,' Hugh conceded, 'but I'm sure he had something to hand to saw away at the girth. No doubt,' he said dryly, 'he thought a bad tumble might finally put Berhane off the area.'

'He must have known better than that,' Anna said sombrely. 'Even I know that a fall from a horse could be fatal, let alone a fall at speed on rocky ground.'

'I suspect that by then Triggs wasn't thinking rationally,' Hugh said. 'If anybody had pointed that out to him at the time he would probably have snapped out of that particular idea. But,' he said crisply, 'Joe didn't discuss it with Susannah. He acted. And when she realised what he'd done, it was too late, Gil was already dead.'

'Joe must have been horrified when he found that it was Gil who had died,' Anna said.

'No doubt,' Hugh agreed dryly. 'And the relationship between Susannah and the landlord was now further complicated. Berhane was to inherit most of Gil's estate, he'd actually told Susannah and Joe that. And Susannah had probably heard from Joe that Gil was proposing Ballamy's Farm being Berhane's training centre.'

'She never understood humour,' Berhane said sadly. 'I don't think Joe did either. Ballamy's would have been suitable, of course, but I've actually already found somewhere better, an old riding school on the high moor. Gil knew that I was starting negotiations for it.'

'I certainly don't think Susannah realised Gil wasn't partic- ularly serious about his proposition,' Hugh replied. 'But it raised a new fear in her mind once Gil was dead. That was why she was keen to suppress his will. If she could have found it, once she knew it hadn't been posted, I'm sure she would have destroyed it. She had, I believe, persuaded herself that in the absence of a signed copy his sister would inherit his estate and sell it off. By then I think Susannah was harbouring plans to buy Ballamy's Farm herself. Probably unrealistic plans,' he said, 'unless she had considerable resources.'

He paused, looking round, but nobody had anything to say.

'Joe initially agreed to this suppression of the will,' Hugh continued, his voice steady. 'No doubt he was horrified at the result of his unscripted action. Susannah would certainly have used her knowledge about what he'd done to put pressure on him.'

'Just a minute,' Mike said brusquely. 'How did she know he'd done it?'

'I should think she guessed,' Hugh said. 'We can't know, of course, but I think she accused him and he just admitted it. He was in the habit of telling her his troubles, and he would have been knocked for six at the consequences of his act.'

'She had the chance to speak to the landlord quite soon after the hunt returned,' Isobel said, startling them. As they looked at her, the little spaniel stirred restlessly at her feet. 'She went up to the inn to take his horse down to Gil's stables. She could have said something to him then.'

'Mmm,' Hugh murmured. 'I'm sure she worked things out pretty rapidly, and readjusted her plans, forcing Joe to fall in with them. But gradually Joe's anxieties over the future of the hunt overwhelmed everything else.' Hugh's twisted smile appeared as he looked at Berhane. 'He knew, you see, that you would keep the hunt going.'

'Did Susannah kill him?' Berhane asked evenly.

'I don't think she intended to,' Hugh said. 'We'll never know for sure, but I think matters between them came to a head near midnight on New Year's Eve. Joe was the hunt treasurer and must have known Gil had a safe. I think he told Susannah about it when she was collecting drinks from the inn. He felt sure the will would be there and meant to produce it, in spite of her arguments.' Hugh sighed. 'Susannah couldn't let that happen. I think she went back, perhaps when the bell ringing started, to persuade him to change his mind. And again she had no effect on him.'

Hugh spread his hands out a little, and let them fall. 'I don't know what happened. I suspect, knowing what I do of the landlord's character, that he dismissed her brusquely and turned his back, swinging round to the barrel he had just raised from the cellar. Susannah, perhaps mindful of the last time he had disobeyed her, reacted against a possible blow, pushing him away from her. She may even have had one of those heavy wooden trays in her hands and shoved him with that. Caught off balance, Joe fell down the stairs and when she looked after him, she could see as well as I did that he'd broken his neck. The wound on the back of his head may well have been caused when he struck the steps on his way down.'

'But she didn't try to help him,' Berhane said bleakly.

'She must have known it was too late,' Hugh replied. 'I don't know whether she accidentally caught the rope holding the barrel up, or whether she sent it down after him deliberately, trying to create the impression of an accident.'

'But it was an accident,' Lucy said. 'She didn't mean him to die.'

'But she meant that Berhane should,' Edith said unexpectedly. 'That was why she sent her up to the moor.'

'I'm afraid so,' Hugh said, regarding Edith with interest. 'Although if the case were going to court, I would be inclined to say Susannah was no longer in her right mind.'

'She certainly seemed very strange in Gil's house,' Berhane admitted. 'I thought her heart was bothering her. After all, she'd taken more pills than usual recently, and should have been seeing the doctor again.'

'Perhaps it was,' Hugh said. 'But when Elliot was talking to us after Joe's death she'd guessed, as you've told us, that you'd suddenly thought of Gil's safe too. So she watched for you to go down to his house.'

'That was why she was sitting by the window,' Isobel said bleakly as understanding dawned. 'And I was so pleased I'd persuaded her to rest.'

'You couldn't possibly have known what was going on, Gran,' Lucy said reassuringly. 'Nobody else did.'

Isobel shook her head, gesturing to Hugh to continue. Solomon moved on her lap, nudging her hand imperatively.

'When Susannah got to Gil's house she found you there,' Hugh said, looking directly at Berhane, 'as she had expected. And you already had his will in your hand. She had to have it, so you had to go, and the sudden memory of Edith wandering off down the lane towards Ballamy's Farm gave her an idea. One that chimed with her deepest fears and wishes.'

'And you were mad enough to go off in the storm at a word from her,' Anna said, glancing at Berhane.

'What else could I do?' she demanded. 'You'd have done the same.'

Anna's brilliant smile flashed out. 'I suppose so,' she admitted. She shot Mike a sideways glance. 'For some people.'

'So she meant Berhane to die,' Edith persisted.

'We can't be sure of that,' Hugh said. 'She was obsessed with her plans for Ballamy's Farm, but I think part of her was horrified at what she had done and was still doing. You know, her doctor says he gave her a new bottle of pills only ten days ago. Even if she was taking them each day, there should still be several left.'

He paused for a second. 'We can't know whether she was in such a state that she was taking more than she realised, and that she forgot she'd need to get another lot. But I wonder if she disposed of them deliberately, putting her fate into the hands of God.'

'The final arbiter,' Anna said unexpectedly.

Hugh smiled. 'Perhaps. In her own mind she may have thought she should expiate what I'm sure a sane corner of her thoughts recognised as her wrongdoing.'

'She had very firm views of right and wrong, of justice,' Berhane said, her face clouded with sorrow.

'And what was it all for?' Edith asked, startling them. 'Three people dead so I would go back to Ballamy's Farm. And it was going to happen anyway. Why did she always have to interfere with fate?'

'Will you still want to go back there now?' Anna asked curiously.

Edith looked at her blankly. 'Of course. If Berhane wants to sell it. I don't want it enough to kill for.'

'You can have it,' Berhane said. 'I don't want it. I never did.'

'I can pay for it,' Edith said. 'I'm going to be rich, you know.' She said it with a surprised pride that made Lucy bite back a laugh.

'No,' Berhane said, 'I don't want to be paid for it. It would seem like blood money. Just make it a happy place.'

'What about those diaries?' Mike demanded, catching Berhane's eye. 'What are you going to do about them? They're a valuable historical resource.'

Anna clicked her tongue in exasperation, but Berhane said calmly, 'If they're mine I'll let you look at them as soon as I can.' She glanced at Hugh apologetically. 'I doubt that I'm going to want to publish them.'

'Will you go ahead with your own plans?' Anna asked, forestalling Mike's attempt to speak again.

Berhane nodded. 'Of course. You must all come over another time, perhaps in the summer, when I may have my training centre site.'

Mike looked at her in horror. 'Bloody hell,' he groaned, 'that's asking for trouble. All of us together.'

'I tell you what,' Anna said sweetly, 'you go and camp on the moor beside your precious sites, and we'll stay in comfort with Berhane.'

'Comfort,' Mike snorted in disgust. 'That's a damn good idea, though. I wonder if I can get enough funding for a preliminary survey of the best site by then.'

Anna stared at him in stunned disbelief, while Hugh suppressed a laugh.

MARY TANT'S Rossington series

The Rossington Inheritance

Lucy Rossington has put a promising career on hold,
so that she can keep the family home going for her
young brother Will. Not an easy task, when home is
an Elizabethan manor that the family have lived in for
generations.

Grandmother Isobel is favourably inclined to Lucy's
plans to keep them afloat and bring them into the modern
world, but the estate manager opposes anything new and
could make progress difficult. Fortunately Lucy has the
support of her elegant and impulsive childhood friend
Anna.

There are newcomers on the scene, though, and Lucy
begins to wonder if they are all that they seem. When the
taint of avarice and deceit from the past seems to stain the
present, it becomes essential to know who she can trust,
not only for her own happiness, but also for the safety of
her family and friends. Will she find out in time?

*One to watch. This is very reminiscent of Agatha Christie
with its West-of-England country house setting. A good
plot, very good dialogue and the first of a series. I can
envisage it adapting well to the small screen...*

5-star rating   Philip Richards
'crime reader' (London) Amazon.co.uk

2007   HARDCOVER   ISBN 978-1-903152-16-X
          PBK   ISBN 978-1-903152-21-8

Death at the Priory

Lucy Rossington doesn't need any more trouble just now. She's got plenty of that already at the family manor in an idyllic West Country valley.

Her recent marriage is already under strain as she struggles to keep the Rossington family home going for her young brother, Will. Her glamorous and charming friend Anna is becoming an increasingly successful actress, so why isn't she happy? Lucy's grandmother, Isobel, seems to be hiding a secret, and is surprisingly unsympathetic about Lucy's personal dilemma.

So the odd incidents plaguing the Priory excavations, under the controversial leadership of the mercurial Mike Shannon, are really the last straw for Lucy. Does the death of an archaeologist really mean more than a temporary disturbance? Is Lucy imagining evil where none exists? She is soon to know.

2008   ISBN 978-1-903152-17-1

Friends... and a Foe

Life looks promising for Lucy Rossington and her family – there is no way they could guess that in just a few days their happiness might be shattered for ever.

All Lucy's hopes are being fulfilled now the future of the family manor in the West Country is secure. Her elegant friend Anna has left dramatic success behind in Paris to start the long-planned theatricals at Rossington Manor – perhaps because the obstreperous archaeologist Mike Shannon is so sure she won't.

Old friends rejoin the family circle – one of them brings in their wake a secret that somebody would kill to keep. How could the Rossingtons know that this secret will cost them dearly?

2009   ISBN 978–1–903152–22–5

Players and Betrayers

The play's the thing. Or is it?

It certainly is for Anna Evesleigh, with her first summer production at Rossington Manor. She needs to prove to herself – and irascible archaeologist Mike Shannon? – that she can succeed with this.

And it is for Lucy Rossington as she watches the crowds descending on her family home – performers and audience, old village neighbours and incomers.

But Mike's attention is elsewhere, and there is somebody else who has a watchful eye on Anna. For behind the scene another hand is gathering a hidden cast to play a drama of deceit and betrayal. A drama whose unplanned highlight is murder.

Since her own near brush with death earlier in the year, Lucy has slowly recovered her strength. By the time she picks up the threads of this latest mystery the shadow of that master hand lays heavily over her family and friends, and Lucy inevitably finds herself in danger – again.

2010   ISBN 978-1-903152-26-3

The Watcher on the Cliff

Who stalks the cliffs of the remote West Country, mysteriously swathed in cloak and hat? Is there a connection with Lucy Rossington's startling discovery? How do the national papers get the story so quickly?

Short-tempered archaeologist Mike Shannon is convinced it's all part of a plot to discredit him. And he can think of plenty of suspects, including Lucy and her husband Hugh, who are staying in the neighbourhood. They fall eagerly on the puzzle, glad of an excuse to evade their boring host.

To complete Mike's unhappiness, the lovely actress Anna Evesleigh is working nearby.

She and the vicar are producing a community play in an old fishing village, covering centuries of local history. Anna and Mike always strike sparks off each other, and she's probably the only person to enjoy the drama of his find – particularly because he doesn't.

Coincidence has brought many of the Rossington circle together again. They can't know that soon they will be drawn into the pageant of death that will stalk the cliffs.

This time Lucy's unerring instinct for evil doesn't plumb the full depth of the plot that threatens those she loves. If she can't unmask the villain, is there anyone who can?

2011   ISBN 978-1-903152-27-0

MARY TANT'S WEBSITE

To find out more about Mary Tant's world, visit her new website www.marytant.com. Read about the background to her books, find out which other authors she likes, visit the teashops she enjoys, know more about the wildlife she watches and follow her blog.

Order any of Mary Tant's books directly from your local bookshop or in case of difficulty from the publishers at www.threshold-press.co.uk or phone 01635-230272.
